ALSO BY SOPHIE LARK

Brutal Birthright
Brutal Prince
Stolen Heir
Savage Lover
Bloody Heart
Broken Vow
Heavy Crown

Sinners Duet
There Are No Saints
There Is No Devil

THERE ARE NO SAINTS

SOPHIE LARK

B*loom* books

Published by Bloom Books, an imprint of Sourcebooks
P.O. Box 4410, Naperville, Illinois 60567-4410
(630) 961-3900
sourcebooks.com

Originally self-published in 2022 by Sophie Lark.

Cataloging-in-Publication Data is on file with the Library of Congress.

Printed and bound in Canada.
MBP 10 9 8 7 6 5 4 3 2

This one is for all my Love Larks who have
struggled with mental health. Writing this
book was intense therapy for me, dredging
up some deep hurts from a long time ago.

I just want to tell you that every part of you, the
things that bring you pleasure and the things that
bring you pain, the parts of yourself you're most
proud of and the parts that seem like your own
worst enemy eating you alive from the inside...it
all makes up your mind, and your mind is beautiful
and perfect because it's the only one like it.

You are irreplaceable. You are one of a kind. You are art.

Sophie Lark

SOUNDTRACK

1. "Freak"—Sub Urban
2. "People I Don't Like"—UPSAHL
3. "Smells Like Teen Spirit"—Malia J
4. "yes & no"—XYLØ
5. "I'm Gonna Show You Crazy"—Bebe Rexha
6. "STUPID"—Ashnikko
7. "Gasoline"—Halsey
8. "lovely"—Billie Eilish & Khalid
9. "Devil's Worst Nightmare"—FJØRA
10. "Sinner"—DEZI
11. "High Enough"—K.Flay
12. "Black Magic Woman"—VCTRYS
13. "Spells"—Cannons
14. "Bad Things"—Cults
15. "Unholy"—Hey Violet
16. "Mad Hatter"—Melanie Martinez
17. "Bang Bang Bang Bang"—Sohodolls
18. "Hurt Me Harder"—Zolita
19. "Die a Little"—YUNGBLUD
20. "Cradles"—Sub Urban
21. "Burning Pile"—Mother Mother
22. "Raging on a Sunday"—Bohnes

23. "Dirty Mind"—Boy Epic
24. "Twisted"—MISSIO
25. "Sick Thoughts"—Lewis Blissett
26. "INFERNO"—Sub Urban & Bella Poarch

Music is a big part of my writing process. If you start a song when you see a 🎵 while reading, the song matches the scene like a movie score.

Spotify   Apple Music

1
COLE BLACKWELL

♫ *"People I Don't Like"—UPSAHL*

I SAW THE HEADLINES THAT A GIRL HAD BEEN MURDERED ON Ocean Beach, her body left floating in the ruins of the old Sutro Baths. I knew it was Shaw as surely as if he'd signed his name to his work. I didn't need to see his smug smirk at the showcase to confirm it. He delights in losing himself in the frenzy of beating and mutilation. His subjects can rarely be identified by teeth or even fingerprints.

I already saw the piece he's showing tonight. Mine is better.

Everything is excess with him. All the color, all the bold strokes, all the symbolism hitting you over the head.

I'm sure he'll sell a thousand prints whether he wins tonight's prize or not. Alastor is nothing if not industrious. His genius for self-promotion far exceeds his genius for art.

He catches my eye as he swaggers into the gallery, giving me the merest suggestion of a smile, a tug of the lips that shows the glint of bleached teeth. I give him nothing in return.

He looks tanned, despite the soup of fog covering the city all week. Women flock toward him, including Betsy Voss, who organized this event. She smiles up at Shaw, resting her hand lightly on his forearm as she laughs at some joke he's made.

Alastor grins back at her, his face boyishly animated.

He reminds me of a pitcher plant, exuding sticky sweetness to lure in flies.

I know most of the people milling around, drinking complimentary glasses of merlot, examining the work on display, and arguing its merit with increasing abandon as the wine takes hold.

It's all the same people, the same ass-kissing conversation.

I'm so fucking bored.

The San Francisco art scene is incestuous. Everyone knows everyone else, in both the common and biblical senses. Betsy and Alastor have fucked before, though she doesn't have to worry about ending up in the Sutro Baths—she's much too useful as a broker for Shaw's art.

In fact, the only person I don't recognize is the skinny girl shoving cheese in her mouth over at Betsy's excellent buffet spread. Betsy never skimps—she's provided a generous selection of fresh fruit, sandwiches, and macarons. The girl is demolishing the smoked Gouda like she hasn't eaten in a week, which she probably hasn't. Another starving artist scavenging on the outskirts.

The girl tried to dress up for the occasion: she's wearing a loose white shift dress, crisp and bright enough that she must have acquired it recently. Her boots tell another story—the battered Docs look older than she is.

I'm about to turn my gaze to a more interesting subject when the girl collides with Jack Brisk, curator of contemporary art at SFMOMA. The fault is his—he was gesturing aggressively with his chubby hands—but it's the girl who pays the price. Merlot splashes from Brisk's glass down the front of her dress, the wine soaking into the white cotton as if it were blotting paper.

"So sorry," Brisk says carelessly, barely glancing at the girl, who is clearly a nobody, before turning back to his conversation.

I watch the girl's face to see if she'll cry or rage or fall over herself apologizing to Brisk in return.

She does none of the above. She examines the stains, a crease forming between her eyebrows. Then she picks up her own glass of wine and strides off toward the bathrooms.

I make the rounds of the pieces I haven't yet seen. It's obvious which will be in the running for the prize. Art may be subjective, but quality shines like brass next to gold.

I'm guessing it'll be me, Rose Clark, and Alastor Shaw as top contenders.

My piece is superior. That should be obvious from the crowd of people around it, lingering longer and whispering more intently than they do for anyone else's work.

The complicating factor is the panel of judges. It includes Carl Danvers, a bitter misanthrope who's never forgiven me for making a joke at his expense eight years ago at a gala. I intended for him to overhear but underestimated his capacity for spite. He's taken every opportunity for revenge since, even at the cost of his own credibility.

Alastor sidles up behind me.

I hear him coming from a mile away. He has the subtlety of a bison.

"Hello, Cole."

"Hello, Shaw."

He uses my given name to annoy me.

I use his surname for the same reason.

He thinks because he knows certain things about me, that there's an intimacy between us.

There is no intimacy. The emotion is all from one side.

"How's your weekend going?" He's barely able to contain his grin.

He desperately wants me to acknowledge what he's done. I prefer to deny him that pleasure. But it's probably better to get this over with so he'll fuck off and leave me alone.

"Uneventful," I reply. "I don't think you can say the same."

Now he allows himself to grin, showing those perfect capped

teeth, those boyish dimples, and that gleam in those warm-brown eyes that make women go weak with the impulse to smile back at him, to run their fingers through his sun-streaked hair.

"I love a college coed." His voice is low and guttural. His thick pink tongue wets his lips, his features dissolving into lust at the memory of what he did.

I take a slow breath to dispel my distaste.

Alastor's need disgusts me. He's such a cliché of himself. College coeds, for fuck's sake.

"You and Bundy," I murmur, my lips barely moving.

Shaw's eyes narrow. "Oh, you're above that, are you? You don't feel a certain…urge when you see something like that?" He jerks his head toward a stunning blond bent over to examine the details of a floor-level installation, her tight red dress clinging to the curves of her ass.

He inclines his head in the direction of a slim Asian girl, her nipples clearly visible through the gauzy material of her top. "Or what about that?"

I don't kill women, typically.

Not out of any petty moral constraint.

It's just too fucking easy.

I could overpower either of those women like they were small children. Where's the challenge? The sense of accomplishment?

"Brave hunter of newborn fauns," I sneer.

Alastor's face darkens. Before he can retort, the skinny scavenger comes striding back into the gallery, her chin upraised, her dark hair streaming behind her.

I thought she was going to the bathroom to attempt the impossible task of washing those stains out of her dress.

Quite the opposite: she's tie-dyed the entire thing.

She used her merlot to make a textile of deep burgundy, magenta, and mulberry in delicate watercolor layers. I'm staring at the dress because it surprises me—not only in the concept but in the execution. It's really quite beautiful. Nothing I would have expected to emerge from a bathroom after eight minutes' work.

Alastor follows my gaze. He sees my interest while completely missing the reason behind it.

"Her?" He smiles. "You surprise me, Cole. I've never seen you take a stroll in the gutter before."

I turn away from the girl, my irritation swelling. "You think I'd be attracted to some filthy little scrabbler with bitten fingernails and raggedy shoelaces?"

Everything about that girl repulses me, from her unwashed hair to the dark circles under her eyes. She radiates neglect.

But Shaw is certain he's made a discovery. He thinks he caught me in some unguarded moment.

"Maybe I'll go talk to her," he says, testing me.

"I wish you would. Anything to end this conversation."

I stride off toward the open bar.

The hours pass slowly from eight o'clock to ten.

I slip in and out of conversations, soaking in the ready praise for my piece.

"You never cease to amaze me." Betsy's pale blue eyes peer up at me through the rims of her expensive designer glasses. "How on earth did you think of using spider silk? And how did you acquire it?"

She's giving me the same look of dazzled admiration she gave to Shaw, but she doesn't dare rest her hand on my forearm like she did to him.

Everyone says the prize is as good as mine—or at least everyone with taste.

Alastor is sulking over by the canapés. He's received a hefty helping of accolades, but he's noted the difference in tone as well as I have. Compliments for him, raves for me.

I want the prize because I deserve it.

I couldn't give a shit about the money—ten thousand dollars

means nothing to me. I'll make ten times that amount when I sell the sculpture.

Still, cold foreboding steals over me when Betsy calls the crowd to order, saying, "Thank you all for coming tonight! I'm sure you're anxious to hear what our judges have decided."

I already know what she's about to say even before she casts me a guilty look.

"After much debate, we've decided to award tonight's prize to... Alastor Shaw!"

The applause that breaks out has a nervy tension. Alastor is popular, but half the crowd casts glances in my direction to see how I'll react.

I keep my face as smooth as still water and my hands tucked in my pockets. I don't applaud along with them because I don't care about looking gracious.

"The rivalry continues!" Brisk says to me, his face florid with drink.

"The Lakers and the Clippers aren't rivals just because they both play basketball," I say, loud enough for Shaw to hear.

The sports metaphor is for Alastor's benefit, digging under his skin like a barb.

Brisk chortles. A flush rises up Shaw's neck. His thick fingers clench around the delicate stem of his champagne flute until I can almost hear the glass cracking.

"Congrats." I'm not even trying to sound sincere. "I know Danvers is a big fan of your work—he struggles when the message is open to interpretation."

"Not every piece of art has to be a riddle," Alastor snarls.

"Cole!" Betsy pushes her way toward me. "I hope you're not too disappointed—I liked your piece better."

"So does Shaw," I reply. "He just won't admit it."

Betsy wheels around, noticing Shaw directly behind her. She gulps, her face turning pink. "Your painting was wonderful, too, of course, Alastor!"

Without bothering to reply, he stalks away from us.

"Put my foot in my mouth, didn't I?" Betsy grimaces. "Well, it's what everyone's saying. These prizes are so political."

"Or personal."

Sure enough, Danvers isn't finished venting his spleen. The following morning, he publishes his review of the showcase, with several poorly veiled barbs thrown in my direction:

> While Blackwell's work continues to exhibit his usual level of precision, there's a cold technicality to his technique that fails to inspire the same level of energy stirred up by Alastor Shaw's frenetic colorful constructions. There's a wild abandon to Shaw's work that Blackwell would do well to emulate.

I can just imagine Alastor smirking over his morning coffee, scrolling through the article on his phone.

Danvers's opinion on my art means less to me than the twittering of the birds outside my window. The rage I feel is entirely generated by the audaciousness of that little worm daring to attack me publicly.

Just as Shaw's belief that we're rivals offends me, so do Danvers's pretensions that he can judge me.

I finish my breakfast, the same meal I eat every morning: an espresso, two slices of bacon, half an avocado, and a perfectly poached egg set atop a slice of grilled sourdough.

Then I wash and dry the dishes before setting them back in their places in the cabinet.

I'm already showered and dressed for the day.

I walk to my studio, which is close to my house on the sea cliffs north of the city. The vast sunlit space once housed a chocolate factory. Now the bare steel, glass, brick, and concrete form an open cage in which I do my work.

I don't commission workmen to execute my designs, though I could certainly afford to do so. Every step of the process is completed by me, even with my most complicated and technical sculptures. I've built custom equipment for welding, gilding, cutting, and soldering. Winches and scaffolding. Even pneumatic lifts for the largest pieces.

I keep no assistants, and I work alone.

I start at ten o'clock in the morning and labor until dinner. The kitchen is stocked with drinks and snacks, though I rarely take breaks for either.

Today I'm beginning a new piece in the same series.

I know how I want it to look—organic and deconstructed. I want the elements of the sculpture to seemingly hang in space.

But when I examine the materials at hand, nothing seems right.

The iron is too heavy. The steel lacks luster.

I picture the precise curved shape I want, like the hull of a ship or the rib of a whale…

Then I smile as inspiration surges through me.

I wait outside the *Siren* offices on Cabrillo Street.

It's a dingy low-slung building with a tin roof on which a light rain patters.

Rain is incredibly useful. It obscures the view, forces people to keep their heads down, and urges them to run from place to place without lingering, without looking around.

Umbrellas are even better.

I stand in the alleyway, watching Danvers through the greasy little window of his office.

You learn everything about a person when they think they're alone.

I watch Danvers take a tin of nuts out of his drawer, open them, and eat a few handfuls before wiping his salty palm on the leg of

his jeans. He pushes the nuts away as if he's not going to eat any more. But a few minutes later, he takes another handful. Then, in a burst of motivation, he puts the lid back on the tin and encloses the tin within the drawer. That lasts even less time before he opens the drawer and takes some more.

Danvers's receptionist comes into his office. She's already wearing her coat and carrying her purse, eager to leave before the weather worsens.

Danvers steps between her and the doorway, blocking her path with his soft-shouldered body, ignoring her several hesitant steps in his direction as she hints at him to release her.

His chatting stretches out agonizingly slow. I see the girl touch the phone in her pocket several times, probably feeling the vibration of text messages from friends who might be waiting for her at some nearby café or restaurant.

Finally, he lets her go. I expect him to follow her out—the receptionist was the last person left in the office besides Danvers himself.

Instead, he stands there awkwardly before sinking into his chair once more.

Frustrated by whatever attention he failed to drain from the receptionist, he pours the remaining nuts directly into his mouth and flings the tin at the wastepaper basket in the corner, missing it by two feet. I see him mouth the word *fuck*, though he doesn't bother to pick up the tin.

He scrolls through Facebook for a while. He's facing the window, his computer screen turned away from me, but I can see its reflection on his glasses. He opens a Word doc, types a few sentences, then closes the document again. Apparently, he exhausted all his creative energy slandering me this morning.

At long last, Danvers powers down his computer, retrieving his coat from a hook on the wall. I'm pleased to see he neglected to bring his umbrella.

Danvers shuts off the last of the office lights before locking the door behind him.

I step out from the alleyway, avoiding the camera perched on the northwest corner of the squat brick building. Once my umbrella is open, I'm nothing but a tall dark stalk beneath its black canopy.

I pretend to hustle along the sidewalk, head down, lost in thought, until Danvers and I brush shoulders.

"Carl," I say in mock surprise. "Didn't see you there."

"Cole." Danvers is little nervous. He's wondering if I read his article—if I'm here to harangue him.

"Is that the *Siren* office?" I say, as if I didn't know.

"That's right." His nod is jerky. He's stiff and wary.

"My studio's right over there." I gesture in the direction of Fulton, where—as Danvers well knows—the rent is triple what the *Siren* probably pays.

"Is it?" Danvers says vaguely, looking the other way toward Balboa, where he often takes the streetcar back to his condo.

The rain is falling harder now, plastering his thinning hair against his skull, bringing out the ratlike quality of his protuberant nose and underbite.

"Share my umbrella," I say as if I only just noticed him getting soaked. I reorient the canopy so it covers us both.

"Thanks," Danvers says grudgingly. And then, because it's human nature to seek conciliation, to give a favor for a favor, Danvers says, "No hard feelings about the showcase, I hope. It was stiff competition."

"I'm not one for grudges."

Danvers squints at me through his foggy glasses. I'm sure he's wondering if I saw the review. Perhaps even wishing he hadn't written it because, at the end of the day, Carl Danvers has a desperate need to be liked. It was my public mockery that first spurred his rage against me. At any time, I could have disarmed him with a compliment. If I could bring myself to lie.

There's nothing I admire in Danvers.

In fact, I've never admired anyone.

"I think you'll find my current project much more absorbing," I tell Danvers. And then, as if I just thought of it, I say, "Would you like to see it? It's still in progress, but it would get us out of the rain."

Danvers is suspicious at this sudden olive branch. He studies my face, which I've carefully arranged to appear casual and almost distracted—as if I'm pulled back to my studio, inviting him along as an afterthought.

I see the greedy gleam in his eye. His distrust of me—sensible and warranted—battles with this undreamed-of offer: a view of my work in progress, which I never share with anyone. Just to see inside my studio, to be able to gossip about it and maybe describe it in an article, is a temptation Danvers can't resist.

"I could come for a minute," he says gruffly.

"This way, then." I turn sharply to cross the road.

The rain thunders down, sluicing through the gutters, carrying trash and fallen leaves. I hardly have to watch for passing cars. The sidewalks are empty.

I cut through the route I've walked several times. The route with no ATMs or traffic cameras. Devoid of sidewalk restaurants or nosy homeless camped in tents.

If we were to encounter anyone along our way, I'd cut this excursion short on the spot.

But no one intervenes. That sense of rightness settles over me—the one and only time I feel a connection to anything like fate or destiny. The moment when everything aligns in favor of the kill.

I let Danvers in through the back door. The lights are low. Our footsteps echo in the cavernous space. Danvers cranes his neck, trying to peer through the gloom, not noticing as he begins to traverse an expanse of thin plastic tarp.

I take the garrote from my pocket. Silently, I unspool the wire.

"I'd like to see your machinery," he says with ill-concealed eagerness. "Is it true you do all the manufacturing yourself?"

He'd love to catch me lying.

I'm closing the space between us, descending on Danvers like a hawk from the sky. He doesn't hear my footsteps. He doesn't feel my breath on his shoulder. He doesn't notice my shadow engulfing his.

I wrap the wire around his neck and pull it taut, cutting off his breath as if I snipped it short with a pair of shears.

His panic is instant.

He scrabbles at his throat, trying to grip the wire, but the razor-fine metal has already sunk into the soft flesh of his neck. He thrashes and bucks. I take him down to the ground, pressing my knee into his back, pulling crossways on the wire in a rowing motion.

Danvers's glasses have fallen off his face. They lay a few feet to the side, staring up at me like a pair of blank eyes.

Danvers himself is facedown; I can't see his expression.

It wouldn't bother me to look into his face. I've done it before. I've watched the fear, the anguish, the suffering, all eventually sinking into dull resignation and then the utter blankness of death. Life over, snuffed out by the endless emptiness of the universe. Back into nothingness, like a spark from a campfire disappearing into the night.

I could taunt him while I kill him.

But what would be the point? In a moment he'll be gone forever. This is for me, not for him.

His struggles grow weaker, the bursts of effort further apart, a flopping, dying fish.

My pressure on his throat is as relentless as ever.

I feel no sympathy. No guilt. Those are emotions I've never experienced.

I'm aware of the full range of human emotions. I've studied them so I can mimic their effects. But they have no power over me.

What I do feel, I feel intensely: rage, revulsion, and pleasure.

Those are elemental forces inside me, like wind, ocean, and molten rock.

I have to keep tight control over them, or I'll be no better than Shaw, a slave to my impulses.

I'm not killing Danvers because I *have* to.

I'm killing him because I *want* to.

He was an irritation, an inconvenience. A worthless, sniveling, envious shit stain. He deserves nothing more than this. In fact, he should be honored because I'll make more of him than he ever could have made of himself. I'll immortalize him so his spark burns bright for a moment in time.

I hear the crack of his hyoid bone fracturing.

His body goes limp. Three minutes later, I release him.

Then the butchering begins.

While I'm working, I feel a sense of purpose. I'm stimulated, interested, flushed with satisfaction.

This is the feeling I always get when I'm creating art.

The sculpture is exquisite. My best work yet.

I show it at Oasis, where I know Shaw will likewise display his latest work.

None of the bones are recognizable as a rib, a mandible, a femur. I filed them down, dipped them in gold, and mounted them in an entirely new arrangement. Still, their linear, organic shape remains. The sculpture lives in a way it never could have had it been constructed of gilded metal or stone.

The response is immediate and ecstatic.

"My god, Cole, you've outdone yourself," Betsy breathes, staring at the sculpture like it's an idol. "What are you calling it?"

"*Fragile Ego.*"

Betsy laughs. "How uncharacteristically self-deprecating."

As usual, Betsy has completely missed the point.

I'm not referencing my own ego, which is indestructible.

Before the night is out, my sculpture has sold for $750,000 to some newly minted tech billionaire.

"Are they planning to melt it down for the gold?" Alastor says sourly.

He's never sold a piece for half that much.

"I don't think anyone's bought a piece of *my* art just to destroy it." I smirk, reminding Shaw that a fundamentalist church bought one of his paintings just to set it on fire. That was in his early days when he was a provocateur, not a salesman.

He's in no mood for mockery tonight. His face looks puffy above the too-tight collar of his dress shirt, his broad chest rising and falling a little too rapidly.

He stares at the sculpture with unconcealed envy.

Shaw has talent, I can admit that.

But I have more.

Then, amid his irritation and resentment, his entire expression changes. Understanding dawns.

"No…" he says softly. "You didn't…"

I don't have to confirm it, and I don't bother to deny it. The truth is plain for anyone who has eyes to see.

Alastor lets out a sensual sigh. "The balls on you…to put it up for display…"

Briefly, he sets aside his jealousy, and I set aside my loathing. We gaze at the sculpture, sharing a moment of deep satisfaction.

Then his impulses take over, and he can't help sneering, "It took the small words of a small man to motivate you to make great art."

Anger bubbles up inside me, thick and hot.

Unlike Shaw, I don't allow my emotions to shape my words. I carefully consider what will enrage him most.

Looking him right in the eyes, I say, "No one will ever talk about your work the way they talk about mine. It must eat you up inside every day, waking up to your own mediocrity. No matter what you do, you'll never be great. Do you want to know why?"

He's fixed in place, the sneer frozen on his lips.

"It's because you lack discipline."

Fury engulfs him, his massive body trembling like a volcano. "You're no different than me," he hisses. "You're no better."

"I am better. Because whatever I do, I'm in control."

I walk away from him so those words can echo and echo in the emptiness of his head.

2
MARA ELDRITCH

I GET UP AT AN UNGODLY HOUR SO I CAN SHOWER BEFORE ALL THE hot water is gone.

I share a moldering Victorian row house with eight other artists. The house was hacked into flats by someone with no respect for building codes and very little understanding of basic geometry. Thin plywood walls divide the rooms into triangles and trapezoids with no consideration for how a rectangular bed is supposed to fit in the space. The slanting floors and sagging ceilings add to the madhouse effect.

I occupy the tiny attic space at the very top of the house—sweltering in summer, frigid in winter. Still, it's a coveted perch because it provides access to a small private balcony. I like to drag my mattress out on cool nights to sleep under the stars. That's the closest I've ever come to camping.

My whole life has been spent in this city, often in worse houses than this.

I've never known anything but fog and ocean breeze and streets that roll up and down in dizzying hills that make your calves burn and your body lean like a tree in wind.

The pipes shudder as I turn on the shower, crammed into a space the size of a phone booth. The water that sputters out is gray at first, then relatively clear. Lukewarm, but that's better than ice-cold.

I shower quickly because other doors are already creaking and slamming as several other roommates roll out of bed. Frank's coffee is burning in the downstairs kitchen. Smells like his toast may be, too.

Artists are not known for rising early, but none of us are successful enough to avoid the shackles of a side job. I've got three.

This morning I'm working a brunch shift. Later, I'll be taking four unruly canines for a run in the park.

I slam my hip against the bathroom door to force it open again, since the steam-swollen wood is jammed into the frame. When it gives way, I almost collide with Joanna, who's heading downstairs in an oversize T-shirt, nothing underneath.

"Mara," she says, her face already screwing up in apology. "I can't sublet my studio to you anymore—my residency at La Maison is over."

"Starting when?" I ask, panic boiling in my guts.

"Next week."

"All right," I say. "Thanks for letting me know."

It is not all right. Not even fucking close to all right.

Studio space is impossible to acquire at the moment. Studio after studio has closed as the rent in San Francisco skyrockets.

When I was growing up, this was an artists' city. Clarion Alley, the New Folk, and wild, chaotic underground art burgeoned everywhere you looked.

My mother wasn't an artist per se, but she liked to fuck a lot of them. We crashed on couches and in little flats above steamy restaurants in Chinatown. Every day I saw grandiose murals, pop-up installations, and performance art on the street.

Life with my mother was chaotic and miserable, but I watched beautiful things being created all around me. It gave me hope that loveliness could bloom out of ugliness and scarcity.

Now it feels like a plug has been pulled. All the artists are draining away, fleeing to Oakland or Portland or even LA, where they can at least find commercial work.

The spaces they rented are snapped up by tech companies and

software millionaires who gut the historic buildings before filling their wood frames with gleaming glass and steel.

Logically, I know I have no right to hold on to any of it—I own nothing myself. I've barely got eighty bucks in my bank account.

But it makes me so bitter to see it all disappear right when I'm finally old enough to take part.

I dress in my work clothes, which are just cutoff jean shorts, athletic socks, and Converse sneakers. So far I've successfully avoided any job with a dress code.

I plop down at our rickety breakfast table, canvasing Frank, Heinrich, and Erin to see if anyone's heard of affordable studio space.

"Not me," Heinrich says glumly. "I'm looking myself."

Heinrich always finds studio space hard to come by because his work is based around electrical illumination. He requires torches and soldering equipment, and he's set at least one place on fire.

"You could try applying to the Minnesota Street Project," Erin says.

"Good fucking luck." Heinrich scoffs. "They've got a hundred applicants for every space."

None of this is improving my mood. I gulp down some of Frank's awful coffee, forgoing the toast in favor of fresh croissants at work. My boss, Arthur, never minds if I steal a few.

"Mara," Erin says. "You owe me twenty-eight dollars for utilities."

Internally groaning, I dig in my pocket and pull out the twenty-dollar bill I was hoping to use for groceries.

"I'll get you the other eight after work," I promise.

I've never known what it would be like to swipe a card without wondering if the balance would clear. I'm on some kind of hamster wheel where the faster I scramble to earn money, the faster the ground slips away beneath me.

On the other hand, I've never starved yet.

I run to Sweet Maple, where I show up sweating and puffing, the effects of my shower already obliterated. Arthur shoves an apron at me, saying, "Move your ass. I just sat three tables on the sidewalk."

San Franciscans' commitment to eating outdoors even in the shittiest weather will never cease to impress me. We've got heat lamps and umbrellas for the chilliest days, but I don't think anything short of a direct lightning strike would keep our diners away.

Granted, we've also got the best goddamned brunch in the city. I carry out heaping plates of asparagus omelets, crab Benedict, and our famous bacon until my arms are shaking.

Whenever I see anybody I know, I sneak them free mimosas. Arthur doesn't mind that either—he may be rude and overbearing, but he's a sweetheart to the core, and this is his way of supporting the community.

When Arthur finally lets me go, a much-needed seventy-two dollars in tips stuffed in my pocket, I'm sprinting to pick up the dogs on time.

I brought my skates in my backpack. I take the dogs all around Golden Gate Park, letting them pull me along, only working on the uphill stretches.

Bruno is being a shithead as usual, trying to tangle the leashes. I rub my knuckles across his thick skull to remind him we're friends. He's an oversize mastiff, too big for the little apartment in which he resides. I don't think his owner ever takes him out beyond our excursions.

The dogs make me happy because *they're* happy. They've got their tongues out, scenting the peppery eucalyptus in the air. I breathe it in, too, closing my eyes so I can taste it in my lungs.

I'm thinking about the piece I'm working on in Joanna's studio, wondering if I can finish it before I'm kicked out of her space. It's too big to move easily. If I could get it into the New Voices show, that would be something…

Something pretty fucking unlikely.

God, I wish I could sell something.

Erin sold a painting for eight hundred dollars last month. Covered almost all her rent. What a dream that would be.

I think about the showcase a few weeks back. Alastor Shaw won a ten-thousand-dollar prize. Now *that's* a fucking dream. I could practically live a year off that.

I wasn't there when they announced the winner—I had to leave early to hit my third job, bartending at Zam Zam.

Before I left, I saw Shaw standing by his piece—a Technicolor painting that practically seared the eyeballs. Erin whispered to me that she wanted to talk to him.

"He's so fucking hot," she murmured. "Look at that body…"

I thought he looked like he should be on the rowing crew for Yale in 1952. He had that square-jawed, sun-kissed, excessively healthy look, with just a dash of misogyny. Handsome, but not my type.

I thought Cole Blackwell should have won. His sculpture had a pale, haunting quality that captivated me, floating in space like a wraith.

Everybody knows about Blackwell and Shaw's rivalry. The art mags love writing up every little tiff between them. Both young, loaded, and fucking everything that moves, all while trying to top each other's increasingly outrageous artwork—it's a columnist's wet dream.

I've never actually seen Blackwell. Erin says he's moody and standoffish. Sometimes he skips his own shows.

We might cross paths tonight—he's supposedly showing at Oasis. Erin is dragging me along because she did indeed chat up Shaw at the last event, and she's hoping tonight will turn into something a whole lot steamier.

She'll have to get in line. As far as I can tell, taking a ride on Alastor Shaw is about as "exclusive" as his endless runs of "limited edition" prints.

———

Once I've dropped the dogs off back at their respective houses, I hurry over to Joanna's studio in Eureka Valley. There I spend the next six hours deeply immersed in my collage.

I haven't decided what medium I'll work in consistently. Sometimes I paint, and sometimes I craft objects that require immense concentration and an insane number of hours. This is not at all a profitable way to make art—you cannot spend two hundred hours on a tiny beaded teacup that no one wants to buy. But I'm addicted to the sensation of minute, repetitive, and even torturous activity.

Occasionally, I take photographs on an ancient Pentacon. I wouldn't consider that my best work—I use the camera only when I want to capture a moment in time, something that actually happened.

Not knowing what sort of artist I'll be makes me feel unformed and amateurish. As if I'm a child playing dress-up; my paint-spattered overalls become cosplay.

Other times I think about how I've poured every spare cent I ever had into raw materials and how almost all the free hours of my life have been spent on art, and then I think if that doesn't make me an artist, then nothing does.

In those moments I experience a burning righteousness that makes me hate people like Cole Blackwell despite never having met him, because he's always been rich and probably has never sacrificed a day in his life.

The Blackwells are an old San Francisco family. His ancestors probably made their money on the gold fields or, more likely, selling shovels to hapless miners. That's always where the real profit lies.

Once I've been working long enough, I no longer think about Blackwell or anybody else. I don't think about the fact that I'm about to lose this cramped but highly useful space and that I don't have enough shifts lined up to make my next rent payment.

All those buzzing thoughts melt away like wet cotton candy, and all the other sensory inputs that prick and poke at me likewise disappear. I don't hear the hum of the halogen lights or the irregular rush of traffic outside the window. I'm no longer bothered by the slice of sunshine that cuts across the room, overheating the back of my arm.

I listen to music on my headphones while sinking into the pod.

The pod is a state of perfect concentration. It's my nirvana, my state of meditative bliss. Nothing can bother me here. Nothing can upset me.

In the pod, I'm my truest self. Alone. Utterly at peace.

I'm so deeply immersed that I don't notice I'm extremely late to meet Erin until she calls my phone for the third or fourth time.

"Fuck, I'm sorry," I say, by way of greeting.

"I left without you," she informs me. "You should get over here. Cole Blackwell made this gorgeous gold sculpture. Everybody's freaking out! It sold for a boatload of cash before the show was even over."

I check my watch.

I've missed most of the show—but if I hurry, I could still make it for half an hour at least. Shows never end on time. The organizers get as tipsy as everybody else, staying for hours afterward, talking and polishing off the drinks.

My stomach growls, reminding me that all I've eaten so far today was a croissant. God, I hope I didn't miss the snacks—parties and shows subsidize half my grocery budget.

I don't have time to change clothes. Joanna keeps a couple of things stashed in the coat closet—I dig out a '90s-style crushed-velvet dress, wrinkled and smelling of turpentine.

I hop a streetcar to the gallery. The floor-to-ceiling windows illuminate the street like the whole building is one vast glowing lamp. Music bursts out the doors when anyone enters or exits.

I slip inside, immediately enveloped by the hubbub of laughter and conversation. You never feel out of place at an art event because everybody is dressed eccentrically. I'm surrounded by every type of attire, from brocade suits to raggedy jeans.

I don't have to ask Erin where to find Blackwell's piece—it glows on its plinth like a collection of celestial bodies rotating in space.

I stand in awe of this beautiful thing that hits me like an arrow shaft to the chest, filling me with a helpless sense of longing.

I wonder if I'll ever create anything this good.

After I've goggled at it for a good twenty minutes, my snarling stomach finally pulls me away.

The buffet table bears only a few scattered grape stems and a couple of cheese rinds.

"The hyenas picked it over," says a gruff male voice.

I turn around, beholding the oxen frame of Alastor Shaw, his broad face devoid of its usual smile.

I might like him better this way. I've never been a fan of people who smile too much. It feels like they're trying to force you to smile back at them.

I shrug. "That's what I get for being late."

"What's your name?" He steps closer. "I haven't seen you around before."

We've crossed paths several times, but I wouldn't expect him to remember. "Mara Eldritch."

"Alastor Shaw." He holds out his hand.

I take it, feeling his thick, calloused fingers close around mine. "Yeah." I laugh. "I know."

He grins back at me, friendly crinkles at the corners of his eyes. "Well, it never seems to get me a table anywhere good."

"It might get you a free mimosa at Sweet Maple. My boss is a big fan of yours."

"Let me guess," Alastor says wryly, "he's forty and balding?"

"Sixty and bald," I confirm.

"I'm never the favorite of the ones I'd like to impress." Alastor leans against the buffet table, and his muscular forearm makes brief contact with my hip. He hasn't broken eye contact.

"I don't believe that for a second."

"Oh, no?" Now he's leaning in all the more. "What would I have to do to—"

Erin inserts herself neatly between us, pretending not to notice Alastor, saying brightly, "There you are! I thought you weren't going to make it?" She gives me a hidden prod with her elbow.

"This is my roommate Erin," I tell Alastor.

"Right—we met at the showcase." Alastor's still smiling, but I think I see a flicker of irritation on his face.

Erin doesn't notice, probably because she's not used to men eluding her advances. Her sleepy smile and luscious body have a near-perfect record of attracting her quarry.

"You offered me a tour of your studio." Erin gazes up at Alastor from under her long lashes. "But we never exchanged numbers…"

"I've gotta pee," I say, slipping away from the pair.

I didn't need Erin's elbow to the ribs to remind me that she has dibs on Alastor. I wouldn't need it either way—I've never dated anybody famous and successful, and I'm probably not secure enough to handle it. Not that Alastor seems like he's much for dating.

For what he wants, I'm sure Erin will suffice just as well as me—probably better. I like sex, but I'm not that great at it. I'm too easily irritated. If a guy eats a slice of pizza and then tries to kiss me, if he makes a clicking sound when he swallows, if a hangnail scratches my skin, if he even fucking thinks about kissing my ears, my pussy clamps shut like a bear trap.

I wander the rest of the galleries, trying to recapture that transcendent feeling I experienced looking at Blackwell's work. Nothing else hits me quite as hard, so I circle back around to take another look at it.

The small placard reads *Fragile Ego*.

I wonder what that means. Blackwell's work is rarely self-referential.

I chat with a couple of other people I know before sneaking out the back of the gallery to take a hit off Frank's vape pen.

It's raining again, a light drizzle that barely dampens us any more than the usual fog. The droplets condense in Frank's tight curls like tiny gemstones. The smoke curls around his face with every exhale until he looks like Zeus with a beard made of clouds.

"I wish I had my camera." I laugh. "You look incredible right now."

"You're high." Frank laughs back at me. "I've looked like shit all week."

Frank's boyfriend broke up with him. He's been miserable ever since.

"You want another hit?" He holds out the vape.

"Nah."

Weed hits me hard. I can already feel that loose warmth working on my body and my sense of time. I'm no longer sure how long we've been standing out here. Only that Joanna's velvet dress is heavy with moisture.

"Some of us are gonna grab drinks at Zam Zam," Frank says. "You wanna come?"

"I've got to work early." The Sunday-morning brunch shift is insane. Arthur won't thank me if I'm late tomorrow.

"See ya, then." Frank leans back against the brick wall to take another puff.

I head off along the tree-lined street, wondering if Erin and Shaw are on their way back to his studio yet. Or straight to his apartment. I'm sure I'll hear all the gory details in the morning.

The route back to my house isn't particularly well lit.

The bodega on the corner sends out a bright beacon of light, but the thickness of the laurels, the tall row houses, and the narrow winding streets obscure the streetlamps.

I'd like to put my headphones on while I walk, but I think better of it, even though I probably look too poor for mugging.

Instead, I examine the facades of the houses I pass, the brightly painted scrollwork and well-tended window boxes giving way to chipped paint, rusted railings, and sagging steps as I draw closer to my own ramshackle house.

Gritty footsteps sound on the sidewalk, too close.

A large dark mass hurtles toward me.

I barely have time to turn before I'm struck across the back of the skull.

I wake in the trunk of a car.

I can tell it's a trunk from the vibration of the engine, the smell of gasoline, and the centrifugal lurch that presses me against the tire wheel when the vehicle takes a hard left turn.

I can't see anything because of the bag over my head.

Thick black fabric presses against my face, sucking into my nostrils with every panicked breath. I shake my head wildly, trying to fling it off, but it's cinched around my neck. Tape covers my mouth so tightly that I can't even rip my lips apart.

My arms are bound behind my back with some thin plasticky material—zip ties? My ankles are bound in the same way, my knees bent, the two points of contact wrenched together in a hog-tie, so I can't even kick.

The position is excruciating. My fingers and toes are so numb that for a moment, I'm afraid they're not even attached anymore.

I can't get enough air. The smothering hood, the sealed trunk, the tape, the gasoline fumes…I'm panting faster and faster through my nostrils, my head swimming. My stomach lurches, and I know that whatever else happens, I absolutely cannot allow myself to puke. With the tape over my mouth, I'll aspirate the vomit.

Everything in me wants to scream. I fight that urge just as hard. I don't want this motherfucker to know I'm awake.

My head is pounding. I'm sure if I could reach up and feel the back of my skull, I'd find a lump the size of a baseball.

Where is he taking me?

Who the fuck is this?

I don't bother to ask myself what he's gonna do to me. I'm already riding the thin edge of hysteria—I don't need to fill my head with visions of what this psychopath has planned.

I have to get out of the trunk. A tumble out of a moving car is the least of my worries right now.

I squirm around, feeling for the hidden latch that's supposed to be inside every trunk. My numb fingers can barely differentiate between the rough material of the lining and the metal lid.

I want to cry. I want to scream. I want to puke.

These impulses cycle over and over, each one harder to crush than the last.

The car slows, and my heart rate spikes.

No, no, no, no, no!

I don't want to get wherever we're going.

I scrabble madly for the latch, still finding nothing.

The car rolls to a gentle stop.

WHERE'S THE FUCKING LATCH?

The engine shuts off, and the driver's side door creaks open.

Too late.

Footsteps circle around to the trunk—slow and widely spaced.

Fighting every impulse within me, I lie perfectly still within the trunk. I want him to think I'm still unconscious.

It takes everything I have not to flinch as he puts his arms under my body and lifts me out.

It's only when the cold air hits my flesh that I realize I'm naked—or at least partly naked. My tits are definitely bare.

The sense of violation is almost enough to make me crack. To say nothing of the agony of being carried in this contorted position.

He walks along at that same steady, measured pace.

I can feel his heart beating against me like a creature inside his chest, pulsing, swelling. I hate the intimate feel of it thudding away, and I hate even more his sour breath against my bare flesh.

Don't puke. Don't fucking puke.

I can't tell how long he's been walking.

I'm praying he'll set me down somewhere, maybe next to a nice, convenient rock I could use to break these ties.

My plans are impossibly weak, I know that, but my befuddled brain can't seem to think of anything better. My head feels like it's split along the back, each of his steps sending another bolt of pain through my skull.

This can't be happening. It's too surreal. I can't be one of those girls raped and murdered in the woods. Nothing exceptional has ever happened to me—the irony that this could be my one claim to fame is too much to bear.

Without warning, he dumps me on the ground.

I fall like a sack of potatoes, unable to put up my hands to protect myself, chin slamming against the dirt. The air wheezes out of my lungs. I taste blood.

"I know you're awake." His voice is so flat, it almost sounds robotic. I can't tell how old he is or if there's any hint of an accent.

I can't answer him because of the tape over my mouth. I can't see him either—the hood is so thick that no light passes through. I know we're outdoors from the sound of his shoes on the rough ground and the dirt and pebbles beneath my bare skin. But I have no idea if we're still in the city or hours from civilization.

He crouches next to me, his knees popping. "Hold still."

I feel his hand on my bare right breast, and I howl against the tape, the sound smothered and trapped inside my mouth.

Red-hot pain stabs through my nipple. I'm choking and screaming, thinking he sliced it right off.

"Oh, shut the fuck up," he says. "It's not that bad."

Before I can draw breath, he roughly seizes my left breast. The same pain stabs through me, and this time I understand I'm being pierced, not severed. This motherfucker put rings through my nipples.

My tits are on fire, the cold metal fixed in place no matter how I squirm. It's so much worse that I can't see what he's done—I can only imagine.

"There," the flat voice says. "Much better."

My control is splintering away.

I'm rolling and wrenching against the ties, thrashing helplessly, howling against the tape. I'm raging, screaming, though hardly any sound leaks out. The hood is wet with tears.

He's standing there watching me, the way you'd watch a worm twitching. I can't see him, but I know it's true. There's no pity there. No hint of humanity.

I scream harder, flail harder, knowing it's all for nothing. I can't do anything to help myself.

I'm about to die, and there's nothing I can do to stop it.

My life has been a fucking disaster, but I wanted to keep it. I always believed it would get better.

I guess I was wrong.

"One more thing," the man says, turning me over on my side, his heavy hand gripping my shoulder.

"*Grahhhhhh!*" I scream against the tape.

A vicious slash burns across each arm as he slits my wrists.

3

COLE

It takes several weeks for the rumors of Carl Danvers's disappearance to begin swirling around the art world.

I'm sure the *Siren* office reported his failure to arrive at work.

Maybe the cops even visited his squalid little apartment in Pacific Heights. They won't find anything there.

I've already heard whispers that he was deeply in debt, that he was depressed, that he once made a joke about throwing himself off a bridge.

Nobody's saying the word *dead*.

That's the thing about murder: no body, no crime.

It's devilishly difficult to prove someone is dead if they simply disappear.

I've made every trace of Danvers vanish.

The last of him resides in the industrial bin I brought out to the mine today. I doused it all in bleach. Not just any bleach—highly concentrated oxygen-producing detergent. It causes hemoglobin to degrade, destroying the ability to harvest DNA.

I drop the bin down a three-hundred-feet-deep shaft, hidden inside a cave. There are forty-seven thousand abandoned mines in California, nine hundred just in the Bay Area.

I doubt my dumping ground will ever be discovered. If it is, the remains I've deposited are unlikely to be identified and impossible to link to me.

The bones within *Fragile Ego* are, of course, a different story.

Creating the sculpture was an act of uncharacteristic flagrancy. Accepting the purchase offer was even more hubristic.

There's no art without sacrifice, without risk.

The fact Danvers's bones will be displayed in the lobby of a tech firm gives me even greater pleasure than removing his irritating existence from my life.

I feel deeply peaceful as the bin disappears down the shaft.

I'm hollowed out, cleansed, ready to rest.

The night is misty and cold. I've never seen another soul within a dozen miles of this place. The bare ground looks blue and ink-soaked, like an alien planet.

Not alien to me. I know every foot of ground, which is why the bundle deposited on the path catches my attention like a flaming neon sign.

There was no bundle when I walked this way before. No cars parked anywhere along the road leading up to the trail.

My pupils dilate; my nostrils flare. I listen for the slightest sound of someone close by. Every blade of grass, every pebble, stands out in acute detail.

The only thing I see is the bundle itself.

It's not a bundle at all but a girl, contorted and bound.

I smell her coppery blood in the damp air.

I know at once who left her here: Alastor fucking Shaw.

Fury consumes me like a pyre.

How *dare* he follow me here.

He crossed a serious fucking line between us, encroaching on my ground, disrupting my process.

He'll pay for this.

The fact he left a woman behind incenses me all the more. I know exactly what he's doing.

I draw closer, expecting to find her already dead.

Instead, she hears my footsteps approaching and turns her head.

I see the silvery band of the tape over her mouth and a pair of wide eyes searching frantically before fixing on my face.

I recognize her.

It's the girl from the showcase. The one Alastor thought had sparked my interest.

She's not wearing a dress now. Alastor has her wrapped up in some ludicrous S&M outfit, all leather straps and steel grommets. He's forced her feet into too-small nine-inch heels. The leather harness encircles her breasts without covering them. Her nipples are swollen, red, pierced with silver rings.

The girl squirms against the brutal hog-tie, her back painfully arched, the bonds cutting into her swollen flesh. She's not fighting very hard anymore. The reason is plain: Alastor cut her wrists, leaving her to bleed out on the cold ground.

It's working. The earth is soaked and dark. I bet the soil would be warm to the touch if I were to lay my palm upon it.

Her struggles cast splashes of purplish blood across her blanched skin. The patterns are not unlike the ones she made on her dress with wine—pretty in the moonlight.

Her body, skinnier than what I like, looks far more sensually curved with her bare breasts thrust forward and her arms pulled back. Her vulnerability overwhelms me—a gift, wrapped in ribbon and set before me. Tender and delicate. In so much pain...

The girl makes weak pleading sounds from behind the tape.

She's begging for help...from the one person who won't give it to her.

I see the confusion in her eyes.

As I stand there watching, my hands tucked in my pockets, her confusion turns to deep disappointment. She stops struggling and lies still, her chest barely moving. Her eyes stare up at me, large and wet and devoid of hope.

I know what Alastor's trying to do.

I cut him too deep when I insulted him, when I called him

undisciplined. He's trying to humiliate me in return. Trying to prove I'm no better.

He knows his lust is a weakness. He thinks this girl will tempt me to be just as weak.

I don't kill on impulse. I prepare my location. And I never lose control.

He hopes I'll break all three rules.

I'll admit, this girl is a hundred times more appealing to me in this moment than she was at the show. She looks delicate and luminous, her flesh so tender that it would bruise at the slightest touch. Her naked limbs, twisted and bound, call out for rearrangement...

I've never killed a woman. I assumed I would at some point, but not some skinny girl, and not in some frenzy of fucking and stabbing like that ghoul Shaw.

I don't even torture my subjects like this. Meticulous preparation has always been the foreplay for me.

Now an endless flow of possibilities passes through my mind, a new door opening inside my brain.

What I could do to her...

What I could make her feel...

Blood rushes through my veins, nerves sparking to life.

For a moment Alastor's plan succeeds.

I am tempted...

Then I slam that door shut.

I'm not killing this girl.

Even if I dispatched her as cleanly as possible, it would still create a bond between Alastor and me, something I've always rejected.

I won't give Alastor what he wants. Not after he intruded on my sacred space.

He'll be punished, not rewarded.

Which leaves only two options.

I could play the hero, save the girl.

That would cause all kinds of unwanted complications. She's

seen my face, and who knows what she's seen of Shaw. She could lead the cops back here.

The other option is to simply…walk right by.

Alastor slashed her deep. The night is cold. We're miles from civilization. She'll bleed to death on the path. Then it's up to Alastor to pick up his own trash.

I don't like the loose ends. If someone finds her body, if the police come poking around, we're only a mile from my dumping ground.

But the mine is well hidden, not marked on any map.

The only way to win this particular game is to refuse to play. That's what will enrage Shaw the most.

I take one last glance at the girl's beautifully tortured body…

Then I step over her and carry on my way.

4

MARA

I LIE ON THE GROUND, MY ENTIRE BODY THROBBING. SOME OF THE hurts flare up—my jaw is particularly painful from its collision with the ground. The rest of me feels so heavy that I might as well be trapped inside a cement suit. I'm weighed down, compressed. For the first time, I understand why it might be a relief to allow the soul to slip from the body. Pain overrides my fear.

I know I'm bleeding from my wrists, but I can hardly feel it, and that scares me worse than anything.

I'm getting colder and colder.

Footsteps come up the path. I stiffen, thinking this fucking psychopath has returned. He pretended to leave just to fuck with me.

There's something different in the stride.

The man who brought me here walked heavily. These steps are so light, so subtle, that for a moment I think I'm imagining them. Hope flutters in my chest, praying it's someone else, maybe even a woman…

I turn my head.

Death himself has come to claim me.

Death is tall and slim and wears a black suit, stark against the pale flesh of his throat and hands. His hair, darker than the night around us, frames the most beautiful face I've ever seen.

An artist is always looking at ratios and proportions.

His almond-shaped eyes, the straight slashes of his brows, the line of his nose, the high cheekbones and razor-fine jaw, all relieved by the flawless curve of his lips—I've never seen such perfect balance.

It's so surreal, I think I must be hallucinating.

Especially once he stops and stands over me.

I've never seen such coldness on a human face.

His eyes roam over my naked body, taking in every detail. The rest of his features are motionless, without a flicker of sympathy.

Still, the most desperate part of me, the part that refuses to believe what's happening, makes me whimper behind the tape, begging for mercy, pleading for him to help.

He doesn't move. Doesn't blink. Just stands and stares, his hands in his pockets.

I'm so fucking confused.

Is this the man who kidnapped me?

He doesn't feel like the same one.

But if this is someone else, why doesn't he help me?

I scream behind the tape, my throat raw, the sound echoing in my mouth.

I glare up at him, bewildered, furious.

He looks at me like his eyes are nothing but holes in his head.

Then he steps over me like I'm a loose bag of trash lying in the road. And he walks the fuck away.

I howl after him, strangled, enraged.

This is the moment I almost give up.

My brain can't understand what's happening, and my body is exhausted, draining out on the frigid ground.

I'm so fucking tired.

My eyelids are lead, my thoughts swirling and breaking apart like punctured yolk.

♫ *"Smells Like Teen Spirit"—Malia J*

I shake my head hard, jolting myself awake with the pain in my jaw. I'm not fucking dying here.

I can't feel my hands anymore, but I know they're covered in blood.

Blood is slippery. Almost as slippery as oil.

I start twisting my wrists, tugging and pulling, trying to slip my hands free of the plastic ties.

The slashes on my wrist fire up in agony, raw and burning. I start bleeding harder, which is both good and very, very bad.

My head is swimming; I'm getting weaker by the moment. But on the plus side, I can feel the warmth on my hands, and I can feel my right wrist turning, the joint of the thumb compressing as my hand begins to slip free.

I yank ruthlessly, my shoulder screaming—my thumb, too.

I've always been skinny. My bones are like chopsticks, and my hand is barely bigger than my wrist. I twist and wrench. Slowly, agonizingly, the right hand pulls free.

I sob with relief behind the tape.

Now I can use my right hand to help with the left.

This tie is tighter. It takes even longer than the first—so much yanking and digging with numb fingers that I'm crying long before it's done.

The relief of pulling both hands loose, of straightening my back from its horrible arched position, is nearly overwhelming. The little blood I have left rushes down through my arms, and my hands ignite as sharp electric pulses jolt through my fingertips.

I pull the tape off my face before gasping the crisp night air, cold as water in my mouth.

I want to scream with all my might, but I try to shut the fuck up instead. My abductor could still be close. He could be watching me right now.

Wildly, I look everywhere at once, expecting to see that massive frame hurtling toward me once more.

All I see is bare ground and the trees behind me.

I need to get my feet free.

I yank off the stupid stripper shoes, then search for a rock with a sharp edge. I try to hack the ties around my ankles, but the rock is slippery in my hand. I only succeed in hitting my shin, taking out a chunk of flesh.

Gritting my teeth, I retrieve the hateful duct tape and use it to wrap my left wrist, which is bleeding hardest.

Fuck. I don't know how much time I have left. My vision tilts every time I move my head.

I wipe my palms off on my bare thighs, leaving streaks of dirt and blood. Gripping the rock, I saw through the ties, then try to stand.

My legs have turned to putty. I collapse hard to the ground, an agony of sparks shooting up and down my limbs.

Sobbing quietly, I massage the life back into my legs.

I'm not dying here. I'm not fucking doing it.

When I can feel my feet a little, I push myself up. Wobbling like a newborn giraffe, I manage to stand.

Then I start to run.

I'm stumbling and lurching, rocks cutting the swollen soles of my feet. The ground pitches like the deck of a ship.

Each step jolts my body, slams my jaw, and rattles my brain around inside my skull. Blood patters down from my right wrist. I clamp my filthy hand over the wound as I run.

I don't know how far I'll have to go.

A cold voice in my head whispers, *If it's more than a mile, you won't make it. You might not make it another hundred feet. You're going to pass out any second.*

"Shut the fuck up," I mutter out loud. "I'll run all night if I have to."

Rationally, I know that's impossible. I'm literally at death's door. Black spots bloom in front of my eyes, disappearing only when I press hard on my wrist. The pain jolts me awake over and over.

Twice I fall, and the second time, I almost don't get up. The ground feels soft and pillowy; my jaw no longer aches. A warm drowsiness descends on me like a blanket, whispering, *Stay here and rest a while. You can get up again after you sleep.*

Sleeping means dying. That's the one thing I know for certain.

Sobbing, I force myself up again.

I've gotten turned around in the fall. I'm not sure which direction is forward and which is the way I came.

I take two steps, reeling and confused, almost missing a dark splotch on the side of the path. Blood. My blood. I left a trail like Hansel and Gretel, marking the way I came. Only I have no intention of following it back.

Giggling hysterically, I turn around and run in the opposite direction.

This time, the voice that speaks to me is crystal clear on the night air, as alive as if she were speaking directly into my ear:

I told you this would happen.

I stop and vomit next to the path. I don't have much in my stomach—what comes out is thin and yellowish, burning like acid.

My mother often has that effect on me.

You go out dressed like that, what did you think was going to happen?

I slap myself in the face hard enough to make my ears ring. "Seriously," I mutter. "Fuck off."

There's a pleasant interlude in which I hear only my own ragged breath and the breeze rustling the trees.

Then, in that sickly-soft tone, always so reasonable even as the words coming out of her mouth are the very definition of insanity, she says, *It's probably for the best. It was only a matter of time for a girl like you...*

"*Fuck off!*" I roar, startling a bird so much, it rockets up out of an aspen tree before disappearing into the dark sky, flapping like a bat.

My heart batters painfully against my chest. The beats are

unsteady—three hard clenches, then none at all while I gasp and reel in place.

The black spots are everywhere now. They don't disappear while I blink.

She's right—I dress like a whore. I'm not that smart. I'm not that talented. I don't take care of myself. I probably *will* come to a bad end.

But there's something else my mother always said about me:

I'm a stubborn motherfucker.

And I don't take advice from anybody, least of all her.

For the last time, I start to run. The next sound I hear is faint but unmistakable: a swift rushing that swells and recedes at sixty miles an hour. A car on the road ahead.

The path widens, sloping downward. I can no longer feel anything beneath my feet. I can barely tell when the path connects with an actual highway.

I come out on the smooth black tarmac, striped down the middle with a single yellow line.

I stand on that line, watching for headlights coming from either direction.

I'm panting and reeling, my heart skipping every second beat. The pressure on my chest increases as black dots expand across my vision.

A white light rushes toward me, gradually separating into two headlights.

I stand right in front of the car, waving my arms, praying to god it stops before it hits me.

5
COLE

I watch the local headlines for several weeks, waiting for news of a girl's body found in the woods or any further developments with Carl Danvers.

He's got no family locally, and a vast amount of police effort is driven by nagging. The cops are spread thin from the protests breaking out all over the city. Without any invested parties prodding for an answer, it appears the members of SFPD are happy to let the file on some minor art critic's disappearance languish at the bottom of the pile.

Getting away with murder is pretty fucking easy.

Only 63 percent of homicides are solved under the best of circumstances—and that includes the cases where the idiot criminal is literally holding the smoking gun. There are precious few genius detectives, despite what network television would have you believe.

I've killed fourteen people, and I've yet to receive a single knock on my door.

A pretty, young girl is a different story—the media loves to sensationalize Alastor's work. They call him the Beast of the Bay for the way he batters his victims and even bites chunks out of their flesh.

He draws too much attention to himself.

If the girl were found, her case would be linked to the seven he's killed over the past three years. He leaves them out in the open, proclaiming what he's done.

I don't like loose ends.

I hope he cleaned up his mess.

He probably didn't, that reckless piece of shit.

I'm not going back to check. I won't go anywhere near the mine in the foreseeable future or possibly ever again. That's what angers me most—the loss of a convenient disposal location that took me a long time to find.

Shaw has successfully thrown a wrench in my process.

I ponder how best to deal with him.

I could just fucking kill him.

He's been a thorn in my side for too long. He knows too much about me, and his careless behavior puts us both at risk.

But Shaw is no oblivious art critic, easily lured and easily disposed of. He's a predator, already on his guard because he'll be expecting retaliation.

Killing within my personal circle is always risky. Even Alastor isn't stupid enough to hunt within the art world. He never slaughters women he's dated publicly.

Our supposed rivalry is so well publicized that Alastor's disappearance would cast a spotlight in my direction, drawing unwanted parallels to Danvers.

I decide to break into Shaw's apartment instead.

He invaded my space—I return the favor by visiting his penthouse on Balboa Street.

I disable his security system, but as soon as I enter his living room, I spot the camera hidden in the face of his clock, doubtless sending a motion alert to his phone, along with footage of me strolling around his space, insolently picking up his tchotchkes and flipping through his books.

I manhandle his belongings before setting them down in different places, knowing it will enrage him.

The penthouse is luxurious in precisely the way I'd expect from Alastor.

The floor-to-ceiling windows offer a postcard view of the Golden Gate Bridge and the flat dark water of the bay.

The walls are hung with massive prints of Alastor's own art. The canvases pop in eye-searing shades of fuchsia, canary, and violet. Shaw can't keep the originals because he has to sell them to pay for his toys.

He's the son of a teacher and a plumber, something he proudly touts in interviews when he's pretending to be the salt of the earth. In truth, he hates that he was ever middle class. He's acutely sensitive to the cars he drives, the watches he wears, and the restaurants he frequents, in case he betrays himself.

His designer furniture is cartoonishly exaggerated—serpentine Wiggle chairs and a Magistretti lamp that looks like a chrome mushroom. His couch is a giant scarlet gummy bear.

A gleaming Harley parks against the far wall, an electric guitar set in a stand next to the bike.

I highly fucking doubt Shaw plays the guitar.

Everything is a performance with him. Everything is for show.

This apartment screams "eccentric artist" because that's how he'd love to be perceived.

I open a bottle of merlot and pour myself a glass.

Twenty minutes later, a key scratches in the lock.

Shaw's heavy tread crosses the open space between the kitchen and the living room.

I'm sitting at the head of his dining table, sipping his wine.

"Hello, Cole," he says.

He's very angry, though he's trying not to show it. The tightness of his lips makes them white all around the edges, while his face is sunburn red.

"Hello, Shaw. Have a drink." I pour him a glass of his own wine.

His hand twitches as he takes it.

It's been years since we were alone in a room together. Not since school.

"This is cozy," Alastor says.

"I was admiring your view. My house is just over there…"

I nod toward my own mansion, perched on the ridge directly above the bay, clearly visible from the living room window. In fact, it cuts off the lower-left corner of Alastor's view.

"I know." I'm surprised he can get the words out with how tightly his teeth are clenched.

I take another sip of the wine, which is thick and plummy.

Shaw does the same, the glass dwarfed by his overlarge hand. His bull-like shoulders hunch almost up to his ears. His biceps bulge as he raises his arm.

I'm sure he's making the same calculation—his strength against my speed. His brutality against my cunning. I see no clear winner—a dilemma that intrigues us both.

Alastor relaxes, his smile widening, tiny threads of wine between his teeth. "How did you enjoy my gift?"

"I didn't."

Shaw frowns, disappointed. "What a waste. I thought you'd do something with those tits at least—so much better than I expected, once I got them out. You never know what you'll find…flat as a board under a push-up bra or a pussy that looks like a handful of roast beef." He laughs crudely. "Sometimes, though…sometimes it's better than you hoped. Sometimes it's near perfect…"

"Not my type," I repeat dismissively.

His face darkens. "The fuck she wasn't. You did something with her before you tossed her down the shaft."

I hesitate a fraction of a second, puzzled by Shaw's words.

I didn't put the girl down the mine shaft. I didn't move her at all. But Shaw seems certain I did.

Mistaking my pause, Shaw chuckles. "I knew it. Tell me what you did to her."

I rise from the table, setting down my glass.

Shaw is ravenous for details, darting his tongue out to moisten his lips. "Did she fight? She looked like the type to fight."

"What was her name?" I ask him, "Do you know?"

Now he's grinning, flushed with triumph. He really thinks he got me. "Mara Eldritch." He walks around the kitchen island to rummage in a drawer. After pulling out a small plastic card, he tosses it across the island so it slides on the polished marble before stopping right at the edge. "I fucked her roommate in the stairwell. Stole her ID out of her wallet."

I pick up the driver's license of a voluptuous redhead with heavy-lidded eyes and a languorous smile. Erin Wahlstrom, 468 Frederick Street.

"I didn't touch her," Shaw says, his voice husky. "I left her fresh for you. As fresh as you can find one these days, when they'll suck and fuck anything that walks. You don't even have to buy them dinner anymore."

His upper lip curls in disgust, both at the promiscuity of women and the loss of the challenge when hunting becomes too easy.

"Please don't tell me you're into *virgins*." I scoff. He really is so fucking cliché.

"Nah." Shaw laughs. "I just don't want to get crabs."

I set the license back on the counter with a soft clicking sound.

I'm not interested in this confrontation with Shaw anymore. A much more pressing concern demands my attention.

I head toward the door.

"I pierced her," Alastor says.

My hand is on the doorknob.

"Made her pretty for you…"

I turn slowly.

Those silver rings through Mara's tight little nipples were fucking beautiful. Far lovelier than anything Alastor's made before.

But his happiness displeases me.

"You know, Alastor," I say. "The way you talk about these women…that's exactly the way I feel about you. You disgust me. Just standing in this apartment makes me feel like I'll catch herpes from the aesthetic."

The smile drops off his face, leaving a vacant absence in its place.

It's not quite enough.

Looking him dead in the eye, I make a promise:

"If we're ever alone in a room again, only one of us will walk out breathing."

The next morning I watch the front door of Erin Wahlstrom's house. So much paint has peeled off the sagging row house that it's difficult to tell if it was originally blue or gray. An obscene number of people seem to live inside, as evidenced by the lights that flick on as the residents haul themselves out of bed one by one. Instead of blinds, half the windows are covered by sheets or, in one case, by a square of aluminum foil.

After a short interval, these residents begin exiting down the steep front steps, some wearing backpacks or shoulder bags, one trundling an oversize portfolio under his arm.

I see the voluptuous redhead, owner of the missing driver's license. She shouts something back inside the house before hurrying down the steps, heading in the direction of the bus stop.

Then, when I think that must be all of them, the door opens once more.

Mara Eldritch steps onto the landing.

I'm seeing a ghost.

She was dying, almost dead. Bleeding out on the ground.

But there's no mistaking the willowy frame, the long dark hair, the wide-set eyes. She's wearing a heavy knit sweater that hangs down over her hands, covering any bandages that might remain on her arms. Beneath the sweater, she wears a ragged pair of jeans and filthy, battered sneakers.

Did someone help her?

It seems impossible, in the middle of the night, in the middle of nowhere.

How did she do it, then?

It was three miles to the nearest road. She couldn't take three steps.

I don't like mysteries, and I definitely don't like surprises. I watch her descend the stairs with a deep sense of unease.

I follow her down Frederick Street, keeping plenty of space between us.

The wind blows in her face, making her hair dance around her shoulders, sending dry leaves tumbling against her legs. When the same air reaches me, I smell her perfume, the low, warm scent mixing with the dusty sweetness of the decaying leaves.

She's covered head to toe in the baggy jeans and sweatshirt, giving no hint of how appealing she looked naked and bound. I wish I took a picture on my phone. Already the details are losing their crispness in my mind. I'm struggling to recall the exact shape and color of her nipples and the curve of her hips.

How is she alive?

Alastor doesn't know.

She must not have seen his face, or he'd be sitting in a cell right now.

She *did* see *my* face; I know that for certain. Either she forgot it in her delirium, or she doesn't know who I am.

Which is it?

I was so certain she was dead.

I hate being wrong.

I hate it all the more for how rarely it happens.

My anger flares at the girl.

This is her fault. Her fault for defying the fate rushing toward her.

We've come to a café. She enters the building and reemerges

with an apron cinched around her waist, her hair pulled up in a ponytail. She immediately goes about the business of serving the guests at the outdoor tables.

I take a seat at a different café across the street, lingering over my coffee and toast so I can watch her.

She's quick and efficient and seems to know most of the patrons. In lulls between service, she pauses to talk with the ones she knows best. She shakes her head and laughs, the sound drifting over the traffic between us.

It baffles me that she's back at work. That she's chatting and laughing.

She's acting like nothing happened. Like the night in the woods was a fever dream. Like she knows I'm watching right now and is taunting me.

That can't be true.

But I'm fixated on her, trying to find evidence of what the fuck happened.

6

MARA

I woke up strapped to a bed in a hospital in Hollister.

The nurse informed me that I'd been given four units of blood and that she couldn't unlock the restraints for twenty-four hours because that was hospital policy after a suicide attempt.

I was exhausted and drugged. It took much longer than twenty-four hours before I finally had a cop in front of me taking down a statement.

I could tell from the start, he didn't believe a word I said. The nurses showed him the outfit I was wearing when I came in. He couldn't seem to grasp the concept that it wasn't something I ordered off Amazon.

"I know you kids get into some kinky shit." His notebook was open on his knee, not a thing written inside it. "What happened? The guy took it too far?"

"Well, he tried to murder me," I snapped. "So, yeah, that was a bit far for my tastes."

The officer stared at me impassively, the pouches under his eyes deep enough to store handfuls of loose change.

"You're saying he did that?" He nodded toward my bandaged wrists.

It took forty-nine stitches to close the gashes.

"Yes," I hissed.

"What about those?" He pointed his pen to the other scars farther up my arm, above the bandages. Thin white slashes, a dozen in a row. "He do those, too?"

I was boiling with rage, incandescent with it. I wanted to rip that pen out of his hand and jam it through his iris.

"No," I said, through gritted teeth. "He didn't do those."

"Uh-huh," Officer Fuckhead said. This time he did scribble something down, and in that moment, I hated him almost more than the man who put me in the hospital bed.

"So where did you meet this guy? Tinder?"

"*I didn't fucking meet him!*" I screamed. "*He kidnapped me off the street!*"

The fact that I never saw his face, that I couldn't describe anything about him, also sounded like bullshit. I thought he might be tall. Strong enough to lift and carry me.

When he removed the hood over my head—when I squirmed and struggled and finally rolled over—he was already gone.

I told Officer Fuckhead the full and complete truth up to that point. But I didn't tell him what happened next.

I said nothing about the figure who came and stood over me—the one with the face of an angel and the eyes of a black hole.

I was afraid it would only make me sound more insane.

I wasn't sure if it was the same person who kidnapped me. Certain details didn't match, though it was so muddled in my head, it was hard to be sure.

Truth be told, I wasn't sure he existed at all. The way he watched me so long with that strange, cold curiosity. The way he finally stepped over me and walked away, as if he'd seen all he needed to see—it didn't make any sense.

I'd already lost so much blood. I heard my mother talking in my ear, for fuck's sake.

It didn't help that the college student who picked me up was drunk. I scared him half out of his mind, appearing in the middle of the road like an apparition out of a horror film. He swerved and almost ran off the road, the car doing a full 360 before it stopped.

I hobbled over and wrenched his passenger door open before collapsing into the front seat. He could barely look at me as I bled all over his parents' Accord—not that I was in a state to care.

After a brief and mumbled explanation to the emergency room nurses, he sped away. By the time the cops tracked him down, all he could tell them was that he picked me up somewhere off the 101.

It was inconceivable to me that the state of my body—the deep marks on my wrists and ankles, the cuts all over my feet, the slashes down my arms—weren't enough evidence.

"*He pierced my fucking nipples!*" I howled at the cop.

Officer Fuckhead sucked on his teeth, a sound that enrages me. Then he wrote a single word in his notepad that probably said *liar*.

At least Erin was worried about me.

"Where the fuck have you been?" she cries when I stumble through the door four days later. "I called your phone like a million times!"

"I don't have a phone anymore," I mumble, remembering that's another thing I'm going to have to replace.

I give her a brief and emotionless description of what occurred, again omitting any mention of a second psychopath.

"You can't be serious." Erin's pretty face crumples, her hands at her mouth.

I know she's feeling guilty that she didn't call the cops herself. I don't blame her for that—it wouldn't be the first time one of our roommates disappeared on a four-day bender.

"Yeah, it's insane," I agree. "Don't know if I should buy a lottery ticket or watch out for lightning strikes."

"Are you okay?" Erin winces like she knows how stupid a question that is.

"Yeah." I carefully avoid looking at the bandages around my wrists. "I'm fine."

I'm not fine, but I learned a long time ago that the only options are to fake it or succumb to a complete breakdown.

To change the subject, I say, "What about you? How did things go with Shaw?"

"You don't want to hear about that." Erin blushes.

"I really do. A lot more than I want to talk about my night."

"Well," she says, trying to hide her grin, "we hooked up in the stairwell."

"You did?"

I'm not really surprised. Erin is gorgeous and Shaw gets around. It was only a matter of time until she punched her ticket.

"It didn't last long, but it was pretty fucking hot." She giggles.

"Great. Good for you."

The words come out dull and emotionless. I'm trying to pretend like nothing happened, but it's fucking with my head being back inside the madhouse walls of the town house with the scent of Frank's burnt coffee and Joanna's oil paints. She has the only room in the house big enough for a bed and an easel.

"So…you wanna go for a drink?" Erin says kindly. "You look like you could use one."

We go to our usual place on Belvedere Street. When we ascend to the rooftop bar, Erin hunts through her purse, swearing softly.

"Oh, fuck. I lost my ID again."

"You probably left it at Zam Zam," I say. "Don't worry about it. Manny's bartending; he won't card you."

The rooftop bar is stuffed with hanging plants and fairy lights and so many people that we can't get a seat and have to stand by the bar. Erin buys the drinks because I'm beyond broke—no purse or cellphone, and god knows what kind of hospital bill coming my way.

"Thanks." I gratefully sip the mule she thrust into my hand. "So, you gonna see him again?"

"Who?" She's scanning the crowd for anyone else we might know.

"Shaw."

"Oh, I dunno." Erin shrugs. "I gave him my number, but he hasn't texted."

I chug my drink before pressing the cool glass against my cheek. "I'm sure we'll bump into him again."

For several weeks I can't sleep outside on the deck.

It's stifling inside my attic room, but dragging my mattress out into the night air makes me feel horribly exposed. Every buzz of an insect, every distant honk of a car, makes me jerk upright, staring wildly around in the dark.

I go back inside, still jolting every time the walls creak or one of my roommates laughs too loud.

When I finally fall asleep, I wake screaming because the room is too dark and I think I'm back in the trunk.

Every dream is a nightmare where a low voice scoffs, *I know you're awake.*

That dark figure rushes at me over and over. I try to fight him off, kicking and punching, but my hands are too weak, fragile as wet paper.

Only once do I catch hold of him, tearing at the mask over his face.

I pull it away, expecting to see those awful, beautiful features once more.

Instead, I see nothing at all: just blank, empty space, into which I fall, tumbling down, down, down…

After a while, it gets better.

I still have nightmares, but in the day, I can smile and carry a conversation. Well enough that people stop asking me if I'm okay.

I go back to work at Sweet Maple.

My boss at Zam Zam fired me for missing three shifts. He hires me back after Erin marches over there and bawls him out, telling him she'll never stop leaving one-star Yelp reviews.

Joanna offers to cover the rent for me as long as I promise to pay her back. That makes me want to cry all over again. I keep the tears behind my eyes, hot and burning, while I hug her hard.

The bandages come off my wrists. The two raised scars, thick and meandering as twin snakes, are pretty fucking ugly. But as Officer Fuckhead pointed out, they're not the only ones I've got.

I'm probably recovering faster than most people.

I'm used to getting over things that really fucking suck.

7

COLE

I take my stalking of Mara online.

Like most people, she's splashed her life all over social media for anyone to see—both on her own accounts and her friends'.

They're an artsy bunch, so the photos they share are more eclectic than average. I have to wade through a number of sepia-toned popcorn machines, pictures of people's feet, and landscape shots to find something useful. Once I do, I find endless portraits of Mara.

Like most struggling artists, Mara's friends have to use their acquaintances as models.

Despite not being as sexy as her roommate Erin, Mara is popular for this purpose because she has that stark bone structure that captures well on film.

Her grungy, neglected air and those sharp, elfin features give her the look of a female Peter Pan, a wild thing left to fend for itself.

I spend a long time examining her face.

The foggy eyes tilted upward at the outer corners. The upturned nose spattered with freckles. The full lips and sharp teeth.

She's a conundrum. Vulnerable yet fierce. Damaged yet stubborn.

Mara doesn't make personal posts—no long, rambling dissertations on her inner feelings under a mirror selfie, no vague captions intended to elicit a flood of comments begging for more details.

She makes no mention of her ordeal in the woods.

Her only recent posts are requests for studio space.

This is a constant problem in San Francisco for those at the mercy of fickle landlords. I own my private studio close to my house as well as a block of studios on Clay Street.

I'm considering offering one to Mara Eldritch. It would make stalking her much more convenient. And I'd see her work up close.

I've already decided Mara and I will inevitably cross paths—the art world is too small to avoid it.

I intend to choose the time and location of that meeting. I'll control the setting and arrange the players like pieces on a chessboard.

It's unlike me to fixate on a woman like this.

I find most people horrifically boring. I've never met anyone as intelligent as me or as talented. Most people are weak and emotional—slaves to their impulses. Constantly making promises they can't keep, even to themselves.

Only I seem to have the power to control my fate.

I can make anything happen if I'm willing to invest the time.

Everyone else is wrapped in chains. Chains they don't even notice, or worse, chains they wear gladly, by choice—chains of laws, religions, social conventions…

I do what I want.

I get what I want.

If there's a god of this world, it's me.

But even Zeus found mortals interesting from time to time.

I want to see Mara again, to speak to her. I want to manipulate her and see how she reacts.

And if I want something…that means it's good.

On a Wednesday afternoon, I break into Mara's room.

She's walking a half dozen dogs in Golden Gate Park, something that usually takes her several hours with the pickup and drop-off process.

It's almost impossible to find a point in the day where none of her roommates are home, so I don't bother waiting. The house is so crowded, with so many people coming and going, I doubt any of them will notice a few extra creaks from a room that ought to be empty.

It helps that Mara's room is on the topmost floor. It's easy to scale the trellis of the neighboring house, drop onto her deck, and force open the flimsy lock on the glass door.

The attic room is certainly not up to code. The ceiling is so low that I can't stand upright, even in the center of the peaked space. Mara's bed is a futon on the floor, her clothes folded in plastic milk crates because she has no closet or dresser.

This is the sort of cramped, chaotic space that usually disgusts me. The dusty air and stacks of battered secondhand books next to the bed—no bookshelf to hold them—reek of poverty.

Curiosity staves off my repulsion. I'm drawn to the hundreds of sketches taped all over the sloped walls.

Most of the drawings are figure studies. Mara has a good sense of proportion, and she's skilled at indicating the direction of the light. Perhaps because most of the subjects are her friends, she's caught a strong sense of personality in their positions, in the expression of their faces. The tall Black girl, Joanna, looks awkward but pleased at being drawn. The boy with frizzy curls is holding back a smirk.

With no place to sit, I sink onto Mara's pathetic mattress. The bed is unmade, her blanket a crumpled pile.

I flip through several of her books. *Naked Lunch*, *The Virgin Suicides*, *Life After Life*, *Troubled Blood*, *Black Swan Green*, *Lolita*, *Cold Spring Harbor*, *Winter's Bone*, *The Cement Garden*...

Butterflied next to the bed is *Dracula*. I pick it up, seeing she's drawn all over the pages, marking passages and writing notes.

She's underlined:

Even if she be not harmed, her heart may fail her in so much
and so many horrors; and hereafter she may suffer—both in
waking, from her nerves, and in sleep, from her dreams..."

I smile to myself.

Poor little Mara isn't impervious to nightmares, whatever she
may pretend during the daylight hours.

I pick up the next novel on the stack, *Prometheus Illbound*, and
let it fall open to a dog-eared page. Here she's marked:

I do not love men: I love what devours them.

That actually makes me laugh. I haven't laughed in some time.

I set the books down.

I can smell Mara's perfume on her sheets, stronger than when I
followed her. I lie in her bed, my head on her pillow. I turn my face
so my nose is pressed against her crumpled sheets and inhale.

Her scent is layered and complex. Warm notes of vanilla,
caramel. A botanical scent—mandarin or black currant. Then
something exotic, spiced—maybe a jasmine soap. Under that, the
light scent of her sweat, which arouses me far more than any of the
others. My cock swells until it's no longer comfortable within my
trousers.

I enjoy the trespass of lying in her bed. Knowing she may catch
a hint of my cologne lingering there tonight. Will it frighten her?
Or will it arouse her, if my chemical composition calls to her, as hers
is doing to me?

The idea of Mara's heart beating fast, startling her awake as she
searches her room for a ghost long gone, amuses me.

Deliberately, I rearrange the order of the books next to the bed.

Then I hunt through her clothes.

She wears cheap nylon underwear, thin and transparent, in
shades of black, gray, and taupe.

Most of her clothes are dirty, stuffed in a drawstring bag to be hauled down to the laundromat.

A single pair of black briefs lies abandoned next to the bed. I assume this is the underwear she shucked off this morning.

Lifting her panties to my face, I inhale the scent of her warm morning pussy.

It smells like her sheets but muskier.

My cock is raging now. I unzip my pants, allowing it to spring free. I stroke it gently while I breathe in the scent of Mara's cunt. I even put out my tongue and taste the cotton strip that nestled between her pussy lips.

I picture her lying on the ground, tightly bound, her arms behind her back and her breasts thrust forward. Her knees were pulled back, her bare pussy exposed. I could have shoved my cock in her. That's what Alastor expected me to do.

If I had smelled this scent, I would have done it.

I've never experienced anything like it. It's addicting. The longer I spend in this room with her sheets, her half-empty perfume bottle, her dirty laundry, the more it fills my lungs, surging through my blood.

I want more. Fresh from the source.

I jerk my cock harder, taking deep breaths of the dirty panties draped over my face.

I imagine her tied down, this time on her back with her legs pulled apart. I imagine burying my face in her cunt, thrusting my tongue all the way inside her while she thrashes against the ropes.

My balls are boiling, my cock throbbing with each stroke.

I wrap the panties around the head of my cock and thrust into them, right against the crotch. My cock erupts, pouring come into Mara's underwear.

I use her panties to catch every last drop, squeezing them around the head.

That skimpy black fabric feels better around my cock than any actual pussy I've ever fucked. Maybe it's the novelty, or maybe it's the way her scent still clings to my fingers, lingering in my lungs. I fucking exploded.

It's not enough. The orgasm was rapid, powerful as a rifle shot. I'm not satisfied.

I want to watch Mara in this space. I want to see how she walks around her room, how she undresses, how she behaves when she thinks she's alone.

I look out her window.

The adjoining row houses offer no line of sight into Mara's room. But the house behind hers—the tall Georgian with the black shutters—offers a perfect view from its own attic space.

Mara has no curtains on her windows. She's so high up, she feels as safe as a crow in its nest.

Crows forget about hawks.

I drop the panties back on the floor where I found them.

Then I leave the way I came, already dialing my estate agent.

8

MARA

BY THE TIME I GET HOME FROM WALKING THE DOGS, I'M LATE FOR a date with Josh.

We've been seeing each other on and off for a couple of months. He's a photographer who likes to take pictures of repurposed buildings. Really, he makes most of his money shooting weddings.

He's good-looking, decent at sex, and better at conversation, though he has a tendency to get preachy. He's judgmental as fuck about me bartending at Zam Zam because he says the regulars are alcoholics and I'm fueling their addiction. Never mind that I met *him* at Zam Zam.

Much like Erin, Josh didn't notice when I disappeared for four days. We only meet up once every week or two, both of us busy with work and side projects.

I haven't fucked him since the incident. I haven't fucked anybody since then, and I'm not sure how I'll react when I do.

Even though that maniac didn't rape me, I feel violated. There's no way to compare trauma, and I don't want to try. But the terror I felt, and the physical pain, can't be that far off.

Sometimes I just want to forget the whole thing.

Other days I'm filled with deep, roiling rage. I want to find that motherfucker. And I want to cut little pieces off him until I start to feel better.

That isn't going to happen.

It's pretty fucking clear the cops aren't doing shit because they don't believe what I told them. My story sounds crazy. Even if they cared, there are no witnesses and no evidence.

I'm not a good witness. I didn't see anything useful—not one goddamned number off a license plate. Where would I even start looking?

Besides…I don't believe in revenge.

This isn't the first time in my life somebody hurt me. Holding on to the anger, stewing in the rage, will only boil me alive from the inside.

What could I do, anyway? I'm five-five, 112 pounds. I've never punched anyone in my life. Even with a Taser and a pile of duct tape, I'd have a hard time subduing a fully grown male. I have no illusions about my ability to fight, to hurt, to kill.

It's hard to let go, but that's what I'm trying to do. I'm trying to tell myself that I'm alive, I'm healing. As long as I'm still breathing, I can keep moving forward. Everything can be overcome except death.

Even if I could find that asshole, all I'd do is get myself killed.

I hurry into the house, knowing how much Josh hates that I'm never on time.

Joanna passes me on the stairs, likewise hurrying to a date, though hers is with her long-term boyfriend, Paul.

"You look gorgeous!" I tell her.

"You too!" she lies.

I laugh. "Don't worry, I'm about to change."

I strip off my clothes, sweaty from skating around the park with the dogs. Though we're well into a cloudy October, it was close to eighty degrees, muggy and humid.

I consider rinsing off in the shower, but I don't really have time. Instead, I pull a black minidress out of the closet.

The glint of silver on my chest catches my eye. I pause for a moment, looking down at my naked body.

I never removed the piercings.

Maybe I should because every time I see them, I remember the blinding, burning pain of that psychopath shoving a needle through my nipple.

But they also remind me that I ran down that fucking mountain, naked and half dead.

I stole these silver rings from him. He thought they'd adorn my corpse.

Well, I'm still fucking here. And they look good on me.

Shimmying into the dress, I hunt for some clean underwear. It's been two weeks since I hauled my clothes down to the laundromat, so I'm in short supply.

Desperate and late, I snatch up the panties on the floor.

Wetness presses against my pussy lips.

"*What the fuck...*" Hooking my thumbs on either side of the briefs, I lower them to knee level. I examine the crotch of the underwear, trying to figure out if I got my period without noticing.

Stepping out of the panties, I rub my thumb across the strip of cotton sewn into the crotch. It feels distinctly slippery. I raise my fingers and inhale a faint bleachy scent.

I drop the panties on the floor, my heart racing.

I know what come smells like.

You've lived in this house for two years, I tell myself. *Nobody comes up here.*

Three of my roommates are men, but two of them are gay and the third, Peter, is engaged to my other roommate Carrie. He's the only one of us who's not an artist, which means he's the only person who pays his rent on time. He's so shy and soft-spoken that we've probably only exchanged twelve words over the past two years.

Of course, the rest of my roommates have friends over constantly. It's possible some asshole could have come up here and poked around my stuff.

I sweep the room, wondering whether I'd notice if anything had been moved.

My copy of *Dracula* is still right next to the bed, open to the same spot as before.

Other than that…how the fuck would I know if someone had been up here?

My hands tremble as I set *Dracula* down once more.

You're being paranoid. So your underwear was wet. It's probably just…you know, discharge or something.

I don't want to be this person. Jumping at shadows and thinking everybody is out to get me.

I can't live like this, terrified and paranoid.

I take several deep breaths, trying to slow my racing heart. Then I look at my new phone, bought with a credit card I've already maxed out.

It's 7:14. I'm really fucking late.

Snatching up my purse once more, I leave the underwear on the floor and hurry out of the room commando. No underwear is probably better than dirty underwear anyway.

Josh is irritated it took me so long to arrive.

"I've been sitting here for twenty minutes with this drink! The waitress is pissed."

Our waitress is leaning against a pillar, flirting with the busboy.

Josh often transfers his own feelings onto other people. Especially me.

"You like the caprese salad, right?" he says, scanning the menu.

"Not particularly."

He's not listening, eager to put the order in as soon as he can catch the server's eye.

"We'll have the caprese and the pork belly to start," he says.

I don't argue because Josh will be the one paying for the meal. I'm still a broke bitch.

Relaxing a little, Josh slings his arm across the back of my chair.

He's five-ten, dark-haired, with a tasteful amount of scruff on his face. He's got classic Polish features, something I've always liked, and he reads and watches an immense number of documentaries, so there's always something to talk about.

"How's Bruno doing?" he asks.

Josh likes animals, probably even more than I do. He sometimes joins me at the park when I'm walking the dogs. He takes his shirt off and jogs beside us. Anytime it's socially acceptable to take his shirt off, Josh will.

"Bruno's good. I fucking hate his owner, though. Buys him the shittiest food. Keeps him locked in that apartment all day."

"Big dogs are expensive," Josh says.

While Josh enjoys attacking people who lack compassion, he will also defend that exact type of person for no goddamned reason at all.

His hand hangs against my bare arm, his fingertips making erratic contact with the skin. Every time they do, I flinch like an insect's landing on me.

"Then he shouldn't have gotten a big dog," I say irritably.

"He already did, though. So…" Josh shrugs, as if that's all there is to say about that.

"Then maybe he should give Bruno to somebody who actually gives a fuck about him," I say through gritted teeth.

"What, like you?" Josh laughs. "You can barely feed yourself."

I scoot my chair forward so his arm falls off the back. "I can feed myself fine. Just not caprese salad every day."

Josh snorts. "I've seen your shelf at the house. You've got, like, half a box of Captain Crunch and a can of soup."

"I love soup," I inform him.

"Poor people always like soup." Josh grins at me.

He reaches out to tuck a piece of hair behind my ear. His finger-tips graze the rim of my ear, the middle one dipping in toward the canal. I jolt like I've been electrocuted.

"Jesus!" Josh says. "What's wrong with you?"

"Don't touch my ears. I fucking hate that," I snarl. "I've told you that before."

"I was touching your hair." Josh rolls his eyes.

"Just stay away from them," I snap.

I lean back in my chair, my arms crossed protectively over my chest, breathing hard. My heart is racing again.

I know I'm being a spaz. I know I'm overreacting. But I can't seem to stop.

The waitress drops off the appetizers.

Josh devours the salad.

I eat half the pork belly, which is hot, crisp, and delicious. You can't beat the food in San Francisco. Unless you want to drive up to wine county, where the farm-to-table food is an hour out of the garden. Josh has taken me to Sonoma when he's flush with cash from a bougie wedding.

The food calms me a little. It seems to improve Josh's mood, too. Or he remembered the reason I might be a little jumpier than usual.

"Hey," he says. "Sorry about the ear thing. You have told me that."

"It's fine. Sorry for snapping at you."

"Why's it bug you so much?" He spears another slice of tomato and pops it in his mouth.

I push my plate away, not looking at him. "No reason. They're just sensitive."

Josh rests his hand on my bare thigh, giving me a half smile. "How about there? Can I touch you there?"

Honestly, even his warm palm against my thigh makes my stomach clench. But I was kind of being a dick before, so I force myself to smile back at him. "Yeah, that's fine."

He slides his hand up a little farther under my skirt, smiling wider. "How about there?"

Now my own smile feels rigid on my face, hardening like plaster.

He slides his hand all the way up to my crotch, his fingers grazing my pussy lips.

"Oh, you naughty little whore…" he murmurs. "You're not wearing any underwear…"

He thinks I did it for him.

I'm in the ridiculous position of wanting to shove his hand away when it appears that this is exactly what I'm asking for.

Under the cover of the table, he rubs his fingers back and forth across my slit, his middle finger grazing my clit. It feels good like it always feels good to be touched there, even though I don't really want this. My throat constricts and my face burns. I feel like everyone seated at the tables around us knows what he's doing, and the waitress knows, too. They can all see me blushing.

Josh leans over and murmurs, way too close to my ear, "Maybe we should skip the rest of dinner…"

I clamp my legs together, shoving his hand away. "Actually, I've got to get back home. I've got this project I'm working on. It's, uh…I just have to go."

I stand from the table, almost knocking my chair backward.

Josh is staring at me like I've lost my mind. I probably have. "You're gonna leave. Right now. In the middle of dinner," he says.

"Uh, yeah. Sorry." I snatch up my purse, throwing it over my shoulder. "Just…here."

I throw down twelve dollars I really can't spare.

It's the wrong thing to do. Josh is more offended than if I'd just stuck him with the check.

I hurry out of the restaurant, back down Frederick Street, all the way back to my house.

I don't know what the fuck is wrong with me.

This isn't the first time I've been irritated by the way a man touches me—actually, it happens a lot. I have sensory issues, sound and touch affecting me the worst. Tonight I'm keyed up ten times worse than usual. I feel like Peter Parker right after he gets bitten by the radioactive spider, when the onrush of super senses almost makes his brain explode.

I can still feel the hot moisture of Josh's breath in my ear and the patch on my arm where his fingers tickled me.

I hear the shrill sound of Frank's electric toothbrush and the irritating buzz of the ceiling fan in the living room. Even the irregular *clank*, *clank* of its little metal chain swinging against the light.

I clamp my hands over my ears, but that doesn't block out the sounds. I can still hear them, buzzing, muffled, insects outside a tent. I'm the tent. The rest of the world is insects.

I grab my headphones and turn on my music to full blast.

Flopping down on my mattress, I try to lie still.

Sweat begins to trickle down between my breasts. This room is stifling; it must be a hundred degrees.

I'm sleeping outside tonight. I have to.

After throwing the glass door open, I drag my mattress out on the tiny porch.

I lie down on my lumpy futon, my headphones on my head, my arms and legs outstretched.

The sea breeze brushes my skin, cool, salty, clean. The sky is thick with clouds, piled up in deep drifts of purple, ash, and indigo.

I close my eyes, sinking into the music, finally finding peace.

9

COLE

I skip a meeting with the SF Artists Guild in favor of further reconnaissance.

The house directly behind Mara's is listed on Airbnb for eight hundred dollars a night. I message the owner, convincing him to cancel his next three bookings so I can take the place for a month.

My desire to spy on Mara is so intense, I probably would have bought the damn thing.

I drive over to the town house early in the evening before parking my Tesla at the curb.

The three-story Georgian isn't nearly as nice as my own house, but it's ten times more habitable than Mara's. The pale oak floors look freshly polished, and the host left a bowl of foil-wrapped chocolates on the kitchen island, as well as stocked the fridge with bottled water.

As long as the house is clean, I don't give a fuck about anything else.

Strike that—it's the view I care about.

I climb the creaking stairs to the third floor, which includes an office, a small library, and a sitting room.

The library window is the one that looks across the back garden to Mara's house. The beveled glass offers a watery view into the protected alcove of Mara's balcony.

She could be forgiven for thinking she has complete privacy in that space. The library window is small, set high up on the wall, divided into a dozen diamond panes.

I cut out the entire window with my glass cutters. Then I cover the space with black paper, leaving only a hole for my telescope.

From a distance, it will look like nothing more than a dark window into an empty room.

My efforts are rewarded when Mara rushes into her bedroom only twenty minutes later, before I've completed my preparations.

She rushes everywhere she goes, running from job to job, always late.

I respect the hustle, but her existence is tawdry and depressing. The thought of waiting tables, taking people's orders, and ferrying their food is offensive to me. Picking up dog shit in the park for mutts is worse. I'm surprised Mara wanted to save herself the night Shaw abducted her, if this is all she had to come home to.

My interest in this hectic, desperate girl baffles me.

My desires have never been mysterious to me. In fact, they've always felt rational and natural.

Danvers irritated me, so I removed him from my sphere. I put his bones inside my sculpture as my own private joke. The art world is always looking for the symbolism behind the work. *Fragile Ego* proclaimed a statement that every viewer felt all the way down to their own hollow bones, without consciously understanding what they were perceiving.

This is the first time in my life I've desired something without understanding why.

Out of all the thousands of women I've encountered, how did Mara catch my attention like a hook through the gills of a fish?

It's not because Alastor threw her in my path.

I noticed her the first moment I saw her, when she spilled wine on her dress. She hardly flinched—just marched into the bathroom, emerging with that makeshift tie-dye that was creative, beautiful, and possessed a spirit of playfulness quite opposite to anything I could have come up with.

Then Alastor knocked her down hard, so hard that I thought he'd killed her. Yet she rose again, stubborn, unbroken.

She has me wondering what it would take to break her. To shatter her into so many pieces that she could never put them together again.

The view through the telescope is so clear that I could almost be standing in the room with her.

I watch Mara strip off her clothes, revealing a lean, taut body with small breasts and narrow hips. I'm intrigued to see she hasn't removed the piercings from her nipples—the twin silver rings remain in place.

As she hunts for clothes, a cold bead of excitement runs down my spine. I already know she has no clean underwear.

Sure enough, she spots the discarded panties on the floor. My heart stops. I can hardly breathe, riveted in place, eye to the telescope, watching…

She picks up the underwear and steps into it.

Blood rushes to my cock so fast, I get light-headed.

She's wearing panties soaked in my come. The most intimate part of me pressed up against the most intimate part of her.

She hesitates, standing still in the center of the room.

She's feeling the wetness of my come against her cunt.

My cock tents the front of my trousers.

I love the thought of my come on her bare flesh. How long does sperm survive? I wonder if those desperate swimmers are trying to wriggle inside her right now.

She yanks down her underwear.

I watch the panic and confusion on her face, my cock harder than it's ever been.

She touches my come. Smells it. Then rips off the underwear and flings it away from her.

My whole body is warm and throbbing. I can't remember when I last felt this level of excitement. I've been so fucking bored lately. Nothing impresses me. Nothing interested me. Until now...

Tormenting Mara without even touching her is so stimulating that I can hardly imagine what it would be like to put my hands directly on her flesh...to circle them around her throat...

Mara shifts her weight back and forth, trying to decide what to do.

She's wondering if she felt what she thinks she felt.

She doesn't trust herself.

Finally, she snatches up her purse and exits the room.

I'm already heading down the stairs. She's not dressed for work—I want to see where she's going.

A date, I suspect.

At the thought, my pupils contract and my throat tightens. My heart slows. I'm cold and focused.

Who does she date? Who does she fuck?

I want to know.

I exit the town house, not bothering to lock the door behind me. I cut across Frederick Street, catching sight of Mara walking ahead in her tight black dress and ankle boots. She doesn't wear heels often. I like how it hobbles her, slowing her pace.

It's easy for me to track her, walking along the opposite side of the street like a disconnected shadow. I follow her to a trendy little restaurant a few blocks away, where she meets some scruffy-faced hipster in a too-tight T-shirt.

Unlike Mara and her date, I don't have a reservation. A hundred-dollar bill pressed into the hostess's palm solves that problem. I probably could have convinced her just by holding her gaze and letting my fingers trail across her wrist. The hostess giggles and blushes as she leads me to the table I requested, tucked away in a corner with several hanging plants shielding me from Mara's view.

I have no problem attracting women. In fact, it's too easy. The wealth, the fame, and the looks suck them in before I say a word. There's no challenge.

Will Mara fall at my feet as easily as that hostess?

I confess, I'd be disappointed.

She doesn't seem particularly enthralled with her date. She twitches irritably as he rests his arm across the back of her chair.

Her date yammers on, oblivious to her expression of boredom. He doesn't seem to notice how she angles her body away from him, only rarely meeting his eye. When he tries to tidy her hair, she jolts away from him.

I feel a strange sense of satisfaction in her rejection of this buffoon. It would have lessened her in my eyes if she were besotted with someone so…pedestrian.

My pleasure evaporates as he reaches under the table to fondle her pussy.

In its place: a sharp spike of fury.

I want to rip that hand off his arm, leaving a ragged stump with a bare glint of bone.

Even in my most extreme moments, like when I've slit the throat of someone I hated and watched their blood run down my arm, my heart rate barely rises.

Now that lump of muscle pounds in my chest like a war drum. This is something new—something that makes me sit back in my chair, breathing hard, my hands clenched into fists on my lap.

What the fuck is happening?

I almost feel…jealous.

I've never been jealous before. Why would I? No one on this planet has anything I covet.

Now I've smelled Mara's scent on my fingers.

And I've decided that nobody should be touching her sweet little cunt but me.

If that medium-shirt-wearing motherfucker doesn't remove his fingers from her pussy immediately, he's going to eat them for an entrée.

Luckily for him, Mara jumps up from the table, shoving back her chair. I hear her hasty apologies as she throws cash by her plate. She leaves, abandoning her disgruntled date.

"Bitch," he mutters after her.

I pass so close behind him, it's child's play to steal his cell phone off the table.

I drop it down the nearest sewer grate as I follow Mara.

The sky is fully dark now, thick with clouds. The wind is colder than before.

I walk back to Frederick Street, curiously elated at the prospect of watching Mara alone in her room.

I like her best in her private space. It's a look inside her mind— her comforts and preferences.

Settling myself behind the telescope once more, I watch her pace. Mara is a skittish horse. When she's calm, she moves with grace. But when she's frustrated or uncomfortable—like in the company of her incompetent date—she becomes stiff and withdrawn, hypersensitive to irritants.

She hauls her mattress out on the small deck attached to her room.

This is all the better for me. I can see her as clearly as a figure in a diorama.

She lies down on the futon, a pair of headphones over her ears. It takes a long time for her breathing to slow, for her to settle deeply into the mattress. Her lips move in time with the lyrics of the song.

Though she's not actually singing, I can make out a few scattered words:

> *Don't know if I'm feeling happy...*
> *I'm kinda confused, I'm not in the mood to try and fix*
> *me...*

I google the lyrics to pull up the song on my phone; it's one I haven't heard before. I play it aloud in the dark library, listening to what Mara is hearing over on the balcony.

♫ *"yes & no"—XYLØ*

She's so still now that I wonder if she fell asleep. Her chest rises and falls with metronome regularity.

The breeze whispers through the hedges in the garden between us. It slides across Mara's skin, making her shiver. Her nipples harden, visible even through the black dress.

Why did she keep those piercings? Does she like them? Is she afraid to take them out?

Thunder rumbles softly overhead.

A few scattered droplets hit the black paper covering the library window.

Mara stirs, feeling the rain on her skin.

I expect her to rise, to pull her mattress back inside.

I'm not good at predicting when it comes to her.

She sits up. Lifts her palm. Feels the rain pattering down.

Then she pulls her dress over her head and tosses it aside. She lies down on the mattress once more, fully nude.

I lean forward, my eye pressed against the telescope.

Thunder rolls, and the rain falls harder. It shatters across her naked skin: on her thighs, her stomach, her bare breasts, her upturned palms, her closed eyelids. It falls in her partly open mouth.

She's soaking it in. Feeling the delicious coolness and the tiny impact of each droplet breaking on her skin.

Her expression is dreamy, floating. Soaked in pleasure. Fully relaxed for the first time since I've been watching her.

That strange squirming returns to my guts:

Jealousy.

The rain rolls over her body, makes rivers around her breasts, streams down between her thighs.

It soaks her hair, drenches the mattress, chills her skin to marble. Mara doesn't give a fuck.

She reaches between her thighs and begins to stroke her fingers back and forth across her pussy lips. Touching herself lightly, delicately.

Her lips part, allowing more rain into her mouth.

The rain beats against the side of the house. A bolt of lightning sizzles across the sky, illuminating her shining body like a camera flash. Every detail stands out in sharp relief: the long column of her throat, the divot of her collarbone, the points of her nipples, the long, flat expanse of her abdomen, the delicate bones of her hands, the slender fingers slipping inside her.

I've never seen anything so beautiful.

She's bronze as a statue in the purplish light. If I could sculpt her exactly like this, it would be my greatest work.

I want to pour molten metal over her, freezing her in time forever.

I put my hand down the front of my pants, feeling the thick rod of my cock, painfully hard.

My skin feels feverish.

I want to be out where she is, drenched in rain, touching that cold flesh...

I pump my cock in time with the motion of her hand.

Her pace quickens, her back arching, her head thrown back.

I fuck my hand harder and harder, imagining I'm about to explode over her body, hot come raining down on her harder than the storm.

Her eyes squeeze tightly shut, her cries drowned out by the rain. Her thighs clamp around her hand, her body shaking.

I'm coming for the second time today, a hot flood that pours over the back of my hand, dripping onto the floorboards.

I can't tear my eyes from the telescope.

I can't stop looking at her for a single second.

10

MARA

Monday morning, Joanna catches me at breakfast.

"Mara," she says, "about your stuff…"

"I know." I wince. "I've been looking everywhere for space."

"You gotta get it out. I need room for my own shit."

"I know. This week, I promise."

That's a promise I have no way of keeping. I've been looking every day, but I'm flat fucking broke. Even if I can find an affordable studio, I don't have money for first month's rent, let alone a deposit.

I borrow Erin's laptop, planning to scan the artists' message boards yet again. Instead, I see I've got a new email from the Onyx Group, whatever that is.

I open it, expecting spam.

The sentences that meet my eye are so serendipitous that I read them four times over, stunned and unbelieving.

Dear Ms. Eldritch,

We received your application for studio space. We're pleased to inform you that our junior studio in the Alta Plaza building on Clay Street is currently available.

The junior studio is offered to upcoming artists at a discounted rate of $200/month, payment due at the end of the month.

I have an appointment available at 2:00 this afternoon if you'd like to view the space.

Regards,
Sonia Bridger

For a second I wonder if one of my roommates would be cruel enough to prank me. But I doubt any of them can spell this well, except maybe Peter, who was born without a sense of humor.

Hands shaking, I type back as quickly as possible.

That would be incredible, thank you so much. I will be there at 2:00.

I want to run over there right this second before they give it away to somebody else.

Two hundred bucks a month is unheard of. I don't remember applying for this place specifically, but I put my name down everywhere I could find. This feels like manna from heaven. I really can't believe it. I'm keyed up, terrified that something will happen to fuck this up.

I can barely concentrate while I race my way through the brunch shift. Arthur can tell I'm excited, or maybe just useless, so he lets me off early to run home and change.

I dress in my most professional-looking outfit, a linen peasant blouse and almost-clean jeans, and hustle over to Clay Street.

Ms. Bridger is already waiting for me. She's tall and elegant, with an iron-gray bob and a long aristocratic nose.

Her handshake should have its own office. "Nice to meet you, Mara. I'll show you the space."

She leads me through the corridors of the Alta Plaza building, which is bright and modern, white paint and blond wood in the Scandinavian style.

"Here we are," she says, throwing open the double doors of the last studio at the end of the corridor.

I gape around at a dazzling sunlit loft. The exposed ductwork soars thirty feet over my head. The floor-to-ceiling windows look out over Alta Plaza Park. The air is fresh and cool, scented by the ornamental lemon trees potted along the far wall.

If this is a junior studio, I can hardly imagine what the rest of the rooms are like. It's easily four times the size of Joanna's space, bigger than the main floor of my house.

I'm stunned.

"What do you think?" Sonia represses her smile.

"When can I move in?" I stammer.

"It's open now. I can get you a key card for the main door. The building is accessible twenty-four hours a day. There's a mini-fridge in the corner as you can see, and the café on the main level makes an incredible iced latte."

"Have I died? Is this heaven?"

She laughs. "Cole Blackwell is very generous."

"Cole…what?" I say, trying to tear my eyes away from combing over every inch of this perfect space. The art I could make in here… I'm itching to get started.

"Mr. Blackwell owns this building. It was his idea to discount the junior studios. He may not have the cuddliest persona, but he supports his fellow artists."

"Right, amazing," I say, only partly following this. "Honestly, he could ask for my firstborn child, and I'd gladly hand it over. This place is just…perfection."

"That won't be necessary." Sonia passes me her clipboard. "All I need is a signature. We can start with a six-month lease."

"Any deposit?" I ask, thinking that will be the killing blow.

Sonia shakes her head. "Just bring me a check at the end of the month."

"Cash okay?"

"As long as it's not all ones and fives."

"I see I'm not the only waitress you know."

"It's almost a prerequisite in this industry." Sonia adds kindly, "I was a waitress, too, once upon a time."

"Thank you," I tell her again. "Really, I just can't thank you enough."

"Will you need moving services? From your old studio?"

I do need that. Badly. "How much is it?" I ask nervously.

"Complimentary."

"Don't pinch me, I don't want to wake up."

Sonia smiles. "Speak with Janice at the front desk on your way out, and she'll schedule it for you."

She leaves me alone to soak in the warm sun, the scent of the wooden cabinets, the endless open space I could run up and down like a bowling alley.

I've never been one to believe that when a bad thing happens, a good thing follows.

But maybe this one time…fate's on my side.

―――――――

By Wednesday, all my supplies have been cleaned out of Joanna's studio, transported with the greatest care to the new studio on Clay Street.

My roommates are so jealous that they can hardly stand it, except for Peter, who says, "That's great, Mara," bringing us up to a grand total of fifteen words of conversation.

"Cole Blackwell owns the place?" Erin moans. "You'll probably see him all the time."

"You wanna fuck him, too?" Heinrich teases her. "Trying to get a monopoly on slutty artists?"

"He's a complete dick," Joanna says. "Not friendly at all."

"Gorgeous, though," says Frank.

"Oh, wow." I laugh. "That's really something coming from you, Frankie. You're picky as hell."

"Not that picky," Joanna says. "He used to date Heinrich, after all."

"Get fucked." Heinrich scowls.

I'm floating on cloud nine all through my shifts, dying to get over to the studio so I can work on my collage.

I stay late every night, working longer hours than I ever have in my life. I finish the piece and jump right into a new composition, even more layered and detailed. I'm experimenting with different materials—not just acrylic but lacquer and corrective fluid and Sharpie and spray paint.

The studios are separate and soundproof. No one seems to mind when I play my music loudly. The nighttime streets are distant, glittering like a jeweled cloth laid out below me.

For the first time in a long time, I feel hopeful. Maybe even happy.

This feeling intensifies tenfold when Sonia taps on my door Friday afternoon, informing me that I've been short-listed for a grant from the SF Artists Guild.

"Are you serious?" I squeak.

"The panel would like to come see your work on Monday. If they like what they see, they're awarding two thousand dollars to each recipient and showcasing a piece at New Voices next month."

I feel like I'm about to pass out.

"What do they want to see?" I ask eagerly. "I just finished a collage. And I started this new piece, but I haven't done much yet..."

"Just show them whatever you've got," Sonia says. "It doesn't need to be complete."

I am equal parts elation and sickening terror. I want this so fucking badly. The money would be great, but a spot in New Voices is even better. It's by invite only, and all the biggest brokers will be there. Getting a piece in the show could really boost me up the ladder.

I look at my work in progress. It's fucking cool; I'm proud of it. But I have another idea percolating in my mind...

A fresh canvas waits, stretched and ready, leaned against the wall. It's massive—eight feet high, ten feet long. It would be the largest painting I've ever done.

Should I start working on it? Sonia said my painting didn't need to be complete to show the panel... This would be more ambitious.

Maybe too ambitious. It could be a fucking disaster.

I shift back and forth, gazing between my collage and the blank canvas.

I turn back to the easel. Starting something new would be a huge risk. I've practiced the collage technique—that's what I should stick with for now.

I'm a nervous wreck over the weekend. Any minute that I'm not at work, I'm laboring feverishly on the new collage, trying to get as much done as possible before the panel comes to see it.

Monday morning, I spend an hour rifling through my closet, flinging clothes around like that will magically transform them into something wearable.

I can't decide if I should wear something "artistic" or something professional. This is a stupid dilemma because I don't actually own anything professional. Most of my clothes are thrifted, very few made in the past decade.

The other issue is these fucking scars on my arms. I'm so pissed that this happened when the others had finally faded. When I was starting to look normal again.

The scars are ugly. They make me look sketchy and unreliable. They make me look like a fucking lunatic, frankly.

I *feel* like a lunatic after trying on yet another shirt, then ripping it off and flinging it across the room.

Taking a deep breath, I tell myself the panel won't be looking at me—they'll be looking at the collage. They'll either like it, or they won't. It's not in my control.

After snatching up my purse, I head to the studio.

The panel is late.

I keep working on the collage, pretending like I can't hear the clock ticking away on the wall. I'm too nervous to play music like I usually would.

Finally, I hear footsteps out in the hall and the low murmur of polite conversation. Someone raps on my door, light and formal.

"Come in!" I croak.

The door cracks open, allowing six people to file inside.

Sonia heads the group. "Everyone, this is Mara Eldritch, one of our most promising junior artists! As you can see, she's hard at work on a new series. Mara, this is the panel of the Artists Guild: Martin Boss, Hannah Albright, John Pecorino, Leslie Newton, and of course, Cole Blackwell."

As she reels off the names, I turn to face the panel of artists, most of whom I've at least heard of before. My eyes slide across five faces before landing at last on the man I've most been wanting to meet: my benefactor, Cole Blackwell.

The room tilts with a sickening jerk.

That face was burned into my brain, never to be forgotten.

Shaggy dark hair. Silvery skin. A soft, sensual mouth. Eyes blacker than sin.

This man stood over me.

This man left me to die.

I'm frozen in place—literally frozen: cold, stiff, petrified.

It feels like twenty minutes pass.

Maybe it's only a moment, because Cole says smoothly, "Nice to finally meet you, Mara. How are you getting along in the space?"

The silence ticks by. Several panel members shift in place.

Finally, I rasp out, "Fine. Good. Thank you."

Thank you?

What the fucking fuck?

Why am I thanking *him? He saw me squirming on the ground like a dying bug, and he walked right over me.*

He's staring at me now in precisely the same way: face cold, eyes bright. The corners of that beautiful mouth quirk up as if he wants to smile...

This fucking maniac is doing it all over again.

He's watching me squirm. And he's loving it.

I want to scream out loud, *I WAS KIDNAPPED! TORTURED! LEFT TO DIE! THIS MAN MIGHT HAVE DONE IT! And if he didn't, he was definitely there...*

"What are you working on today?" Leslie Newton says. Her voice is high and bright, as if she's trying to smooth over the awkward moment.

I've got to pull it together. They're here to see my collage. Everything is riding on this moment. If I start shouting like a madwoman, I'll lose everything.

I turn toward the canvas, reeling like I'm drunk.

"Well." I pause to clear my throat. "As you can see, in this new series, I'm experimenting with nontraditional artistic materials. Seeing if I can create a luxe effect by layering and manipulating alternative substances."

"And where did you get that idea?" Martin Boss demands. He's tall, skinny, and bald, dressed in a black turtleneck and Buddy Holly glasses. His voice is sharp and challenging, like he's accusing me of something.

"I grew up in the Mission District." All I can think about is not looking at Cole Blackwell. "I'm inspired by murals and graffiti."

I can feel his eyes burning on my back. Sweat breaks out beneath my long rope of hair. My heart is racing, and I'm terrified, fucking terrified. I can't believe he's standing five feet behind me. Why is this happening? What does this mean?

It's him. I know it's him.

He's wearing a dark suit just like that night, with a cashmere polo in place of a dress shirt. That's not common attire. I didn't make that up; I couldn't.

Another panel member, a woman in a red wrap dress and chunky bracelets, is asking a question. I can't hear over the pounding in my ears.

"I—I'm sorry, could you repeat that?" I stammer. I have to turn and look at her, which means turning toward Cole.

He's definitely smirking now. Watching me sweat.

"I asked if that figure is a reference to Japanese Neo-Pop," the woman says kindly.

"Yes," I say. "The juxtaposition of cute and sinister."

I don't know if that makes sense. Nothing is making sense right now.

"I like the peeled-off layers," the last panel member says. I think his name was John, but I can't remember now. "You should consider a piece focused on that technique."

"Right." I push my hair back out of my face. "I will."

My cheek feels wet where the back of my hand touched. Fuck, did I just smear paint all over my face?

My skin is burning, I want to cry. Everyone is staring at me, most of all Cole. He's draining the life out of me with those black eyes. Sucking me in.

"Well, if no one else has any questions, we'll move on to the next studio," Sonia says. "Thank you, Mara!"

"Thank you. All of you," I reply awkwardly.

My eyes fix on Cole Blackwell once more, on that malicious and utterly stunning face.

"Good luck," he says.

It sounds like a taunt.

They file out of the studio, with Sonia in the rear this time.

I watch them leave.

I'm gasping for breath in a room that suddenly seems devoid of oxygen.

What just happened? What just happened? What just happened…?
I should stay right here. I should keep my fucking mouth shut.
Instead, I kick open the door and chase after Blackwell.

11
COLE

The group is filing into the junior studio on the opposite side of the building when Mara catches up.

"Excuse me!" She pants, her cheeks flaming pink. "Could I speak to Mr. Blackwell for a moment?"

The other panel members turn to look at me.

Sonia is particularly curious. She knew something was up the moment I told her to offer Mara the studio. The discounted rate was a fabrication, invented by me on the spot. The same with this grant. It's all leverage to get Mara right where I want her: completely at my mercy.

"Of course," I say. "The rest of you go on. I'll join you momentarily."

I lead Mara down the hall to an empty studio. I step into the clean, deserted space. She hesitates in the doorway, afraid to be alone with me.

"Are you coming?" I ask, my eyebrow raised.

Pressing her lips together, she marches into the room before closing the door behind her.

I wait for her to speak, watching the rapid rise and fall of her chest, thrilling at the hectic spots of color on her cheeks.

She's illuminated with fury, her eyes blazing, her cheeks flaming. Her dark hair swirls around her face, defying gravity from the pure electric tension between us. Her thin hands tremble. She digs her nails into the thighs of her jeans.

"I know it was you." Her eyes are feverish, her voice low and hoarse.

I'm enjoying this so much, I can hardly stand it. Her rage, her fear, and this delicious predicament are a cocktail I want to drink to oblivion.

Her expression of shock when she saw my face and the awful struggle as she tried to discuss her work with the panel while her brain twisted and turned in her skull…

I'm so glad I have it all recorded. I can't wait to watch it over again tonight.

"What was me?" I say mildly.

"*You know*," she hisses.

Her whole body is shaking. I'd like to hold her against me, to feel those tremors vibrating through my frame…

"Please explain."

Her eyes glint with tears of fury, but she refuses to let them fall. Her lips are swollen and chapped as if she's been biting at them.

"Someone snatched me off the street. They tied me up, cut my wrists, and left me in the woods. You were there. I saw you. You stood over me, staring at me. You saw I needed help. And you walked right over me. You left me there to die."

"What a bizarre accusation," I say. "Do you have any proof?"

I know she doesn't. I just want to see how she'll respond.

"*I saw you*," she hisses. "I'll tell the cops."

"That's not a good idea." I tuck my hands in my pockets, tilting my head as I look at her. "That would cause a lot of problems for you. You'd lose the studio, of course. The grant, too."

"Are you threatening me?" Her voice rises, the edge of hysteria as sharp as razor wire. "Why are you doing this? Why did you do this to me?"

She holds up her arm. Her loose bell sleeve drops away, revealing the long, jagged scar across the wrist. The scar is still healing, raised like a welt.

"I didn't do that." I scoff.

Mara falters, her upraised hand dropping an inch.

Interesting—she doesn't actually know who cut her.

"You were there," she insists.

"So what if I was?"

She startles, shocked that I admitted it. "Then you did this!" she shrieks.

"No," I growl. "I didn't."

In one swift step, I close the space between us. Mara tries to turn and run, but I'm much too fast for her. I seize her by the arm before yanking her toward me, holding up that accusing hand and branded wrist.

I look down into her terrified face, pinning her in place with my gaze as much as my fingers locked around her wrist.

"There's no limit on predators in the world," I hiss. "And no lack of damaged girls to attract them. I doubt this is the first time some man homed in on those bitten-raw nails and that flinch when anybody gets near you. Just those fucking scars on your arm are a billboard screaming, 'I like to hurt myself. Come hurt me, too!'"

"Wh-what are you—" she stammers.

"*Those*," I bark, yanking up her sleeve, exposing the other scars, the old ones, the thin silvery crosshatches that weren't caused by anyone but herself.

Now the tears run down both sides of her face. She stands very still, looking up at me, furious and defiant.

"I bet you've been preyed on by every Cro-Magnon with a cock since before you started menstruating," I sneer.

"Get fucked," she snarls back at me.

"Let me guess." I laugh. "Alcoholic father?"

She wrenches her arm out of my grip, stumbling back, breathing hard.

I let her go because she has no idea of the real grip I have on her—she's a rabbit wrapped in my coils, and she doesn't even know it.

"Alcoholic mother, actually." She tilts up her chin in defiance. "Shithead stepfather—but hey, at least he was creative. Mom was just textbook, wasn't she?"

Her voice is steadier than I expected.

She's shaking harder than ever, but she still hasn't run.

"If you didn't attack me," she says, "then why didn't you help me?"

I shrug. "I don't help anyone."

"You offered me a studio."

I laugh. "I didn't give you that studio to help you."

"Why then?" She looks up at me, almost pleading, desperate to understand.

I don't mind telling her. "I did it for the same reason I do everything: because I wanted to."

To Mara, that makes no sense.

For me, it's the ultimate reason for anything.

"You can't bribe me," she says. "I'm not going to keep quiet."

I snort. "It won't matter. No one will believe you."

Her face blanches, her breath catching in her throat. That touched a nerve. Poor little Mara has been disbelieved before. Probably in relation to the "creative" stepfather.

Stepping close once more, I look down into her terrified face, and I tell her the brutal, unvarnished truth:

"I own this city. With money, with connections, and with pure fucking talent. You try spouting off about me, and see what happens...you'll look unhinged. Unstable."

"I don't care," she whispers.

I let out a low laugh. "You will."

12

MARA

I stumble back to my own studio before closing the door behind me and locking it, leaning back against the wood with my heartbeat scattering frantically across my ribs.

I'm breathing hard, clutching the front of my shirt, sweating more than ever.

He's lying! He's fucking lying!

He's not gonna gaslight me. I know what I saw that night. He was standing there, staring down at me. I didn't make that up—I couldn't. How could I have imagined his face before I ever saw it?

Maybe you had seen it before. In a photograph. In a magazine.

No, fuck that. I didn't see his picture and forget about it. That's not what happened.

What can I do? Who can I tell?

He kidnapped me. Did he? Someone did. And Cole was there.

Bits of memory cut at me from all sides, jagged as shattered mirror. I see little flickers, fragments. I want to cry, but I know he's still somewhere close by; he could hear me. He owns this building. *He owns the fucking building!*

What's happening? The coincidence, the situation, it's making me feel like my head is splitting apart. I don't know what to believe.

Maybe I could have imagined it.

But the way he reacted when I confronted him…he wasn't

surprised. His eyebrows dropped, his pupils contracted, and he didn't hesitate for a second—he bit right back at me, attacking like a snake. That's not normal.

He says it wasn't him.

Is that true? Could it be true?

That would mean there were two soulless psychopaths in the woods that night. That doesn't make any sense. None of this makes sense.

I'm pacing back and forth, still strangling my shirt, sometimes lifting it over the bottom half of my face and breathing into it.

What am I supposed to do?

What about the grant? What about the fact all my stuff is here now?

Does any of that matter? There might be a murderer walking around. There is for sure; I've seen it in on the news: girls beaten and hacked to bits by the Beast of the Bay, which is a fucking upsetting nickname by the way—like the media itself wants to give him power over us. Turning him into some supernatural force before which we can only be prey.

Did the same person snatch me off the street? Was it Cole Blackwell? Is he the Beast?

Questions shout at me from every corner of my mind. I can't get a grip on myself. I don't know what to do. I feel frantic and powerless and like I really might be crazy.

That's what Blackwell said. He called me unstable.

That's what people will think if I accuse him publicly. Hell, even the cops didn't believe me, and that wass before they heard some famous rich guy was involved.

No one believes me because my story makes no sense.

Why would someone snatch me off the street and cut my wrists, then leave me there? Only for a completely different guy to appear ten minutes later?

Blackwell said it wasn't him. But he also said he wasn't there at all, and that's fucking bullshit. I know what I saw.

I know what *I think* I saw.

Could I really be unstable?

That stirs up some deeply buried shit for me. I'm talking the stuff you pack way, way down in the back of your mind and never look at ever, under any circumstances.

Your mom is so nice.

How can you hate her?

She just wants what's best for you.

I know you're lying.

She told me what you said about me.

She told me what you did.

You're disgusting...

And then, even deeper down, the voice that makes up the worst fucking part of me. The part I wish I could tear out and burn on a bonfire, but I never can because she's a part of me. All the way down in my DNA.

You can't escape what you are...

I'm just doing what any good mother would do.

You can't imagine what it's like, having a daughter like you.

All mothers love their children. All of them. If I don't love you, what do you think that means?

I read your journal. I know what you think, secretly, when you're pretending to be so sweet.

I know what you do alone in your bed.

You're disgusting. Disgusting.

I slap myself across the face once, hard.

Then I grab my own wrist to stop myself from doing it again.

You're not going to do that anymore.

When you hurt yourself, you leave marks. Then nobody believes a word you say. *All* the marks look like you did them.

I have a better way now.

I just have to remember to use it.

Breathe. Take the feeling. Turn it into something.

I look at my half-finished canvas, at the collage I was so proud of this morning.

It's not bad. But it's also not great.

It's…safe.

Safe is pointless. Safe is an illusion.

I wasn't safe when someone snatched me off the street. And I sure as fuck am not safe here, now, today, in Cole Blackwell's studio.

I'm not getting the grant; that much is obvious. Blackwell is jerking my chain.

Well, fuck it, then.

I take the half-finished collage off the easel and rest it against the wall.

In its place I set the larger canvas, the one that intimidated me, the one I don't actually have time to complete.

I pick up a bucket of dark wash and throw it against the canvas, letting it rain onto the floor.

If this fucker plans to evict me, I'm not gonna baby the hardwood.

I'm so tired of fighting. Every time I feel like I'm getting just a tiny bit ahead in my life, something happens to slap me down again.

Maybe the common denominator is me.

Maybe I am fucking crazy.

And maybe that's just fine. I'd rather be crazy than be like half the people I meet.

I pick up my brush and start painting with wild abandon, with vast strokes and no hesitation.

♬ *"I'm Gonna Show You Crazy"—Bebe Rexha*

I think back to that night. I remember the things I know were real: the cold ground beneath me. The agony of my arched back, bound hands, and bleeding wrists. I remember the lonely rustle of wind in the trees, the black, empty sky.

And then footsteps…

Lighter than the ones I'd heard before.

The hope that fluttered in my chest.

And the sickening dread of Cole Blackwell's face staring down at me.

Merciless. Pitiless. Curious…but uncaring.

Like I was worthless.

Like I might as well die.

I pick up my pencil and sketch an outline on the canvas: a girl's body, bent and bound. My body.

He can deny it all he wants. I know what happened. I can draw it as clearly as a photograph.

I work on the new painting feverishly, until I can hear lights switching off all over the building, people bidding each other good night as they leave.

I check the studio door once more to make sure it's locked. Then I return to the painting and keep working.

I work all night long.

13

COLE

As soon as Mara and I part ways, I make an excuse to the panel and head back to my own office on the top floor so I can watch what she does next.

All the studios have security cameras mounted above their doors.

The feed from Mara's streams directly to my computer. When she's working, I can see her every move.

I watch as she paces the studio, freaking the fuck out.

She held it together in front of me, but now she's hyperventilating, pulling on her shirt and biting at her nails.

I savor her distress. I want to see her break down.

Or at least part of me does.

The other part wants to watch her fight.

I enjoy her stubbornness. And I want to crush it out of her.

She pauses in the middle of the studio. Slaps herself hard across the face. The crash echoes in the empty room. I think I'm witnessing the moment of fracture.

And maybe I am.

Because Mara cracks. I witness it. But something else steps out from her shell. Someone who stands still, not fidgeting, not tearing at her nails. Someone who doesn't even glance toward the windows or the doors.

She grabs the half-finished collage and yanks it off the easel. In its place, she throws up a fresh canvas, double the size, and flings a dark wash across it, letting paint dripping onto the floor.

She goes to work, rapidly and rabidly. She's feverishly focused, paint streaked across her face and down her arms, her eyes fixed on the canvas.

I watch the composition take shape.

She has an excellent eye for proportion, everything in balance.

It's rare for me to admire other artists' work. There's always something to criticize, something out of place. But this is what I noticed about Mara from the moment she dyed that dress: her aesthetic sense is as finely honed as my own.

Watching her work is like watching myself work.

I'm glued to the computer screen, watching for hours as she sketches out her composition and begins to block in the color.

Sonia's knock on the door startles me. I sit up, frowning as she pokes her head inside.

"You can come out now," she says. "The panel's gone."

"Good. I hate all of them."

She steps into my office, almost tripping over the golf bag set directly behind the door. "You don't actually enjoy that game, do you?"

"It's a game of the mind, not the body. So, yes, I enjoy it. You should take it up yourself. You know damn well how much business gets done on the golf course."

"I know," Sonia sighs, giving my clubs one last venomous glare. "Do you want to look over their scores for the finalists?"

"No. I've already decided."

Sonia grips the stack of folders containing all the applicants I'm supposed to review, her expression resigned. "Let me guess…"

I nod. "It's going to Mara Eldritch."

"That's going to irritate the panel. You know they like to have their say…"

"I don't give a fuck what they want," I snap. "I'm funding the grant and half their budget for the year, so they can suck it up and do as they're told."

"I'll tell them," Sonia says, amenable as always. She knows that the primary points of her job description are obedience and discretion.

Still, she lingers in the doorway, her curiosity too powerful to restrain. "For what it's worth, I would have picked Mara, too."

"That's because you have taste. Unlike the rest of them."

"How did you find her?" Sonia asks with pretend casualness.

"She was recommended by another artist."

I can tell Sonia's dying to hear more, but she's already pushing the limits of my patience.

"I'm excited to see what she comes up with for New Voices," she says.

I've already turned back to the computer screen, watching Mara's slight figure bend and stretch to cover the vast canvas with paint.

Sonia hesitates in the doorway.

"By the way...Jack Brisk increased his offer for your Olgiati. He's willing to pay two point four million and trade you his Picasso as well."

I snort. "I bet he is."

"I take it that's a no, then?"

I gaze up at the gleaming solar model hung in pride of place directly in front of my desk. Where I see it every minute, every day, without ever tiring of it.

"This is the only surviving piece by the greatest master in Italian glass. His techniques have yet to be surpassed in the modern era. And besides that, it's fucking beautiful—look at it. Look how it glows. I wouldn't sell it to Brisk if he cut his heart out of his chest and handed it to me."

"Okay, Jesus," Sonia says. "I'll tell him it has sentimental value and you're not interested in selling."

I laugh. "Sentimental value? I suppose you're right—I did buy it with the inheritance when my father died."

Sonia falters. "Oh, you did? I'm sorry, I didn't know that."

I smile. "You could say I was celebrating."

Sonia considers this. "Great men don't always make great fathers," she says at last.

I shrug. "I wouldn't know. I don't know any good fathers."

"You're so cynical." She shakes her head sadly.

My eyes are already drawn back to Mara's figure on my computer screen.

Tolstoy said happy families are all alike, but unhappy families are unhappy in their own way.

I want to know exactly which ways Mara's grungy little childhood fucked her up. I want to know why I can't quite predict her like I can everyone else.

She sparks my curiosity when I can't seem to muster interest in anything else.

As if she knows what I'm looking at, Sonia says, "Do you want to deliver the good news to Mara, or should I do it?"

"You tell her. And don't let her know it's from me."

Sonia frowns. "Why are you always so averse to anyone knowing you're a good guy?"

"Because I'm not a good guy," I tell her. "Not even a little bit."

14

MARA

Early in the morning, I finally rinse out my paintbrushes and wash my hands at the sparkling stainless steel sink in the corner.

I worked all night long, and now I have a brunch shift to cover. But I don't regret a thing. This painting is coming alive in a way I've never experienced before. I wish I could keep working on it right now.

I gather my scattered belongings, then pause in front of the large mirror hung on the wall so I can tidy my paint-streaked bird's nest of hair.

As I'm doing so, I spot something in the reflection that I hadn't noticed before: a camera mounted above the door, pointed into the studio. I frown, turning to face the blank black lens.

Why is there a camera in here?

Is it recording all the time?

Something tells me yes, it is.

I'm suddenly self-conscious, replaying my manic behavior all night long as I labored away on the painting. Was I talking to myself? Scratching my ass?

I'm paranoid that Cole Blackwell is watching me.

He unnerves me, and I don't fucking trust him. I don't know what his intentions are, but experience has taught me that when a man takes a special interest in me, it's never fucking good.

As I'm leaving, I stop at the café on the ground level, treating myself to one of the iced lattes Sonia promised were so good. She's not wrong—the coffee is rich as chocolate.

Sonia herself comes through the front doors as I'm exiting.

I kind of wish she hadn't caught sight of me, since she's dressed in a scarlet pantsuit, her hair freshly blown out, and her lipstick immaculate. Whereas I look like I spent the night riding around in the back of a garbage truck.

Also, if she's talked to Cole, there's a good chance she's going to give me my walking papers.

"Mara!" she calls. "You're here early."

"Hey," I say nervously. "Just leaving, actually. I was working late—I hope that's okay."

"More than okay." She smiles. "That's why you have twenty-four-hour access."

"Yeah... Actually, I was curious...I noticed a camera in the studio. Right above the door."

"Oh, yes," she says. "All the studios have them. It's for security purposes only—we've had issues with theft in the past. Don't worry, no one has access to the feed. It would only be reviewed in cases where an incident has occurred."

I nod. "Sure."

I don't believe a word she's saying. Cole owns this building, and those cameras are there for a reason.

"I have good news for you," Sonia says.

"You do?" I'm still thinking about the camera.

"The guild reviewed all the applications... You've been chosen for the grant!"

I stare at her, dumbfounded. "Are you serious?"

"Completely." She passes me a slim envelope with my name neatly typed on the label. "That's your check. And you'll be showing at New Voices in a couple of weeks!"

I clutch the envelope, stunned. "I'm starting to feel like you're my fairy godmother, Sonia."

She laughs. "Better than a wicked stepmother."

She strides away cheerfully, heading up toward her office.

I open the envelope and take out the check, which has my full name on it, made out for two thousand dollars, right there in black and white.

What the fuck is going on?

There's no way I should have gotten that grant after confronting Blackwell. In fact, I expected Sonia to tell me to pack my shit and get out.

Instead, she handed me a check.

Which means Blackwell is doing me another favor.

Favors *always* come with strings.

What the fuck does he want?

I hurry home so I can shower and change before my shift. Already my tiny room feels cramped and dingy compared to the luxurious studio space. My roommates pepper me with questions as I hastily stuff my face with a piece of toast.

"You met Blackwell?" Erin says. "What was he like?"

"A dick," I mumble around the toast. "Just like Joanna said."

"What did you talk about?" Frank demands.

They're all wide-eyed and eager, thinking we discussed color theory or our greatest influences.

I'd like to tell them exactly what went down. But I find myself hesitating, remembering Cole's threat. *No one will believe you... You'll only look more unstable.*

These are my best friends. I should be able to tell them exactly what happened.

Instead, I'm stammering and twisting in my seat, unable to meet their eyes.

I've had a long and ugly history of people not believing me. Stories twisted, facts changed, people who weren't what they seemed to be.

It really starts to fuck with your sense of reality. Every time someone tells you you're wrong, it didn't happen like you said it did, it couldn't, you're a liar, you're a child, you don't understand…

Each hack of the hatchet takes a chunk out of your confidence until you don't even believe yourself anymore.

"We talked about a grant." I shove the check across the table at Joanna. "I'll sign that over to you—I know I owe you for this month's rent and last."

"I told you I could swing it for a few weeks…" Joanna's elegant features screw up in a scowl.

"I know. And thank you—but I have it now."

Frank rips open the envelope before pulling out the check. "*Two thousand dollars?* Are you fucking kidding me?"

"I know." I blush. "Finally getting lucky."

"It's not luck," Joanna says. "You're talented."

Erin yanks the check out of Frank's hand so she can ogle it, too. "Is he…into you?" she says.

"Erin!" Joanna chastises her.

"No!" I shake my head vehemently.

"How do you know?" Frank says.

"Trust me, Blackwell doesn't like me. In fact, he might hate my guts." I shiver, remembering the coldness of his eyes…dark, empty space. No sign of life.

"Then why does he keep helping you?" Erin says.

I bite my lip too hard. "I really don't know."

———

Three hours later, I'm deep in the brunch shift, hauling out platters of sweet potato hash and artfully arranged avocado toast, when Cole Blackwell sits at one of my tables.

I almost drop my tray of mimosas.

Cole cuts such a striking figure that almost everyone at the sidewalk tables stares at him. Every straight woman in a hundred-yard

radius is suddenly compelled to smooth her hair and check her lip gloss. Even my boss Arthur squints and frowns, wondering if somebody famous just sat down.

Cole has that look of effortless celebrity, like certain models and rock stars. Tall, lean, and elegantly dressed in clothes you know cost five figures. It's his careless arrogance that really tops it off. Like you could get hit by a bus right in front of him and he wouldn't even notice.

He's also drop-dead gorgeous. So stunning that it only increases my distrust of him. Nobody that beautiful can be good; it's impossible. Power corrupts, and beauty warps the mind.

He looks even more handsome out in the open, the gray light glowing gently on his pallid skin, his dark hair wind tossed, and the collar of his jacket turned up against that razor-sharp jawline.

He saw me long before I saw him. He's already smirking, his dark eyes glittering with malice.

"Bring me one of those mimosas," he orders.

I think I hate him. A wave of fury surges inside me at the sight of his haughty face. "You're supposed to wait for the hostess to seat you," I mutter.

"I'm sure you can handle one more table."

"Here you go." Ungraciously, I thrust a menu into his hands.

When I return a few minutes later with his drink, he says, "I want you to eat with me."

"I can't. I'm in the middle of a shift."

"Bring me a coffee, then, and I'll wait."

"No," I snap. "You can't sit here that long."

"I doubt your manager will mind. Shall I ask him?"

"Look," I hiss, "I don't know what you're trying to pull, giving me that grant. You can't buy me off that easily."

"I'm not buying you off," Cole says, his black eyes fixed on mine. "I already told you I don't care what story you tell."

"Then why did you give it to me?"

"Because your work was the best."

That hits me like a slap, even though it's supposed to be a compliment. He sounds completely matter-of-fact. And god, I'd like to believe it. But I don't trust him, not for one fucking second.

"Finish your shift," Cole says, dismissing me imperiously. "Then we'll talk."

I finish out the brunch shift, feeling his eyes on me everywhere I turn. My skin burns, and I fumble through tasks I could usually perform in my sleep.

"What's with the camper?" Arthur asks me.

"Sorry—he's waiting to talk to me. He owns my studio."

"Oh, a rival boss, eh?" Arthur snickers, peeking around the corner to observe Cole closer.

"He's not my boss." I toss my head, irritated.

"He looks rich," Arthur says. "You should ask him out."

"No fucking way."

"He *is* rich, though, isn't he?"

"Yeah," I admit.

"I knew it." Arthur nods wisely. "I can always tell."

"He's wearing a Patek Philippe. You're not exactly Inspector Poirot."

"You better lose the sass, or he'll never date you."

"*I don't want him to date me!*"

Arthur looks at me pityingly. "Women always say that."

I wish I could slap Arthur and Cole at the same time, with both hands.

"Well, go ahead, then," Arthur says. "I'll handle your closing duties."

"Thanks," I say, not actually grateful.

Taking off my apron, I plop down in the seat opposite Cole.

"What should we order?" he says.

"I'm not hungry."

"Liar. You must be starving after working all night."

I narrow my eyes at him, trying to ignore the sensual shape of his lips and those outrageous cheekbones. Trying to focus only on the cold brilliance of that stare, harder than diamond.

"I knew you were spying on me," I say.

Cole shrugs, unabashed. "It's my studio. I know everything that goes on inside."

"What do you want from me?" I demand. "Why are you fucking with me? I know you are, so don't deny it."

"*Fucking with you?* That's a funny way to say 'thank you.'"

"I told you, just because you gave me that grant doesn't mean—"

I'm interrupted by Arthur, who has apparently decided to wait a table for the first time in a decade so he can have the pleasure of observing my annoyance up close.

"*Good* morning!" he trills. "What can I get for you two fine people?"

Cole turns toward Arthur with a smile of such startling sincerity that I can only gape. His entire face transforms, suddenly animated. Even his voice softens, becoming warm and humorous.

"Mara was just telling me how hungry she is," Cole says. "I want to treat her to all her favorites—I'm sure you know what she likes."

"My goodness," Arthur says, eyes wide behind his spectacles. "How incredibly *generous.*"

If I weren't sitting down, he'd be elbowing me in the ribs right now.

"I *am* generous," Cole says, his grin widening. "Thank you for noticing."

Arthur laughs. "And to think Mara didn't want to eat breakfast with you."

"Silly Mara," Cole says, patting my hand in a way that makes me feel murderous. "She never knows what's good for her."

Arthur is enjoying this so much that he doesn't want to leave to punch in our order. I have to clear my throat several times, loudly, before he departs.

As soon as he's gone, I snatch my hand back from Cole.

"I don't need you," I inform him.

Cole snorts. "The fuck you don't. You're flat broke, no studio, barely making rent. No connections and no cash. You absolutely need my help."

I really wish I had an argument for that.

All I can do is scowl and say, "I've gotten along just fine so far."

Cole lets out a long sigh of annoyance. "I think we both know that's not true. Even putting aside how we first met—which was hardly your finest moment—you're not doing so great in the real world either. But now you've met me. And in a few short weeks, you'll be showing at New Voices. I could personally recommend you to several brokers I know. You have no idea the doors I could open for you…"

I cross my arms over my chest. "In exchange for what?"

Cole smiles. This is his genuine smile—not the one he showed Arthur. There's nothing warm or friendly about it. Actually, it's pretty fucking terrifying.

"You'll be my protégé," he says.

"What does that mean?"

"We'll get to know each other. I'll give you advice, mentorship. You'll follow that advice, and you'll flourish."

The words he's saying sound perfectly benign. Yet I get the feeling I'm about to sign a devil's bargain with a hell of a hidden clause.

"Is there some kind of sexual implication here I'm missing?" I say. "Are you the Weinstein of the art world?"

Cole sits back in his chair, sipping his mimosa lazily. This new position shows off his long legs and his powerful chest flexing beneath his cashmere sweater, a display that is absolutely intentional.

"Do I look like I need to bribe women for sex?"

"No," I admit.

Half my roommates would fuck Cole in a heartbeat. Actually, all of them would, except maybe Peter.

I bite the edge of my thumbnail, considering.

"Don't bite your nails," Cole snaps. "It's disgusting."

I bite my nail harder, scowling at him.

He's going to be bossy and controlling, I can already tell. Is that what he wants? A puppet dancing on his strings?

"Can I come see your studio?" I ask.

This is an audacious request. Cole Blackwell doesn't show his studio to anyone. Especially not when he's in the middle of a series. I have no right to ask—but I have the strangest sense that he just might agree.

"Already making demands?" Cole says. He stirs his straw through his ice with a cold clicking sound.

"Surely a protégé gets to see the master at work," I reply.

Cole smiles. He likes being called *master*.

"I'll consider it," he says. "Now…" He leans forward on the table, steepling his slim pale hands in front of him. "We're going to talk about you."

Fuck. That happens to be my least favorite topic.

"What do you want to know?"

He looks at me hungrily. "Everything."

I swallow hard. "All right. I've lived here my whole life. Always wanted to be an artist. Now I am—sort of."

"What about your family?"

Come to think of it, *that's* my least favorite topic.

I put my hands down on my lap so I won't start chewing my nails again.

"I don't have any family," I say.

"Everyone has family."

"Not me." I glare at him, my lips pressed together, stubborn.

"Where's the alcoholic mother?" Cole says.

To me, our conversation at the studio was a blur of shouted accusations and utter confusion. Cole apparently remembers every word, including the part I blurted out and now fervently regret.

"She's in Bakersville," I mutter.

"What about the stepfather?"

"As far as I know, he lives in New Mexico. I haven't talked to either of them in years."

"Why?"

My heart hammers, and I feel that sick, squirming sensation in my stomach that always arises when I'm forced to think about my mother. I like to keep her trapped behind a locked door in my brain. She's emotional cancer—if I let her out, she'll infect every part of me.

"She's the worst person I've ever met," I say, trying to keep my voice steady. "And that includes my stepfather. I ran away the day I turned eighteen."

"Where's your actual father?"

"Dead."

"So is mine," Cole says. "I find it's better that way."

I look at him sharply, wondering if that's supposed to be a joke. "I loved my father," I say coldly. "The day I lost him was the worst day of my life."

Cole smiles. "The worst day so far."

What. The. Fuck.

"So Daddy died, leaving you alone with Mommy dearest and not a penny between you," Cole prods, wrinkling his nose like he can still smell those awful years on my skin.

"There are worse things than being poor," I inform him. "There was a period of time when I had my hair brushed, a clean uniform, and went to a private school with a lunch packed every day. It was hell."

"Enlighten me," Cole says, one dark eyebrow raised.

"No," I say flatly. "I'm not a sideshow for your amusement."

"Why are you so combative?" he says. "Have you ever tried cooperating?"

"In my experience, when men say 'cooperative,' they mean 'obedient.'"

He grins. "Then have you ever tried being obedient?"

"Never."

That's a lie. I have tried it. All I learned is that no amount of submission is good enough for a man. You can roll over, show your belly, beg for mercy, and they'll just keep hitting you. Because the very act of breathing is rebellious in the eyes of an angry male.

Cole's dark eyes rove over my face, giving me the uncomfortable sensation that he can see every thought I'd prefer to keep hidden.

Thankfully, I'm saved by Arthur depositing several platters of steaming food in front of us.

"All the greatest hits," he says, grinning broadly.

"Looks phenomenal," Cole says, turning on the charm with the flick of a switch.

Only after Arthur leaves us does Cole examine the food with his usual critical glare.

"What is this?" he demands.

"That's the bacon sampler platter," I say, nodding toward four marinated strips of premium pork belly labeled with fancy script like each is a guest at a wedding.

Cole frowns. "It looks...intense."

"It's the best thing you'll ever put in your mouth. Look." I cut off a bite of the rosemary balsamic bacon. "Try this one first."

Cole takes a bite. He chews slowly, his expression melting from skepticism into genuine surprise. "Holy shit," he says.

"I told you. Try this one now. Brown sugar cinnamon."

He takes a bite of the second strip, his eyebrows rising and an unwilling smile tugging at his mouth. "This is so good."

"I know," I snap. "That's why I work here. It's the literal best brunch in the city."

"Is that really why you work here?" Cole asks, watching me closely.

"Yes. The smell of food—I can't stand it if it's not good. The food here smells incredible because it *is* incredible. Here, try this now—take a sip of the mimosa, then eat one of the spicy-sweet potatoes."

Cole does exactly what I said, taking a small sip of his drink, then quickly biting into the potato.

"What the fuck," he says. "Why is that so good?"

"I dunno." I shrug. "Something about the sour citrus and then the pop of salt. They amplify each other."

Cole is watching me as I eat my own food, taking a small bite of one thing and then another, cycling through my favorite combinations.

"Is that how you eat?" he says.

I shrug. "Unless I'm in a hurry."

"Show me more combinations."

I show him all my favorite ways to eat the magnificent brunch spread Arthur laid before us—lemon curd layered with fresh strawberries and clotted cream on the scones, blueberries between bites of maple bacon, a dash of hot sauce mixed in with the hollandaise...

Cole tries it all with an unusual level of curiosity. I'd assume somebody as rich as him has eaten at a million fancy restaurants.

"Don't you eat out all the time?" I ask him.

He shakes his head. "I don't spend much time on food. It bores me."

"But you like this?"

"I do," he says, almost as if he hates to admit it. "How do you come up with all this?"

I shrug. "When I was little, we never had fresh groceries. Dinner was whatever I could scrounge from the kitchen without mold growing on it. A can of corn. Boiled egg. Dry cereal. I never tried most foods until I started working at restaurants. I'd never tasted steak, or cilantro, or avocado. I wanted to try everything—it was like discovering a whole new sense."

"But there was a time when you weren't poor," Cole says, harrying that point like a dog with a bone. He's really not gonna fucking drop it.

"Yes," I say testily. "When we lived with Randall."

"That's your stepfather."

"Yes."

"What did you eat then?"

"Not fucking much. He used to scream at me if my spoon clinked in my cereal bowl."

"How old were you?"

"Eleven."

"He didn't like having a stepkid?"

"No. He didn't. And by that point, he had learned a thing or two about my mother. She's very good at fooling people for a while. By the time he realized, they were already married."

"Realized what?"

"That she's a parasite. That her only ambition is to latch on to people and bleed them dry."

Cole nods slowly. "Including you," he says.

"Especially me."

———

I leave brunch in a kind of a daze, wondering how in the fuck Cole Blackwell now knows more about my sordid history than my closest friends. He's relentless…and hypnotic, the way he fixes me with those deep, dark eyes, never looking away for a moment. The way he absorbs everything I say with none of the usual displays of sympathy or irritating commiseration. He just soaks it in and demands more, like he plans to drill down to the core of me, strip-mining my soul.

He insisted on paying for the meal, leaving an extra hundred-dollar bill as a tip for Arthur.

I can already see how he uses his money to manipulate

people—including me. I cashed that two-thousand-dollar check because I had to, because I owe Joanna for rent and utilities, and because I have to pay the credit card bill for the replacement cell phone, and my hospital bill, too.

Cole knows exactly how much leverage he has over me, and he isn't shy about leaning on the lever.

And yet, despite the fact he's clearly callous and manipulative, and he left me to fucking die in the woods, I still find myself walking with strange lightness down the hilly streets to my sparkling new studio.

Maybe because he wasn't *trying* to make me feel better. In fact, it's the first time I've ever mentioned this topic without hearing the words *but it's your mom...*

Cole offered no sympathy. He also offered no excuses. No fucking platitudes. No lies.

I spend the afternoon working on my new painting. I've never felt such confidence in a piece of my own work. It seems to come alive under my hands, like it has a mind of its own. Michelangelo used to say that—that the sculpture was always there inside the marble. He just had to release it.

That's how I feel today. The painting is already there, inside the canvas and inside my brain. My brush is exposing what already exists. Perfect and whole—all it needs is to be unveiled.

15

COLE

THIS OBSESSION WITH MARA CONSUMES ME.

It's all I think about. It directs every action I take.

I've never felt so out of control—which upsets me.

My fantasies have always been a stage where I'm the director, arranging the story at will.

Now I find myself fantasizing about Mara with no intent or control. Without even realizing I'm about to slip into another daydream realer than the world around me.

I see her face, her body, the way she moves…

When I first laid eyes on her, I barely found her tolerable. Her raw nails and grungy clothes disgusted me.

Now some bizarre alchemy is at work. Every part of her is becoming increasingly attractive to me. The slimness of her figure and the dreamy way it moves when she's lost in thought. Those birdlike hands that seem to enact the cleverest impulses of her brain with no barrier in between. The mix of innocence and wildness on her face—that expression of rebellion that creases her eyebrows, that bares her teeth…

She's determined to defy me at every turn, though it's obvious I have all the power and she has nothing.

She's stubborn. Self-destructive, even. But she's not the pathetic victim I expected her to be. She has a will to live, to thrive. A relentlessness in pursuit of her goals that I find…familiar.

I've never seen myself in another person before.

Much as Shaw desperately wants to believe we are one and the same, I've never felt kinship with him. Very much the opposite.

There's only one god in my world. I was alone in the universe.

And now I see...a spark.

A spark that interests me.

I want to hold it in my hands. Manipulate it.

Mara has a kind of power separate from mine. I want to know if I can harness it. Or consume it.

I visit her studio regularly. I don't knock—she knows I'm watching her through the camera mounted above her door. There is no appearance of privacy.

I walk into the studio I own, that I supply to her, and I see the rebellious ways she's altered the space—how she's somehow managed to throw open the high upper windows, how she's scattered her clothes and books around and used an injudicious amount of her grant money to fill the space with plants—leafy tropical flowers, vine-like hanging baskets, and potted trees to supplement the ornamental lemons already in place. She's taken my carefully curated English garden and turned it into a jungle.

Mara's appearance ranges from unkempt to deranged—torn overalls, bare feet, paint-streaked face and hands, brushes thrust into her hair for safekeeping.

And yet her painting glows like the pietà. Illuminated from the inside.

I examine every millimeter of it.

"The hands need work."

"I know," Mara says. "The nails..."

"This edge could be sharpened." I point the handle of a paintbrush toward the figure's left shoulder. "Here."

I take the palette from its resting place and dip the brush, intending to darken the edge myself.

"*No!*" Mara snaps as I raise the brush toward the canvas. "I'll do it."

I set the palette down, narrowing my eyes at her. "You should be so fucking lucky as to have it known I touched my brush to your work."

"I'm aware of your many talents. You can paint rings around me. I don't give a shit—nobody touches this canvas but me."

She faces me down, physically blocking me from the canvas, her eyes wild, paintbrush gripped like she wants to shank me.

She's so passionate about everything.

"You look like you want to stab me. Have you ever hurt anyone, Mara? Or only imagined it…?"

Her fist trembles, clenched around the brush.

That's not a tremble of fear.

It's rage.

At who, Mara? Me? Alastor Shaw? The mother, the stepfather? Or the whole fucking world…?

"I've never hurt anyone," she says. "And I don't want to."

"You don't wish anyone ill?"

"No."

"What about the man who kidnapped you?" I step close to her, looking look straight down into her face. "What about him?"

Her chest rises and falls, faster and faster. She won't step back.

Softly, I say, "You must want revenge. He tied you up. Pierced your nipples."

I look down at her chest. Mara never wears a bra. Her small breasts and pert little nipples are regularly visible beneath her crop tops and dresses. All the more so because of the silver rings through those nipples that she has yet to remove.

"Why haven't you taken those out, Mara? I think I know why…"

She gazes up at me with those wide wild eyes, that impudent nose and vicious little mouth. "Why?"

"As a reminder," I whisper, stroking my finger gently against the side of her cheek. Mara shivers. "You don't want to forget. Which means you don't want to forgive."

Her pupils expand like a drop of oil spreading on water. I'm speaking the thoughts right out of her brain.

"He cut your wrists. Left you for dead. No…worse than that. Left you as a mockery. A fucking joke. He didn't finish killing you—that's how little you meant to him. He didn't even stay to watch you die."

The truth is that Alastor didn't linger because he knew he couldn't conceal himself from me.

But I'm telling Mara what she knows to be true…the man who attacked her sees her as less than garbage. Less than dirt. An insect, struggling and dying on the windowsill, not even worthy of his notice.

"You *would* hurt him, Mara. You *want* to hurt him. And he deserves it. If no one stops him, he'll *keep* hurting people. It would be more than justice…it would be *good.*"

Mara faces me, her eyes blazing, her face flushed. A righteous angel in the face of a demon.

"Evil men always want to justify what they do," she says. "And it's not by telling you all their reasons. No…they want to push you, and bend you, and break you until you snap. Until you do something you thought you'd never do. Until you can't even recognize yourself. Until you're as bad as they are. That's how they justify themselves… by trying to make you the same as them."

There's no space. My face is inches from hers, our bodies so close that her heat and mine radiate in one continuous loop, feeding the inferno between us.

"You wouldn't kill him? If he were here, now, as helpless as you were that night?"

She meets my gaze, unflinching. "No."

"What if he *weren't* helpless? What if it was him or you?"

She stares into my eyes. "Then I would tell him…you're not going to sneak up on me this time. We're face-to-face now."

She still thinks it might have been me.

She thinks I did that to her.

And yet she's here, now, alone in this room with me, inches away, her lips as swollen and flushed as mine...

She's more twisted than I ever dared to dream.

16
MARA

THE NIGHT OF NEW VOICES, I'M SO NERVOUS THAT I VOMIT IN THE gutter on the way to the show.

Cole said he'd send a car for me at 9:00.

At 8:20 I leave on foot.

I've come to know Cole Blackwell more intimately than I would ever have imagined these past few weeks. I honestly think I might know him better than any person in this city because it's only around me that he lets the mask fall. And it's not one mask—there are dozens.

I watch him lift each to his face, one after another, each tailor-made for the person with whom he converses.

The mask for my boss Arthur is that of a fellow businessman with an emotional attachment to his young protégé—in Cole's case, bolstered by a pretend crush.

The mask he wears around most of his employees is of a distant, autocratic artist. He has them jumping at his wild demands, making just enough outlandish requests to disguise what he actually wants…

The mask he wears for Sonia is the most fucked up of all because it *appears* the most intimate. Around her, he shows his ruthlessness and wicked humor. He'll even admit unflattering things to her. But then he turns to me, and I see the animation fall from his face, revealing the absolute blankness beneath—a sight Sonia never glimpses, not even for a fraction of a second. He's too careful. He never slips.

He shows me on purpose.

The rest of the time could just be another mask. The most deceptive of all because it most approximates reality.

He knows how good I am at spotting irregularities. I'm jumpy, sensitive—tiny details are glaring sirens to me. He knows this mask has to be good, a real work of art, or it won't fool me.

I watch Cole as closely as he watches me.

I watch while he mentors and instructs me, ripping my painting to shreds and demanding I work and rework it, making me labor constantly, continuously, perfecting it for the show.

He's right; that's what fucking kills me. The things he points out, the things he tells me to change, I see them, too. I know what I have to do.

We both see the painting as it *will* be. As it *has* to be.

We see the perfect vision.

The closer it gets to perfect, the tighter Cole slips his noose. He thinks he has me tied up, completely under his control: in his studio, in his show, publicly proclaimed as his protégé.

He's getting bossier by the day. Trying to take more and more of my time. Showing up outside my work, waiting when my shift is over, walking me to his studio, taking me home again at night. Making sure I never go anywhere outside his sight, without him knowing.

I see what he's doing.

He's planning to pick me up in that limo tonight, him wearing whatever he's picked out for himself and me in the dress a courier brought over this morning: a stunning silk gown slit to the navel. Elegant and dangerous. Something that would have turned every head in the gallery.

Well, fuck him. I pick out my own clothes.

Nobody's gonna look at me tonight because of a low-cut dress. They're going to stare at the painting. Because the painting is fucking gorgeous.

I stomp over to the gallery wearing a '70s minidress and my favorite boots.

I get there a half hour early instead of fashionably late. I could have strolled in on Cole Blackwell's arm. Instead, I'm going to see people's reactions to my work. Their *real* reaction, when they don't know I'm here.

The half-moon of people around the canvas stand quietly like worshippers.

The painting is lit as all paintings of saints should be: by a single brilliant overhead light.

The figure's face is upturned to that light, her body positioned in a way that is simultaneously elegant and broken, contorted and free.

She's pierced with knives, arrows, bullets, boards…a stone has caved in half her skull. Her pale flesh strains against the leather harness, smooth as alabaster.

Yet her expression is ecstatic. Beatific. Grateful, even.

The title reads *The Mercy of Men.*

The painting is exactly life-size. It's hung as if you could step right through the canvas and take her place in the frame.

The new critic for the *Siren* points at the figure's face.

A perfect portrait.

My portrait.

"Who the fuck is that?" she says.

17

COLE

My rage upon arriving at Mara's house and finding her already gone is only surpassed by my disgust at myself for not anticipating this.

I was counting on her understanding how advantageous it would be to arrive together. Cameras flashing as we stepped out of the limousine, each oozing the glamour, wealth, and cachet I've been carefully curating for this moment.

Instead, the obstinate little idiot ran off on foot.

I *hate* when she walks.

As much as I've tried to conceal my mentorship of Mara, it's only a matter of time until Alastor sees us together. When he does, there's no hiding who she is. He'll recognize her. And for the first time in my life…I'm not sure what to do about that.

I don't want Alastor anywhere near Mara.

I don't want him to know she's even alive.

And yet the only way to hide her from him would be to never interact with her myself, or only do so in the most mundane ways.

I want her with me constantly.

I want to do every fucking thing I want to do with her.

The conflict between this need and its inevitable consequences infuriates me.

I want her always under my eye. Always under my control. I

want cameras in her room, on her fucking body. It's not enough, watching her at the studio, at work, from the house behind hers...

"*Get to the fucking gallery!*" I bellow at the driver.

The moment we pull up, I shove my way inside without any of the usual glad-handing.

The only person I greet is Sonia, and only to snarl, "*Where is she?*"

"Mara?" Sonia says, her eyebrow raised.

She knows damn well I mean Mara. She just wants to make me say it.

"Yes," I hiss. "*Mara.*"

Sonia points wordlessly with her pen.

If I hadn't been so enraged, I could simply have followed the concentration of noise. Mara is already surrounded by journalists, critics, and newfound friends.

I shove my way through all of them before seizing her by the arm and snarling into her face, "*How fucking dare you not wait for me.*"

Dozens of eyes fix us, a sudden frantic silence falling as everyone strains to overhear with all their might.

Mara is just as conscious of these elements as I am. Maybe even more so.

She faces me boldly.

Because she anticipated this. Planned it, even.

"I missed you, too, sweetheart," she says.

And she kisses me on the mouth.

18

MARA

A HUNDRED EYES SURROUND US. CAMERAS EXPLODE IN FLASHES OF blinding light. The air is so thick, you could slice it.

Cole is so angry that his whole body is a live wire, a thrumming electric line.

Our mouths meet, and the entirety of that current passes into me.

I'm jolted awake, my brain opening like a portal into the universe. I kiss him, and I taste his mouth. I taste *him*.

Not the mask, not the pretender.

I taste the fucking animal.

That animal is hungry. It attacks my mouth. It bites my lips. It swallows me whole.

Cole is kissing me like the fucking monster he is, right here, right now, in front of all these people.

He's eating me alive while they all watch.

When we break apart, my mouth is bleeding. I feel the warmth sliding down my chin.

My blood dots his full lower lip. I can see it in the threads of his teeth.

He says, "Don't you ever keep me waiting."

He seizes me by the arm and begins the forceful process of parading me in front of every single influential person in that room.

He introduces me to every last one, telling them I'm his student, his protégé. That we're working on a new series together, and they can see its first example right now, the fucking masterwork of the show.

Whatever I imagined it would be like walking around with Cole Blackwell, the reality is tenfold. He's a dark star at the center of the universe, pulling everyone in. Everybody wants to see him, speak with him. Even the most conceited and influential players become giddy sycophants in his presence.

Even Jack Brisk—who barely noticed when he dumped his wine all over my dress—acts like an eager schoolboy when Cole spares him a glance.

"Did Sonia tell you my new offer?" he says.

"You know she did. And you know what I replied."

"I could make it an even three million—"

"Not interested."

When Brisk stalks off, offended, I ask, "What was that about?"

"I only own a few things I actually give a shit about," Cole says. "I'm not selling any of them to Brisk."

"What do you give a shit about?"

I'm genuinely curious. Though everything Cole owns is expensive—his car, his watch, his clothes—he doesn't seem attached to any of it. Even his fancy suits are dark and simple, worn like a uniform every day.

I don't expect him to answer. But Cole will do anything to shock me.

"I have a garden at my house. Self-contained. Self-perpetuating."

"A mini ecosystem?" I ask, unable to contain my curiosity.

"Not mini."

I have a hundred more questions on this topic, but we're immediately interrupted by Erin and Frank. While all my roommates have shown up to support me, it's those two who shoulder their way through the crowd so they can demand an introduction to Cole.

They're both doing their damnedest to hit on him, Frank by

asking probing questions about Cole's latest sculpture, and Erin by making innuendos and trying to touch him on the forearm.

Cole is remarkably patient with this, though I can tell he's itching to show me off to more important people.

Not wanting to piss him off any more than I already have, I shoo Frank and Erin away and wave to Joanna on the opposite side of the room. Joanna grins, raising her champagne glass in my direction in a silent toast.

She brought her boyfriend, Paul, along with his roommate Logan. Logan is a tattoo artist—in fact, he did the snake on my ribs.

"Who's that?" Cole snaps, following my gaze.

"My roommate Joanna."

"I know that," he says testily. "I meant the other two."

Before I can respond, we're interrupted by Sonia bringing over another round of brokers and curators who want to talk to Cole and, by extension, to me as well.

At the beginning of the evening, I noticed a strange tension in Cole, separate from his annoyance at me. He was scanning the room. Looking for someone.

That person never seemed to materialize.

As the night wears on, as the time passes that anyone important would have come, I see him relax.

I can read Cole. When he wants me to...and sometimes when he doesn't.

He doesn't want me to know he was watching; he tried to hide it. Which instantly makes it the most intriguing aspect of the evening.

Who the fuck is he waiting for?

The accolades pour down on my shoulders. Not because of Cole or his influence. I saw it for myself before he ever arrived—the work is *good*.

The feeling of achievement, of making something worthwhile, eclipses everything else that happens that night and all that *will* happen in the next few days.

Profiles, posts, reposts, and an online viral spread of my name are all coming. I feel the first breath of it in that moment.

But as the show wraps up, there's only one thing I keep thinking, over and over:

I fucking did it.

I made art.

As the night wraps up, alight with happiness, I turn to Cole. My bliss is so complete that it illuminates everything around me, giving every single person their own interior glow. Even Cole.

I think of all the criticism he gave me. All the advice. I think of the studio space itself, which I only have because of him.

And I look at his face. That beautiful fucking face.

I feel grateful to him, genuinely grateful.

Below that…a deeper, darker emotion lurks beneath the surface. It's been there from the moment I laid eyes on him, even in my most extreme and awful circumstance, when I viewed him as the angel of death.

I wanted death.

I wanted *him.*

Every moment of our kiss is seared in my brain. His taste, his scent, those full, strong lips, and the teeth beneath…

The flavor of my own blood in my mouth.

I want more.

I drag him into the empty offices next to the gallery. My mouth is all over him; my hands, too. I shove him against a desk and drop to my knees before him, opening the buckle of his belt.

We're interrupted by the sound of someone clearing their throat.

"As much as I'd like to keep observing in secret, that awful conscience of mine just won't let me keep quiet."

It's Simon Grundy. Cole introduced me to him earlier in the

evening. He's a buyer for the Jolie and Voss—a sardonic bearded man of about forty-eight, smelling faintly of cigars.

He grins at me, seeing me kneel before my teacher in precisely the position he'd have expected to find me if he ever came to visit our studio.

My face burns.

I want to tell him I've never done this before, never even *considered* doing it. I've never sucked cock for a favor, not even at my most desperate.

But in this case…the gratitude was great. As was my impulse to suck Cole's cock.

"No need for embarrassment." Cole's dark eyes flit between me and Simon. "Mara was just about to express her thanks for everything I've done for her. And since she's so extremely…grateful…I'm sure she'd be happy to include you."

Simon takes a step closer, trying to conceal the emotions flushing into his face. Excitement. Lust. And glee… He can't believe his luck in this moment. The fortuitous hand fate is dealing him.

"Here she is, already on her knees." Cole's voice sounds as expensive as his clothes, thick and silky. "I'm sure you'll find her an extremely capable student…"

I'm on a rocket right now, flying to a certain destination. If I want to ride it all the way there, I can't do anything to light the fuse. I can't risk blowing it all early.

This is the deal with the devil:

He owns me.

He controls me.

Slowly, I rise to my feet.

I ignore Simon like he's not even there.

Looking right in Cole's eyes, I say, "I wanted you. Genuinely. Because I admire you, and you attract me. I *wanted* to fuck you. But you don't tell me what to do."

He stands there, pale and still. A dark, swirling fury fills his features. His eyes are glittering chips of black in a sea of flat white.

I don't wait for his response.

I blaze through the crowd of partygoers like a comet in the sky.

A satellite intercepts my path.

It's Logan, shy and out of place in his ripped jeans and T-shirt, showing the thick swirls of ink running up and down his arms. He steps in front of me, stammering something about my painting.

I seize him by the collar, dragging him into my orbit. "You're coming with me."

19

COLE

Mara storms out of the room.

Simon turns, grinning toothily.

"Well, it was worth a try." He snickers.

I shoot him a look that wipes the smile off his face.

"I better get back to the party..." He tries to edge past me out of the room.

I shove him out of the way, striding after Mara myself.

I can see her tangled dark hair disappearing out the front doors of the gallery.

To my utter fury, she's grabbed the hand of some random fuck boy and dragged him along with her.

What the fuck does she think she's doing?

Her stubbornness is really starting to piss me off.

I wanted you. Genuinely.

My head twitches, shaking off the memory of those words like a fly buzzing next to my ear.

I embarrassed her.

She was so vulnerable, kneeling before me...I couldn't help myself. I wanted to see how far I could push her.

The more she rebels, the more I want to crush her.

And the more she clings to her convictions, the further I'm compelled to drag her down dark and twisted pathways...

By the time I reach the front doors, Mara and her hapless companion have already climbed into a taxi and pulled away from the curb.

Where the fuck is she going?

I'm putting a tracker on her phone. First thing tomorrow. I should have done it already.

Sonia intercepts me. "Marcus York is looking for you."

"What?" I'm distracted.

"He's right over there." She points. "Come on, I'll bring you over. He says he has something 'huge' to tell you."

"I bet," I say irritably.

York is a city planner and self-proclaimed patron of the arts. He's influential in this city, but he was also close with my father, which means I can't fucking stand him.

"Cole!" he says in his booming voice, clapping me hard on both shoulders.

York is apple shaped, with outrageously frizzy hair and a florid face. His teeth are long and ivory colored, always on display because he's always smiling. The clownish hair and avuncular tone are meant to disarm the people he meets. I know better—York is a shark, taking greedy bites out of every construction contract and zoning deal that passes over his desk.

"I ought to come visit you," he says. "It's been too long since I came to Sea Cliff."

He was one of the many associates who used to visit my father's private office on the ground floor of the house. Most of the movers and shakers of San Francisco passed through those oak doors at one time or another. Now no one comes to my home, ever. And I intend to keep it that way.

"I do all my business out of my studio."

"But we're old friends." York raises his grizzled eyebrows.

"Friendships founded on business are superior to businesses founded on friendship."

"Spoken like your father." York laughs.

I loathe comparisons to my father.

A savvy operator, York sees my lips tighten and swiftly changes the subject.

"I was telling Sonia here that we have an exciting opportunity in the offing. The city is putting up two million for a monumental sculpture for Corona Heights Park. We'll be accepting designs all next month. I expect you'll want to throw your hat in the ring. Shaw, too, I'd wager."

"Where is Shaw?" I interject, glancing at Sonia. "He never misses New Voices."

Because he'd never miss fucking one of those new voices.

Sonia shrugs. "His name was on the guest list…"

Though I'd rather delay Shaw's collision with Mara, his unexplained absence is worse.

I'm in a foul mood, more agitated than I've been in months. Where's Mara going? What's she doing right at this moment? I could not give less of a fuck what York is yammering on about.

"This is your chance to put your mark on this city once and for all," York says pompously. "Get your name out there."

I smile thinly. "I'm not sure how widely I want my name to be known."

"Then you shouldn't be so damn talented." York guffaws. "You've got a month to draw up your proposal—don't miss the deadline. You know I'll put in a good word for you."

I suppress the sneer that arises at the idea that I need Marcus York to talk up my design.

My phone buzzes in my pocket. I snatch it out, besieged by the irrational idea that Mara might have texted me.

Close…it's a motion notification for the camera inside her studio.

Good. She ditched the guy and decided to get some work done. How industrious of her.

It's not enough to know where she is—I need to see her.

"Excuse me," I say to Sonia, interrupting York midsentence. York frowns, a hint of the shark peering out from under his lowered brows.

I slip past them both, heading back into the empty galleries that were roped off for the show. I weave my way through abstract sculptures on plinths and color-blocked canvases.

I want to be alone so I can watch her. Is she starting a new painting? I told her she should continue her series of saint-inspired portraits. My curiosity to see what she comes up with next far outstrips my interest in any of the art hanging all around me.

My eyes are glued to the phone screen.

The security camera feed loads at last, providing a live stream of Mara's studio in full color, right before my eyes.

She's not alone.

She's brought that fuck boy into her studio. *My* studio.

My fingers clench around the phone so hard, I hear the glass screen groaning.

Mara and the guy are talking. She's taken two beers out of the mini-fridge. They sip the drinks, Mara gesturing with her free hand as she traces in the air the shapes that she intends to draw on the fresh canvas set upon its easel.

Is she telling him about the series? Telling him what she plans to do next?

I hear the low murmur of their voices but can't make out the words.

Mara opens several canisters of paint, showing him the colors inside. He dips his finger into the violet paint and dabs it on her nose. Mara laughs, wiping it off with the back of her hand.

I'll fucking kill him.

Mara sets down her beer. She strides over to the stereo and turns on her music, much too loud as usual.

♫ *"STUPID"—Ashnikko*

The pounding beat is easily loud enough for me to make out the lyrics.

Stupid boy think that I need him...

Molten heat rises up the back of my neck, all the way to my ears. My hands go cold.

Mara marches back to the center of the room, directly in front of the camera. She seizes the guy by the shirt and yanks him toward her, kissing him ferociously.

The kiss seems to go on forever.

It's wild and deep, not unlike the one Mara and I shared only an hour ago.

In fact, I almost feel like I've stepped back in time. With his back to me, his shaggy dark hair, and his black T-shirt, her date could be me. And Mara—eyes closed, head tilted back, body pressed against him—looks just as irresistible as she did up close.

I feel like I'm floating inside the room with them.

I watch, transfixed, as Mara pulls his shirt up over his head, baring an athletic body covered in tattoos. She pulls down the shoulder straps of her tiny floral minidress, letting the dress puddle around her boots. She steps free, slim and nude, the silver rings glinting in her nipples.

Even from behind, I can tell the guy is gawking at her body.

So am I.

Mara's figure is so smooth and lithe that I want to draw it without ever lifting my pencil from the page. Her skin is luminescent. She shaved her pussy bare, something I've never seen before in my time spying on her.

Who did she do that for?

Was it for me?

Now this fucking nobody is looking at her instead. He's putting his hands around her waist. Drawing her close to kiss him again.

I want to drive over there. Rip them apart. Smash his head into the wall a hundred times until his skull cracks like a melon and his brains leak out his ears.

But I'm frozen in place, unable to look away from the screen even for a second.

Mara drops to her knees before him. She unbuckles his jeans and yanks them down, letting his cock spring free, already hard. Mine is bigger. That's no fucking consolation when she takes him in her mouth, enveloped between her soft full lips, running her pink tongue up and down his shaft, then swirling around the head.

She's voracious, enthusiastic, playful. Giving him the kind of blow job men only dream of receiving.

I'm engulfed in jealousy. Inflamed with it. It's a bonfire all around me, and I'm a heretic tied to the stake, burning and burning and burning.

That mouth belongs around *my* cock. Those slate-gray eyes should be looking up at *me*.

Despite my fury, despite my raging jealousy, my own cock is stiffening inside my trousers. It jabs painfully against my zipper, demanding to be released.

I can't stop watching.

Mara stands. The guy swoops her up before lowering her onto his wet, shining cock. She wraps her arms around his neck, riding up and down on him, making her little tits bounce.

She fucks like a demon, biting his lower lip, clawing his back with her nails.

The guy looks like he's died and gone to heaven. He's doing his best to keep up with her, sweating, his arms shaking while he fucks her as hard as she demands. He fucks her against the wall, against the windows, the glass steaming up behind them, their bodies leaving a vacant silhouette when they pull away again.

They knock over one of the open canisters of paint, spilling violet across my hardwood floors. I hear the guy swear and apologize.

Mara just laughs. She places her palms flat on the paint, then smears them across his chest, leaving long streaks of color. Now he's laughing, too, dipping his hands in two more canisters before printing coral and chocolate handprints on her breasts.

They kiss again, bumping the canvas off its easel so it falls flat on the floor.

The guy lies down in the spilled paint. Mara mounts him. He smears paint up and down her naked body in long swoops while she rides him.

The sight of Mara's body streaked in citron, scarlet, and sienna is more than I can stand. I rip down my zipper before taking my throbbing cock in my hand. I start pumping up and down, so rough that I'm almost ripping skin off the shaft. I've never been so angry. Or so aroused.

They're rolling around in the paint until they hardly have an inch of bare skin left. They roll over the canvas and fuck on top of it. He spoons her on it, fucking her from behind.

Mara climbs on top again, and now she's riding him harder and harder, charging down the raceway to the finish line. Her breasts are bouncing, her hair flying, her face flushed and sweating.

Right then, right as she's about to come, she looks directly at the camera. She stares at me like she's looking in my eyes. Her expression is wild and defiant.

In that moment I realize this whole thing has been a performance.

She knew I would watch.

She's been fucking him *for* me, *at* me.

To get revenge on me.

And I realize…she's everything I dreamed of and more. More vengeful. More strategic. More effective.

More fucked up.

I watch her body bouncing, gyrating. I see the wicked smirk on her face as she starts to come.

It makes me explode. Come rockets out of my cock, spurting so

far that I hit the edge of a landscape, spraying the painting and the frame.

I don't give a fuck.

I don't even clean it up.

I simply yank up my zipper, vowing to myself that the next time I unleash a load like that, it's going on Mara's face.

The next morning I arrive at the studio two hours earlier than usual.

I barely slept.

Every time I dozed off, I dreamed of Mara's paint-streaked body writhing and bouncing, so beautiful in motion that it became a living work of art.

I kept jolting awake, sweating, my cock a red-hot iron bar.

I couldn't even jerk off, thanks to my hasty vow last night.

Too bad for me…once I make a promise to myself, I never break it.

I stride into the studio, startling Janice. She wasn't expecting me so early.

"Good morning!" she chirps, hastily tidying her desk, swiping an entire armful of scattered pens and papers into a drawer.

"Get me coffee," I bark. "Iced."

"Right away." She stands up so quickly that her glasses slide down her nose and her pantyhose tear up the back. She pushes the glasses up with her index finger, blushing and likely hoping I didn't notice the stockings. Pausing a moment, she ventures, "Are you all right?"

I must really look like shit if she has the balls to ask me that. I'm flushed and sweating. Feverish.

But I'm getting control of myself. Slowly, by sheer force of will. Formulating new plans for how I'm going to bend Mara in half and crush her under my heel.

"I'll be great when I have my fucking coffee."

"Right! Sorry," she squeaks, hurrying off.

I take the stairs up to the top floor, the entire space given over to my office.

As soon as I step through the door, my nostrils flare, picking up a distinctly sweet and peppery scent.

Mara.

I whirl around, expecting to see her sitting at my desk.

Instead, a freshly hung painting awaits my view. Abstract, with large streaks of violet, scarlet, and sienna...

She fucked on that painting, and then she hung it on my wall.

I'm struck anew by the absolute insanity of this girl.

I admire her audacity. While planning how I'll punish her for it.

Stepping closer to the frame, I examine the painting. The shape of the strokes.

I see a distinct nipple print stamped into the crimson paint, situated where Mara rolled across the canvas. Below that is a heart-shaped mark that almost certainly came from her naked buttocks.

I'd know the shape of that ass anywhere. That perfect fucking ass.

She's signed the painting in Sharpie and titled it *The Best Night of My Life.*

I'm hit with an emotion I've never experienced before. It rolls over me, heavy, smothering, nauseating. It takes the heart out of me. It makes my guts churn. It gives me a deep ache in my chest.

The feeling is so abrupt and unfamiliar that for a moment I think I really am sick. Or having a coronary.

I sink into my desk chair, still staring at the painting.

Slowly, with great difficulty, I examine this feeling that sits on my chest like a fucking gremlin, weighing me down.

I think...it's regret.

The title of the painting is a taunt. But it stabs me all the same.

It could have been the best night of her life.

It could have been me fucking Mara on that canvas. Me smearing paint all over her tits. Rolling around with her. Kissing her like I did at the show.

I wanted you. Genuinely.

She would have taken me back to the studio if I let her.

Instead, in that moment when she knelt before me, my impulse was cruelty. I wanted her—badly. And because I didn't like that feeling of need, of weakness, I tried to humiliate her.

I wanted to force her to submit. I should have known she wouldn't do it. She wouldn't submit even while bleeding, bound, at the point of death.

I could have spent the night with her instead of watching it on a phone screen. Tasting her, smelling her, touching her. Making art with her.

I wish I had.

I've never regretted anything I've done.

It's an ugly feeling. Depressing and unending because you can never go back. You can't undo what's been done.

But I can't shake it off. I can't get rid of it.

My heart rate spikes. I'm sweating harder than ever.

I jump to my feet, looking wildly around my office.

I don't want to feel regret. I don't want to feel anything I don't want to feel.

This is the singular factor separating me from everyone else in the world: I choose what to feel. They're puppets to their emotions. I'm master of mine.

I'm superior to everyone else because I choose not to feel the things that weaken me.

In this moment, I'm weak. Mara is making me weak.

With a howl of rage, I yank the driver out of my golf bag. I whirl around looking for a target, any target.

The solar system catches my eye: gleaming, glittering, the jewel-toned orbs rotating in space.

I swing the club through the air.

It crashes into the model, exploding the glowing Venetian glass into a million pieces. The shards pour down on me, cutting my skin in a dozen places, a rainstorm of shattered glass.

I keep hitting the model over and over and over, beating it, rending it, destroying it.

When at last the club falls from my numb hands, the solar model is nothing but a twisted ruin. Beyond recognition. Utterly destroyed.

I loved that piece.

Sometimes you have to kill what you love.

20

MARA

When I'm done fucking Logan, I tell him to go home.

"Can I get your number first?" he says, his grin a white slash in his paint-covered face.

"I don't think so," I say as kindly as I can. "That was just a one-time thing."

"Oh," he says. "Well, it was a great time. At least for me."

I smile without answering.

I'm already feeling guilty that I basically used him as a prop in an act of spite that's beginning to feel more insane by the second.

But not insane enough to stop.

After he leaves, I still carry that painting all the way to the top floor and hang it in Cole's office.

He doesn't even lock his door, the arrogant fuck.

He'll see me entering his office on the security cameras, but since I'm pretty sure he watched the whole damn event, the painting will hardly remain a mystery either way.

Riding the last waves of malice, I take an Uber home. The driver doesn't want to let me in the car when he sees the amount of paint remaining on my arms and legs and hair.

"It's already dry," I say crossly.

"Sit on this," he orders, throwing a garbage bag into the back seat.

"Fine," I sigh, seating myself on the slippery plastic and leaning my head against the window in utter exhaustion.

By the time I get back to my house, the manic high I've been riding has almost entirely dissipated. I'm starting to realize the level of *fuck you* I just threw in Cole's direction.

And look, he definitely deserved it. Trying to make me suck off that dealer was degrading and outrageous.

But I took it to the next level. I gave him both middle fingers, right to camera.

And I'm starting to think that was a huge mistake.

Cole Blackwell is not somebody you want to fuck with.

I should know that better than anyone.

He is neither reasonable nor forgiving.

And he's gonna make me pay for this, I know it.

After a few fitful hours of sleep, I stumble downstairs.

My roommates are gathered around the table, looking at Erin's phone. The mood in the kitchen is strangely somber. Heinrich and Frank are staring at the screen while Erin slowly scrolls. Joanna stands over by the sink, her arms crossed over her chest, looking faintly nauseated.

"What's going on?" I ask them.

"They found another body," Heinrich says.

"Another girl," Erin clarifies.

A hook lodges in my stomach, reeling me slowly toward the phone. I bend over the screen, my head between Frank's and Heinrich's.

The images are gory and graphic—a headless torso with its breasts torn off. Scattered limbs. A severed foot still wearing a high-heeled shoe.

"What the fuck!" I cry. "That's on the news?"

"It's not the news," Joanna says disgustedly from the sink. "It's that true-crime site. They must have bought the pics from one of the cops."

"I don't want to look at that." I back away.

My stomach is rolling.

The girl was slim, with a tattoo of a phoenix on her ribs. I have a tattoo in that exact same place. Without her head…she could well be me.

"None of us should look at it," Joanna snaps. "It's disrespectful. I hope they find whoever leaked those pics and fire his ass."

"I'm not gawking," Erin says. "They found her right over on the Lincoln Park golf course. That's only a couple of miles from here! This psycho could live right by us."

My stomach is now doing the death roll of a crocodile.

Cole lives in Sea Cliff. He golfs on that course.

"When did she die?" I ask.

"They think after midnight," Erin says. "She was still warm when they found her."

I left the show at 11:00.

I grabbed a date on the way out the door.

What if Cole did the same?

It sounds ludicrous. I've been spending hours at a time with Cole. We're often alone. If he wanted to turn me into mincemeat, he could have done it by now.

He really doesn't seem crazy. Controlling and manipulative, sure. Intense, absolutely. But could he actually put his hands on a woman and rip her to shreds?

I force myself to bend over the phone once more.

Erin scrolls down a little farther.

There's the girl's head, her features strangely unmarked, her eyes wide open, milky as glass marbles.

She was beautiful.

And very, very afraid.

I run over to the sink and vomit.

21
COLE

Sonia comes running into my office. She stands in the doorway, transfixed by the destruction inside.

"Oh my god, what happened?"

I already set the golf club back in its bag. Still, there's no hiding what I did. "I smashed the solar model."

Sonia stares at me, horrified, tears filling her pale blue eyes. "How could you?"

"It belongs to me," I snarl. "It's mine to keep or mine to destroy."

She stares down at the thick drifts of shattered glass, the downward tilt of her head causing the tears to spill down her cheeks.

In all the time she's worked for me, I've never seen Sonia cry. She's competent and capable and keeps her emotions securely buttoned down. That's why we get along. I would tolerate nothing less.

I don't blame her for the tears in this moment, however. The solar model was one of the most stunning works of art I've ever seen. Truly unique and irreplaceable.

I destroyed it on impulse.

Something is happening to me.

Something is taking me over—twisting me, changing me. I've been infected.

Mara is the disease.

"Get someone to clean that up," I order.

I storm out of my office, heading down to the main floor. I don't bother stopping at Mara's studio—I know she isn't here. She's probably still at home sleeping.

As I pass Janice's desk, I see several artists crowded around her computer screen. They break apart as I approach, hurrying off in every direction except mine.

Janice tries to close her browser window. I knock her hand aside. "What are you looking at?"

"A-another girl's been k-killed," Janice stammers. "It happened last night."

I lean over her desk, unpleasantly enveloped in her sickly-sweet perfume as I examine the computer screen.

She's on some trashy true-crime site. The page is covered in full-color photos of the murder scene.

Alastor's work.

His bodies are far more distinct than his paintings.

And yet…this is a new level of violence, even for him. I see the frenzy in the scattered body parts. This wasn't just lust… It was rage.

I stand again, my heart already returning to its steady beat.

This explains why Alastor wasn't at the show last night. He must have gotten distracted on the way over.

He missed something he really should have seen.

Lucky for me—his absence bought me a little more time.

———

I walk over to Mara's dingy Victorian. I hammer on the door, startling her roommate Frank, who answers after a long delay, looking high and paranoid.

"Oh," he says, seeming partly relieved and partly even more confused. "It's you."

"Where's Mara?"

"I dunno," he mumbles, running his hand through his wild curls. "Work, maybe?"

The second I get my hands on her phone, I'm putting a tracker on it.

This intention becomes an absolute fixation as I unsuccessfully visit Sweet Maple and Golden Gate Park in turn, without finding her.

WHERE THE FUCK IS SHE?

Several fantasies play through my mind as I search the park. The first is how I'm going to drag her into the trees and strangle her. But when I picture wrapping my hands around her throat, I instead see them sliding down her body…cupping her breasts…squeezing her tiny waist as hard as I can…forcing her down on my cock over and over and over…

Fucking her in the woods isn't good enough.

I want her somewhere isolated, where we can be utterly alone together. Somewhere I'll have every tool I desire at my fingertips. Somewhere I can spend all night long having my way with her…

I want to bring her to my house.

No one but me has stepped foot through the front door since my father died. The house has been my cave. My one place of absolute privacy.

My desire to bring Mara there shows me how far this obsession has grown. Bringing her into my house is like bringing her inside my own body. A far more intimate act than simply fucking her…

Where could she be?

Did she meet up with that fuck boy again?

Is she at his house right now, letting him put his hands all over her?

The thought is so enraging that I have to lean on my knees, breathing heavily.

No. She wouldn't do that. She only fucked him to get back at me. Because she knew I was watching.

That's what I want to believe. But I have to know for certain.

I pull out my phone, accessing Mara's social media once again.

By now, I know every photograph, every caption. I have them all committed to memory. And I think…possibly…I've seen that guy before.

I scroll through the images, searching.

At last I find it: a post from the day Mara got the tattoo of a snake on her ribs. There he is, standing right next to her, latex gloves on his hands.

Logan hooked me up today—finally got my little hiss.

I touch my finger to his name, switching over to his profile.

Logan Mickelson, Paint It Black tattoo parlor.

Found you, motherfucker.

The parlor is only twelve blocks from the park. I walk over, instinctively avoiding any record of where I'm going. Leaving my options open to deal with Logan as I see fit.

This is the wrong time of day for an acquisition. I'd be better off coming in the evening when he's likely to be working alone, finishing up his last client of the day. I could pose as a walk-in. After checking the building for cameras, of course.

But I'm impatient. I don't want to wait until tonight.

I want to know the precise nature of this bastard's relationship with Mara. Right this fucking second.

I wait around the back of the building. He'll come out for a smoke. These fuckers always smoke.

After I spend nearly an hour patiently watching, he shoves his way through the back door, already sparking up, his hand cupped around his mouth to protect against the wind blowing gusts of dry leaves down the alleyway.

I heave him up against the wall, my forearm against his throat before he's drawn a single breath of smoke into his lungs.

He goes still, not fighting, not struggling. Looking at my face with as much curiosity as fear.

"Oh, shit," he says. "I know you."

I'm becoming entirely too recognizable in this town.

"Then I'm sure you can guess why I'm here."

It still takes him a second to put it together.

"Mara," he says.

"That's right," I hiss. "Mara."

"Sorry, dude, I didn't know she had a boyfriend…"

I could cheerfully decapitate him just for that comment.

"I'm no one's fucking *boyfriend*," I snarl. "She belongs to me. She's my property. You put your disgusting inky hands all over something I own. What do you think I should do about that, Logan?"

The sound of his own name is the alarm that alerts Logan to the fact I'm not here to have a pleasant conversation. The continued existence of that name is a fine thread upon which my arm against his throat operates like a sharp set of shears.

He cuts the bullshit immediately.

"I barely know her. I don't even have her phone number."

"You tattooed her, though."

"Yeah—that's how we met. I did a grim reaper for her roommate. She asked if I'd do the snake. It was her own design—she drew it."

"What other tattoos have you done for her?"

"None. It was just the one."

I ease the pressure off his throat. Slightly.

He isn't stupid enough to think that's the end of it. He looks into my eyes, into those black pits that could never be filled by apologies alone.

"Is there…anything else?" he asks.

"Yeah. Where's your tattoo gun?"

22

MARA

I CONSIDERED GIVING COLE A COUPLE OF DAYS TO COOL OFF.

I could avoid him reasonably well—sleeping over at a friend's house. Not coming into the studio to work.

The effort would be pointless.

Cole ain't ever cooling off. I'm not stupid enough to think that a couple of days apart is going to ease his fury at what I did. Not after I literally hung a reminder on his wall.

Besides, I want to work. I don't want to take a week off from painting, or even a single day.

Which is why I find myself back at the studio a little before midnight, praying Cole might possibly be asleep and not angry enough to haul himself out of bed to mete out what's coming to me.

Janice isn't at her desk. The building has a roaming security guard at night, but I suspect he spends most of his time walking as slowly as possible so he only has to make a few rounds before his shift ends.

The silence of the usually bustling space puts me on edge as I climb the stairs to the fourth floor.

I didn't use to be a jumpy person.

Getting snatched by a monster straight out of a nightmare changed that forever.

I'll never forget that dark figure hurtling toward me. Somehow that was the worst part: realizing the things you fear are very much real. And they're coming for you.

Cole asked me why I kept the piercings. I told myself I was doing it for me—an act of defiance.

But Cole is right.

I like the reminder. I need it.

So I never get too comfortable again.

Sometimes I think it was Cole who kidnapped me. Sometimes I feel sure it wasn't.

Nothing about that night makes sense to me. It feels like one of those perspective paintings where if you look from the wrong angle, it's just a jumble of shapes and lines. But if you move to the right point in the room, the shapes align, and you can see the image clear as day. I could see exactly what happened...if I just knew where to stand.

For now, I know one thing for certain: Cole is dangerous.

I should run far away from him.

I know this, rationally.

Yet I want the exact opposite.

I'm fascinated by him. Drawn to him in every possible way: physically, mentally, emotionally.

I've been reading *Dracula*. It's a cautionary tale. A warning to young women not to give in to the seduction of a man who wants to devour you.

And yet...not all of us were drawn to Prince Charming. Some little girls ate up the stories of ball gowns and castles and knights who slayed the dragon...

While some little girls read the stories of a dark pathway into the woods...a twisted mansion with black windows and fog covering the grounds... That's where we wanted to go. No matter what we might find inside...

I've started my second painting.

It will be just as large as the first—life-size. The primary figure is part human, part animal, with a ram's horns and bat-like wings outstretched on either side. Four arms and two sets of hands. One pair of hands are slim, pale, elegant. The other hands are thick, coarse, brutish.

I put on my music, as loud as I want because there's no one else in the adjacent studios.

♫ *"Gasoline"—Halsey*

The canvas seems to expand until it appears as large as the room. It fills my whole field of view; it becomes my whole universe. Each tiny detail unspools from my brush, bursting into life.

I forget about Cole.

I forget about everything outside the painting.

Time flows by while I stand still.

I don't even realize someone has walked through the door until Cole says, "First a saint; now a demon."

He's standing right behind me. I don't know how long he's been in the room.

I whirl around, brush upraised.

Cole looks down at me, our faces only inches apart. He's paler than usual, dark circles under his eyes. He definitely wasn't asleep. He might not have slept last night either.

It must be raining outside. His clothes are damp. Droplets glint in his thick black hair, the tips wet like my brush.

The rain amplifies his scent. He smells cold and clean like a windswept street. His eyes are black as asphalt.

"I was looking for you," he says.

"I was hiding," I reply.

"I know that. I know you were hiding. I also knew you wouldn't be able to stay away for long."

His voice is as cold as his clothes. It makes me shiver.

He knows me too well.

"It's not a demon," I say. "It's the devil."

"What's the difference?"

"There's only one devil."

He smiles. Cole's real smile is very different from the one he gives to everyone else. It's slower. It doesn't crinkle his eyes. And it ends with him biting down on the edge of his lip. Hard.

"You left a gift in my office."

The chill runs from the base of my skull all the way down my spine. I try not to flinch. I try not to let him see how hard my heart is pounding. "How did you like it?"

Cole steps closer, slipping his right hand under my hair, gripping the back of my skull. With his thumb, he forces my chin up even farther. "I didn't like it at all. In fact, it made me jealous."

My skin goes from chilled to burning hot, all in an instant. My nipples stiffen under the thin material of my top. The rings stay cold like ice.

He's jealous. He's admitting he's jealous.

Cole runs his thumb across my lower lip. My sweat is gasoline. Every place he touches ignites.

I hear a sharp click and the cold clasp of a manacle closing around my wrist.

Before I can move, before I can even glance down at my own wrist, Cole takes three swift steps, dragging me toward the wall. He yanks my arms over my head and handcuffs me in place, the chain wrapped around an exposed pipe.

"*What the fuck?*" I shriek.

I yank on the cuffs, the metal biting into my wrists.

"This will go a lot smoother if you hold still," Cole says.

He plucks the paintbrush out of my hand before setting it aside.

"*What* will go smoother? What the fuck are you doing?"

I'm starting to hyperventilate. The wrist ties are bringing back horrible memories, all in a rush.

Cole doesn't answer me.

Instead, he pulls over a stool and sets down the bag he was carrying—a black leather bag that opens at the top like an old-fashioned doctor's satchel.

He unclips the straps of my overalls, letting the bib fall to my waist. Then he grabs the front of my tank top with both hands before ripping it apart. My breasts fall free, my nipples rock-hard, my chest bared to his view.

We both look down, staring at my tits. At the silver rings, each with a single bead in the center, glinting like the rain in Cole's hair.

His gaze crawls down my body. To the tattoo on my ribs.

"Logan did that to you," Cole says softly.

It's not a question.

"How do you know that?"

Cole rests his hand against the wall, his lips almost touching the rim of my ear. Almost, but not quite.

"I know everything about you, Mara. *Everything.* I know you fucked him to defy me. To show me that I can't control you. And maybe I can't control you—not all the time. But you were given to me."

I was given to him?

What the fuck does that mean?

"I own you now, Mara. You belong to me, whether you like it or not."

He trails his fingers lightly down the side of my chest, along the curve where the breast meets the ribs. My nipples are harder than diamonds. They could cut his face if he leaned too close.

He traces the serpent's body with his fingertips.

"I can't have another man's mark on you."

"*I* designed that tattoo."

"I designed a better one."

He reaches inside the doctor's bag. Pulls out a tattoo gun.

"Are you insane?" I shriek.

"Don't worry," he says. "I've been practicing the past few hours."

"On who?"

He just smiles. "Steady now. I'm still perfecting my technique."

Cole cleans my skin with green soap, also taken from the bag. He really has everything he needs in there.

"Don't you fucking dare—"

He fires up the gun with that high buzzing sound that's all too familiar.

I shriek, trying to twist away from him.

"If you don't hold still, you won't like the result," he says.

He presses the tip of the gun against my ribs, turning my shriek into a piercing scream.

The needle pricks my skin, depositing the ink deep down where it can never be removed.

Instinctively, I freeze.

I can't stop Cole. And I really don't want a fucking mess all over my ribs.

The gun moves slowly, surely. Though I know a tattoo gun operates much like a sewing machine, plunging the needle down under the skin at regular intervals, what it actually feels like is someone drawing on you with a sharp pen.

I look down, trying to figure out what he's drawing.

It's impossible to tell from this angle, upside down.

Cole's hands move over me, strong and capable. Warmer than I would have guessed. In fact, his bare hands on my flesh feel surprisingly pleasurable, in contrast to the bite of the needle.

Every time he exhales, his breath slides across my waist. It runs along the line where my denim overalls meet my bare skin.

Cole is left-handed. I never noticed that before.

His left hand operates the gun with smooth, sure motion, while his right rests against my hip. Gripping me tight. Holding me in place.

I've never had the chance to look at him so close.

His hair is thick like animal fur. When he tilts his head, it brushes against my skin, soft and slightly damp.

Though I know he's older than me, his skin is remarkably smooth. Maybe because he only forms expressions when someone is watching.

Almost all the animation in his face comes from those straight dark brows. They remind me of *shodo* on pale white paper. In Japanese calligraphy, no two brushstrokes are ever the same. So it is on Cole's face—those brows are the ink strokes that give meaning to his bottomless black eyes.

He's utterly focused on me, his gaze lasered in, his jaw tight. My breathing slows, matching pace with his. Inhale. Exhale. Inhale.

His beauty is mesmerizing. I'm watching him, not the tattoo gun. Feeling his touch, not the touch of steel.

He can feel me relax. He looks up into my face.

"I don't know why you always want to fight me. It's so much more pleasurable to give me what I want..."

"More pleasurable for whom?" I gasp.

"For both of us."

He slips his hand down the front of my overalls.

I'm not wearing any underwear. I never did get around to washing my laundry.

His touch is gentler than I expected. I thought it would be as brutal as his kiss. Instead, it's almost soothing...

His fingers slide over my pussy, searching, exploring. Testing...

He touches me here, there, waiting for a reaction. Seeing how I respond. When I lean against him, when my lips part, when I moan...he knows he found the right spot. He soaks his fingers inside me, then rubs me every place that feels the best...

The tattoo gun buzzes angrily against my ribs. It nips and bites, over and over, up and down, across the bone.

I hardly notice the pain. I'm leaned against the wall, my head tilted back, my thighs parted. Letting Cole touch me wherever he wants.

He strokes my pussy like it's his own personal pet. He runs

his fingers up and down my slit, sometimes plunging inside me, sometimes rubbing circles around my clit.

All the while he's drawing on my ribs, his left hand working separately from his right.

The pain enhances the pleasure, and the pleasure enhances the pain.

I'm sweating, waves of sensation rolling over me.

I rock my hips against his hand.

I'm moaning. I don't know how long I've been making that sound.

He's found the spot right under my clit, the most sensitive bundle of nerves on my whole body. He's stroking it with the ball of his thumb, over and over.

"Oh my god…" I moan. "Don't stop…"

"Tell me you're mine…" he hisses. "Tell me I can do whatever I want to you…"

I press my lips together, refusing to say it.

He bears down hard on the tattoo gun, biting into my flesh. "*Say it.*"

I shake my head, my eyes closed, my mouth clamped shut.

He presses harder with the tattoo gun and with his fingers under my clit. He strokes me hard, while drawing god knows what on my flesh.

"*Say it, Mara. Tell me you belong to me…*"

I want to say it.

I want to give in.

His hand is stroking, rubbing, exactly the way I like. Better than a man has ever managed before. Better than I can do it myself…

The pleasure is a need, a demand. An itch that *has* to be scratched…

"*Say it,*" he snarls.

"No fucking way," I bark back at him.

He finishes the tattoo with a vicious slash down the bone.

I shriek. Every muscle of my body tenses, including my thighs clamping hard together. That's what makes me come, as much as

Cole's fingers pressed against my clit. The orgasm is a blazing shock that rips through me from chest to groin.

I turn my head, biting hard on my own shoulder, leaving a wreath of teeth marks.

My weight hangs from the cuffs, my body limp and wrung out. I'm still twitching as the aftershocks spark through me.

Cole wipes the excess ink off my skin with the same green soap. The soap Logan uses.

"You didn't hurt him, did you?" I demand.

"He's not your concern." Cole seizes my face once more. Forcing me to look at him. "You need to worry about what *I* think. What *I* want."

I look into his eyes. "What happens if I don't?"

"Next time I won't be so forgiving."

I laugh out loud, standing up straight now, rattling the cuffs. "This is you being nice?"

Cole looks at me steadily. "Yes, Mara," he says quietly. "This is me being kind. Being merciful. You need to understand that—because if you try to crack me open, you won't like what crawls out."

He unlocks the cuffs. I rub my wrists, trying to bring sensation back into my hands. Then, slowly, I walk over to the full-length mirror hanging on the wall. I stand before it, turning slightly so I can see the tattoo that runs from just under my right breast all the way down to my hip bone.

He branded me. Put his mark on me forever.

And it's beautiful. Truly fucking beautiful.

Cole is an artist in every sense of the word. The composition, the smooth flow of the lines, the way the flowers and leaves follow the curves of my breast, my ribs, my hip bone. Perfectly formed to my shape, undulating with every twist or bend of my body. As I move, the tattoo comes alive.

A wild garden. A riot of ferns, foliage, and flowers, between which my little snake peeks out.

"Jesus Christ," I breathe. "You really are talented."

Cole stands directly behind me.

He's taller than me, and broader. I fit entirely inside his silhouette, Cole a dark halo all around me. As if he's already swallowed me whole and I live inside him now.

"Your turn," he says.

I lock eyes with him in the mirror. "What do you mean?"

He holds up the tattoo gun.

"Are you serious?"

In response, he puts the gun in my hand and reaches over his own shoulder, grabbing a handful of his shirt and shucking it off over his head. He stands upright after throwing the shirt aside.

I stare at his naked torso.

In all my years of figure drawing, I've never seen a body like his.

The closest comparison would be a gymnast or a dancer—lean, tight, fluid muscle, a coiled spring, ready for release.

Even gymnasts aren't this aesthetic. The slabs of muscle across his chest, the perfect V of his waist, the way the ripples of muscle seem designed to draw the eye down, down, to button of his trousers...

His flesh is pale next to the loose dark waves of hair that fall almost to his shoulders. There's no hair anywhere on his body. No ink either. His skin is smooth and unmarked.

"You want me to tattoo you?"

He nods.

"Do you have other tattoos?"

"This will be the first."

I swallow hard.

Cole's beauty is way past intimidating—it's fucking flawless.

I've never given a tattoo in my life. If I fuck this up, I'll feel worse than if I scrawled a mustache across the Mona Lisa.

"I don't think I should."

Cole's brows drop low across his eyes, narrowing them to slits. "I don't give a fuck what you think."

My fingers tighten on the gun.

Now I want to write *FUCK YOU* in six-inch letters across his back. "I hope you have enough ink."

"I have exactly what I need," he replies.

I bet he does.

I grab the stool and drag it over in front of the mirror. "Sit down."

Cole sits, leaning forward with his elbows resting on his knees. Without discussing it, we've both intuited that his back is the best canvas—smooth and relatively flat. Actually, it's as muscular as the rest of him. As soon as I hover the needle over his skin, I can see that I'll have to navigate the scapula, the ribs, and the long sheets of muscle that radiate out from the spine.

"You want me to...sketch it out first?" I say weakly.

Cole doesn't move. He doesn't even turn his head.

"I trust you," he says.

Nobody has ever trusted me, especially not with something as irreversible as this.

Taking a deep breath, I fire up the gun.

By the time I'm finished, the first morning light is streaming in through the floor-to-ceiling windows. It illuminates Cole's skin, turning marble to gold.

I've fallen so deeply into the design that all I can see is those flowing black lines, running like a river down the right side of his back. With a little practice, I've even figured out the shading.

He's bleeding in a couple of spots. He never flinched. Never asked me to stop. He hardly seemed to feel it at all.

I clean his back with the green soap, just as he did to me. Then I stand back to view it all at once. "It's finished."

Cole stands with his back to the mirror. He looks over his shoulder to see the design.

Two snakes: one white, one black. Twisted and entwined around each other, their alternating coils tightly wrapped, their mouths open to show snarling fangs.

I branded him just as he did to me.

23

COLE

THE TATTOO'S COMPLETE. I FEEL STRANGELY PEACEFUL.

The sun is rising. The sky outside the window looks transparent as glass.

Mara notices the same thing, pressing her palm flat against the window as if she could reach through and touch the clear space beyond.

"No fog today," she says.

"Do you want to go for a walk with me?"

She turns her head, her dark hair sliding across her bare shoulder in a way that makes me want to trace my fingers over the same spot. The light illuminates her profile, a burning line down her forehead, the bridge of her nose, the indent above her upper lip...

"Yeah," she says. "I do."

We leave the building together.

I tore off her top. The overalls barely cover her tits. Mara doesn't seem to notice. I've never seen someone so careless of other people's opinions.

Her attention is entirely consumed by the world around her. She looks at everything we pass: The vintage Mustang pulled up to the curb, top down to show off its creamy leather seats. The laurel dropping its leaves onto the street in slow, lazy drifts. The raven breaking open a snail by beating its shell against the cornice of a bank.

This is why Mara is so easy to stalk. When I'm outside, I'm

constantly scanning the street. Watching for cameras, cops, anyone who might be following me. Looking for people I know, people I don't know. Watching everyone all the time.

Mara is consumed by whatever catches her attention. Anything beautiful, anything interesting.

♫ *"lovely"—Billie Eilish & Khalid*

She points it all out to me. A rose-covered trellis on Scott Street. The stained glass window of a church. A girl gliding down the hill on Roller Derby skates.

"Those are Eclipse," Mara says. "They're the best."

My back burns. I bet her ribs are burning, too.

I like that we're feeling the same pain at the same time.

I like that I marked her and she marked me.

We're bound together now, her art on my skin and mine on hers.

I ask her, "Would you let me tattoo you again?"

She looks up at me. In the pale early light, I see there is blue in her eyes after all. Blue like a gull's wing, like a bruise, like Roman silver with a little lead in it.

"Yes," she says.

"Why?"

"Because the tattoo you gave me is beautiful. And because…" She bites the edge of her lip, her eyes dropping to our feet, which tread the pavement in sync. "Because I like when you pay attention to me. I like when you put your hands on me. The other night at the show…I felt like you were pushing me away. It hurt."

Her gaze is naked. Painfully vulnerable.

My natural reaction is to recoil from her.

I despise weakness. Neediness, too.

But this is what I've been trying to get from Mara all this time. She has the hardest shell I've ever seen—I want to peel off her armor. I want her naked. I want to know who she is, all the way down.

So I answer honestly. Though I'm only saying what she already knows, it feels dangerous…walking a thin wire across an unknown abyss.

"*I was* pushing you away," I admit.

"Why?"

"Because I didn't have control."

"Over what?"

"Over how much I wanted you."

Mara searches my face.

Other people look at your expression to make sure it matches what they want to believe. Mara never believes. She always checks.

"What do you see right now?" I ask her.

"I see you," she says. "I'm just wondering…"

"What?"

"If it's another mask."

My face goes cold and still. "And if it is?"

"Then you use the best one on me."

My skin feels stiff like plastic.

"What if I took it off? And you didn't like what you saw underneath?"

Mara slips her hand into mine. Our fingers interlock, fitting together like links in a chain.

"I shouldn't like you now," she says. "But I do."

I shouldn't like her either.

But I do.

I walk along beside her, holding another person's hand for the first time in my life.

It feels outrageously public, like we're shouting for attention. But also intensely intimate, our linked hands a bond more powerful than sex.

Mara often makes me feel two things at once. I'm not used to that. My emotions have always been simple, easy to understand. I've never been confused about what I want.

We're passing Alta Plaza Park. A woman sits on a public bench, her stroller parked beside her. She's taken her infant out of the stroller and set it against her breast. She nurses the baby, singing down to it softly.

Mara turns away from the sight, her lips pressed together.

"You don't think she should nurse in public?" I'm surprised by her prudishness. Mara seems actively antagonistic to the concept of modesty.

"It's not that." Her eyes look nowhere but the ground. "It's the singing."

"Explain." My curiosity is piqued.

Mara takes a deep breath. "My mother's a piano teacher. That's how she makes money—when she's working. If I was sick or hurt, she'd sing to me. It was the only thing that comforted me."

She swallows hard, her skin pale and sickly looking.

"Those were my best memories. When she sang to me, I thought she loved me. But later I realized...she just likes singing. It was never for me. It was only to shut me up.

"Randall would make me stand with my nose to the door for hours. I don't mean it seemed like hours—I watched the time pass on the clock. If I annoyed him, if I was too loud, if I talked back to him—and talking back just meant answering any way he didn't like—then it was an hour against the door. If I moved for even a second, if I had an itch or I just got dizzy, the hour started over again. No food. No drinks. No going to the bathroom.

"While I was standing there, I'd hear my mother singing in the house. In the kitchen, upstairs, out in the backyard...

"It would be two, three hours later, and I'd hear her voice drifting through the air, perfectly content. She wasn't singing for me, to make me feel better. She forgot I was standing down there at all, my legs shaking, trying not to piss myself or move my nose a millimeter from the door so the hour wouldn't start again."

Mara glances back toward the park bench, her white lips pressed tight.

"The things she's said to me. Always in that soft, sweet voice… She poisoned it, like she poisons everything. I can't even listen to a mom in a movie anymore. It makes me want to puke."

We're walking toward the marina. I can see all the way down to the water. The sun breaks above the bay, blazing up the road, glinting on the chrome bumpers of the parked cars, flaming on glass windows.

It burns on Mara's skin, in the tiny filaments of hair that float above the rest.

The sadness on her face doesn't match her beauty in this moment.

And my disgust at her mother doesn't match what I feel in my chest. I'm used to anger and repulsion. The emotion gripping me is something different. A heat in my lungs, a burning behind my eyes…a desire to squeeze her hand tighter in mine.

I don't know what to call this one. I've never felt it before.

I look at Mara, and I don't know what to say.

My lips form the words anyway.

"I'm sorry."

It startles her as much as me.

She turns and faces me, dropping my hand. "What do you mean?"

"I just…I'm sorry."

She shakes her head slowly, her lips parted, her eyebrows raised. "You surprise me, Cole."

I'm surprised, too.

Surprised at the sound of my name on her lips. How it rings like a bell, clear and true.

She stands on tiptoe, stretching up to kiss me. Soft and slow.

Warmer than the rising sun between us.

24

MARA

I have to work late at Zam Zam tonight.

I know I'll be exhausted. I've been putting in long hours at the studio, sucked into my latest painting.

Cole comes to see it in the early afternoon.

The painting is steeped in deeply shadowed tones of charcoal, merlot, and garnet. The figure is monstrous with its gleaming bat-like wings and thick, scaly, muscular tail. But his face is beautiful—a dark angel, fallen from grace.

Cole stands in front of the canvas for a long time, a hint of a smile playing on his lips.

"Well?" I say when I can't stand it anymore. "What do you think?"

"The chiaroscuro is masterful. It reminds me of Caravaggio."

I flush with pleasure but try to hide it. "*Judith Beheading Holofernes* is one of my favorite paintings."

"I prefer *David with the Head of Goliath*."

"You know that's a self-portrait, don't you?" I smile. "Caravaggio used his own face as the model for Goliath's severed head."

"Yes. And his lover was the model for David."

"Maybe they were fighting at the time." I laugh.

Cole looks at me with that steady dark gaze. "Or he knew that love is inherently dangerous."

I mix white and a fractional portion of black on my palette. "Do you really think that?"

"All emotions are dangerous. Especially when they involve other people."

I dip my brush in the fresh paint, not looking at him. My heart is already beating fast, and it's impossible to look at Cole's face and form a coherent sentence at the same time. "Have you always been this way?"

"What way?"

He knows what I mean, but he's making me say it out loud. He knows he can't trick me as easily as other people—which irritates him.

He wants to know exactly what I can see and what I can't. Probably so he can learn to trick me better.

"Cold," I say. "Calculated. Uncaring."

Now I do look at him because I want to see if he'll admit it.

"Yes," he says, unblinking, unashamed. "I've always been this way."

I dab the paint on my demon's tail, bringing out the highlights on the scales. I can feel Cole pacing behind me, though I can't actually hear his light footsteps on the wooden boards. He's disturbingly quiet. It unnerves me when I can't see where he's at in the room. But it's worse trying to talk with that burning black stare drilling into me.

"Have you ever loved anyone?" I ask. "Or were you just voicing a theory?"

I can sense him going still, considering the question.

This is one of the things I like about Cole: he doesn't just say whatever pops into his head. Every word that comes out of his mouth is deliberate.

"I don't know," he says at last.

I have to turn then, because that answer surprises me.

He's got his hands in the pockets of his fine wool trousers, looking past me out the window, lost in thought.

"I might have loved my mother. She was important to me. I

wanted to be near her all the time. I'd go in her room in the morning, when she was still sleeping, and curl up on the end of her bed like a dog. I liked the smell of her perfume on the blankets and on the clothes that hung in her closet. I liked the way her voice sounded and how she laughed. But she died when I was four. So I don't know if that would have changed as I got older. Children are always attached to their mothers."

I feel that sick, squirming sensation in my stomach that always accompanies conversations about mothers. As if my demon's tail is whipping around down in my guts.

"You loved your mother," Cole says, reading my thoughts. "Even though she was a shit parent."

"Yeah, I did," I say bitterly. "That's what's fucked up about it. I wanted to impress her. I wanted to make her happy."

"Loving someone gives them power over you."

When we talk like this, I feel like he really is the devil, battling for my soul. Everything he believes is so opposite to what I do. Yet he can be horribly convincing...

I hate that my mother had power over me. I hate that she still does.

I lift my brush to the painting so I can lose myself in the beautiful colors while I let the ugly words flow out.

"She trained me from the time I was little. She was always the victim. Everything bad that happened in her life was someone else's fault—especially mine. And the thing that makes me angriest is that it fucking worked—I still feel guilty. Every time I ignore her emails or block her calls, I feel guilty. Rationally, I know she's the fucking worst and I don't owe her anything. But the emotion is still there because she conditioned me like a rat looking for pellets. She manipulated me and fucked with me every day of my life until I got away from her."

"Distance is meaningless when she still lives in your head," Cole says.

"Yeah," I admit. "She dug trenches out of me. I keep waiting for it to go away, but it doesn't. Because scars don't heal—they're there forever."

Recklessly, I swipe my brush through the black, adding billowing smoke flowing up from the bottom of the canvas.

"I fucking hate her," I hiss.

I've never actually said that out loud. Usually, I don't talk about her at all.

"She's a perversion of nature," Cole says, in his calm, reasonable tone. "Mothers are supposed to be nurturing. They're supposed to protect their children. Sacrifice for them. She isn't a mother at all."

I turn around, annoyed that he's finagled me into discussing this yet again.

"What about fathers?" I demand. "What are they supposed to be?"

I'm already well aware that Cole loathes his father. Despite the fact Magnus Blackwell has been dead for a decade. And the fact he was the Thomas Wayne of this city—his name is on a dozen buildings, including a wing of the MOMA.

Cole says, "Fathers are supposed to teach and protect."

"Did yours?"

"He did one of those things."

When Cole is angry, his lips go pale and his jaw tightens, sharpening the lines of his face until he hardly looks human.

He frightens me.

And yet it's the terror that heightens every moment in his presence. I smell his scent, hot and exhilarating. I see the veins running up his forearms, the pulse of pumping blood.

I want to kiss him again.

It's a terrible idea, but I fucking want it.

Unfortunately, I've got to get ready for work.

I start gathering my brushes and paints.

"Where are you going?" Cole demands.

"Zam Zam."

"You need to quit that job. You're an artist, not a bartender."

"Right now I'm both. I need the money."

Cole frowns. I think it irritates him that I'm poor. Or that he likes someone poor. Assuming he likes me at all—obsession is not the same thing as affection.

"I'll walk you to work," he says.

I shake my head at him, laughing. "I've lived in this city for twenty-six years, and I've walked every inch of it. Alone."

"I don't give a shit what you did before you met me. It's different now."

"Why?"

He doesn't answer. He simply takes his peacoat from the hook by the door and silently waits for me.

I wash my brushes and my hands, then pull on my battered leather jacket. I bought it at a flea market in Fisherman's Wharf, and it looks like its previous owner was mauled by rabid dogs.

"That jacket is hideous," Cole says.

"Oh, shut up. You're spoiled."

"If we dated, I'd have to buy you an entirely new wardrobe."

"That's why we'll never date."

I don't know if Cole's being serious.

I know I certainly am. I want to fuck him, not date him.

I can't imagine being his girlfriend. He just told me he doesn't support the concept of love. What's that saying? *When people show you who they are…believe them.*

Never mind my lingering suspicions he might be a murderer.

It's insane that I even talk to him, under the circumstances. But it's human nature to believe the best instead of the worst. To allow yourself to be convinced. To give in to seduction.

My brain tells me he's dangerous. My body tells me to stand closer to him, to look up into his eyes, to put my arms around his neck…

"Let's get going." I stride ahead so he won't see me blush. "I don't want to be late."

Cole doesn't mind walking along behind me. I can't quite tell if he's stalking me or watching over me. The night is dark and foggy—I am glad he's here.

That feeling persists as he takes a table at Zam Zam and orders a drink. He sits facing me, sipping his gin and tonic, watching me set up my bar.

If any other man behaved this way—showing up unannounced, following me to work—it would infuriate me.

I don't get sick of Cole like I do other people. In fact, if he doesn't come to the studio every day to check up on my painting, I feel oddly empty and the work doesn't go as well.

Knowing that he's close is comforting.

Before long, I lose him to the crowd. It's Saturday night. Zam Zam is stuffed with programmers, marketers, and students. It's standing room only, people lined up six deep at the bar, shouting at me for drinks.

I like bartending. I get in a flow state where my body moves faster than my brain and I feel like a robot specifically designed for this purpose. I channel Tom Cruise in *Cocktail*, flipping bottles and pouring a whole line of shots at once, because it's fun and it earns me extra tips.

The air gets thick and muggy. I'm sweating. I pull my hair up in a ponytail and strip off my sweater. I catch one glimpse of Cole, his eyes narrowed at the sight of my skintight crop top, before he's swallowed by another swell of customers.

A group of twentysomething guys down at the end of the bar keep shouting for more shots. Based on the matching polo shirts and their extraordinarily boring conversation, I'm guessing they work for some biotech firm.

I bring them another round of B-52s.

"Hey," one bleary-eyed guy says, grabbing my arm. "Can you do a Blow Job?"

His friends all snicker.

"What about a Slippery Nipple?" his buddy says.

They're not the first geniuses to realize that some shots have dirty names.

"Do you actually want either of those?" I say.

A dozen more people are shouting for me all down the bar. I don't have time for stupid jokes.

"What's your rush?" the first guy says. "We're tipping you, aren't we?"

He throws a handful of crumpled bills at me, mostly ones. Half the bills land in my ice well, which really pisses me off because money is filthy—I'm gonna have to dump that ice and fill the well up fresh.

"Thanks." I weight that word with about ten pounds of sarcasm.

"Fuck you, bitch," the second guy sneers.

I look him up and down. "Nah. I don't do charity work."

It takes him a second to get it, but his friends' howls tip him off that it's definitely an insult.

I've already turned away, so I don't hear whatever he shouts back at me.

I dump the ice and run to grab a fresh batch. I'm hoping by the time I get back, those idiots will have found somewhere else to congregate. Unfortunately, when I return, puffing and sweating under the weight of the ice bin, they're still clustered in the same spot. Mr. Blue Polo Shirt glowers at me.

I pour the ice into the well, pointedly ignoring him. Then I turn to set down the empty bin.

The moment I bend over, I feel a sharp slap on my ass. I wheel around, catching Blue Shirt on top of the bar.

I'm about to shout for our bouncer, Tony. Cole is faster. I barely have time to open my mouth before he appears behind Blue Shirt like a pale grim reaper. He doesn't grab the guy's shoulder—doesn't even offer a warning. Faster than I can blink, he snatches up the closest beer bottle and smashes it across the back of Blue Shirt's skull.

Blue Shirt jolts, his eyes rolling back. He collapses, hitting the side of his head against the barstool on his way down.

His friend, the one who threw the money at me, gives a strangled yell. He rushes at Cole, not realizing Cole is still holding the neck of the shattered bottle.

Cole slashes him across the face, opening his cheek from ear to jaw. Blood splashes across the oak bar and into my fresh ice.

The other polo shirts gape at Cole, none too eager to jump into the fray.

I'm likewise staring in shock.

It's not only the violence that stuns us. It's the eerie speed with which Cole moves and the cold indifference on his face. I know he's angry because I know what it looks like when something pisses him off. To anyone else, he might as well be a statue for all the emotion he shows.

He faces the other men, still holding the neck of the bottle, its glinting points wickedly sharp and darkly wet.

Quietly, he says, "Where's the courage you had five minutes ago? Or were you cowards all along?"

This time, I'm faster than the polo shirts. I jump over the bar, grabbing Cole by the arm.

"Let's go!" I yank at him. "You've got to get out of here."

His body is stiff as steel. He's still staring at the other men, daring them to take a step toward him.

"*Come on!*" I bellow, dragging him away.

I pull him all the way outside into the thick fog, then several blocks down the street, expecting to hear sirens any minute.

"What were you thinking?" I cry when I finally catch my breath. "You could have killed that guy!"

"I hope I did."

I turn to stare at him, gasping in the thin damp air. "You can't mean that."

"Absolutely I do. He disrespected you. Put his hands on you. I'd kill him for much less."

I can't believe how calm he is right now. The blood on his hands looks black as pitch on the shadowed street. He's still holding the neck of the broken beer bottle. Cradling it lightly in his fingers, the way I'd hold a paintbrush. As if it's a tool of his trade. An instrument of his art.

Cole sees me staring. He tosses the broken bottle aside. It shatters in the gutter with a high musical sound.

"Why?" I ask. "Why do you care how some guy in a bar behaves toward me?"

"I told you." He steps close to me as he always does, so I'm forced to look up at him. My heart pounds in my ears so loudly that I can hardly make out his words. "I've acquired you, Mara, like a painting, like a sculpture. Anyone who tries to damage what's mine will face consequences."

"I'm an object to you?"

"You're valuable."

That's not an answer. Not really.

"I don't need your protection. I handle guys like that every day at work."

"Not anymore," Cole says. "I'm guessing you're fired."

My cheeks flame with fury. He doesn't give a fuck that he cost me my job—why would he? He's not the one with bills to pay.

"I needed that job!"

"No you don't," he says carelessly. "Betsy Voss just sold your painting for twenty-two thousand dollars."

I stare at him, my mouth open. "You're joking."

Cole smiles thinly. "You know me better than that."

That's true. Cole is humorless. Which, paradoxically, makes his comment its own kind of joke.

"When did you find out?"

"She texted me an hour ago."

I'm light-headed. The swing from horror to elation is so extreme that I think I might be sick. I've never had twenty grand in my bank account in my whole life. I've never passed four digits.

"Cole…" I breathe. "Thank you."

I'm well aware that the painting sold because Cole got me in that show. Because he enlisted Betsy Voss as my broker. Because he talked me up to everyone we met. The painting is good, but in the art world, somebody has to say it out loud. Cole pushed the first domino, and the rest fell in turn.

His smile is triumphant. "I don't back a lame horse."

I can't help grinning back at him. "First I'm a sculpture, and now I'm a horse?"

He raises one black slash of an eyebrow. "What do you want to be?"

"I want to be talented. Powerful. Respected. Successful. I want to be like you."

"Do you?" he says quietly. "Do you really?"

"Isn't that what you want? You said you'd be my mentor. You'd make me in your image."

Cole is silent, as if he's never fully considered what that might mean.

Finally, he says, "The Artists Guild is throwing a Halloween party next Saturday. I want you to come with me."

Unable to resist teasing him, I say, "That sounds suspiciously like a date…"

"It isn't. Do you have a costume?"

"Yeah. I've been making one with Erin."

"What is it?"

"Medusa."

Cole nods. He likes that.

"What are you going to be?" I ask him.

"You'll see on Saturday."

25

COLE

With all the time I've been spending watching Mara, I've barely been paying attention to my own work.

Marcus York rings me up to "remind me" to submit my design for the sculpture in Corona Heights Park.

"Alastor Shaw sent me his early sketches," York says, trying to stoke my competitive fire. "They were impressive...but I'm sure you've got something even better percolating in that brain."

Actually, I don't.

I'm not uninterested in the project. It would be the largest piece I've ever done, which makes my mind run wild. However, this is one sculpture I won't be able to build alone. I'm not sure how much I'd enjoy designing something I can't manufacture myself.

I've always been fascinated by machines. Figuring out how to create the sculptures I see in my mind is half the fun. I've built more custom machinery than I have actual art. My studio is full of my own inventions.

Machines are complicated, but when built right, they work precisely as intended. They're much more useful assistants than I could ever hire from the Artists Guild.

And unlike human assistants, I don't mind sharing my space with them.

Mara's been hinting that she wants to come to my studio.

I'm tempted to let her. I'd be curious to hear her opinion on some unfinished pieces that never quite took shape.

I've never shown them to anyone before. In fact, I wouldn't like to admit that I *have* unfinished work—sculptures I can't complete to my liking that I've made and remade several times, never finding satisfaction in their final form.

Mara sees the same imperfections I do. She has a finely tuned sense of balance; she can tell when something's off.

She'll see what's wrong with them. And she just might know how to make them right.

The thought of bringing Mara here gives me a burst of motivation. I throw all the dust covers off the machinery before oiling and tightening and polishing any pieces that need it.

My work space is clean, but I clean it again, sweeping the wide wooden planks of the old chocolate factory, clearing space in the center of the room as if I'm about to begin a new project.

You can still smell the lingering scent of cocoa from the tiny nibs that fell between the boards. On warm days, the bitter buttery scent mixes with sawdust and steel to create one of my favorite perfumes.

Mara would notice it. She's sensitive to scents. I wouldn't even have to tell her this was a chocolate factory once upon a time—she'd already know.

I picture her standing here in the diffused light, cut with slanting shadows from the muntins between the windows. I imagine the sparkling motes of dust settling among the freckles on her cheeks. How she'll try to appear calm and composed, while bouncing on the balls of her feet.

She'll bring her fingers to her mouth, wanting to bite the edge of her nail, then quickly drop her hand again because she knows that infuriates me.

I imagine her warm, peppery scent mixing with the smell of chocolate.

My mouth salivates.

I drag a flat drafting table to the center of the space. I imagine Mara lying upon it...her arms and legs outspread...a spotlight trained on her naked body...

I imagine her tied down the way I'd secure any object before going to work upon it.

What kind of machinery would I need for this project?

What I have won't do.

No common drills or saws or sanders for Mara.

She needs something special. Something custom. Something built just for her...

26

MARA

THE NIGHT OF THE PARTY, ERIN AND I PUT THE FINISHING TOUCHES on our costumes.

Erin is going as Poison Ivy, so she's been sewing hundreds of artificial leaves all over a fabulous disco jumpsuit. Over the years, she's dressed up as practically every famous redhead in history: Lucille Ball, Jessica Rabbit, Ariel, Wilma Flintstone… I think my favorite was Joan from *Mad Men* because only Erin has the curves to truly pull that off.

I've been hand painting tiny green snakes made of modeling clay to form my Medusa headdress. This might not be the most productive use of my time, but I fucking love Halloween, and I'm no longer so broke that I can't spare a few hours for a silly project.

When I'm finally finished, I spend another two hours on my makeup. I use smoky olive eyeshadow and contour my face with the same shade, painting my lips a deep emerald green. A fishnet stocking forms the perfect stencil to create a scaly pattern around my hairline.

Once I've added the snake headdress and a seaweedy gown, I'm feeling pretty fucking good about myself.

Erin shakes her head. "You look scary."

"Yeah, that's the point."

"Remember that scene in *Mean Girls* where Cady shows up to

the party dressed as the Bride of Frankenstein with big ol' janky teeth, 'cause she doesn't know Halloween is supposed to be sexy? That's you right now. You're Cady."

I scoff at her. "It's not that bad. Besides, it doesn't matter what I wear—I'm never gonna look like you in that jumpsuit…"

Erin grins. "When god handed out tits, I got in line three times."

I laugh. "Apparently, I slept in and missed the whole thing."

Erin scored an invite to the party through Jamie Wiederstrom, an installation artist she met at New Voices.

"What's this, your third date?" I ask her. "Getting pretty serious…"

Erin shrugs. "It's two more than usual. I like to fuck up front. I don't want to waste my time if the chemistry isn't there. But I dunno, maybe I'm giving guys the wrong idea, like that's all I want."

"Don't ask me. I've never had a real boyfriend in my life."

"Josh is out of the picture?"

"I haven't seen him since I ditched him at the restaurant."

Erin pauses a moment before asking, "What about Cole?"

She's been trying not to grill me on the subject of Cole Blackwell because she knows it irritates me when the rest of my roommates do it. In return for her unusual levels of restraint, I feel like I owe her an update.

"I'm not trying to be cagey. I honestly have no idea how to describe our relationship. He's helped me more than anyone ever has. But he's also out of his fucking mind—half our conversations are arguments, and we've had some pretty crazy conflicts."

I already told her how I got fired from Zam Zam, so she knows I'm not talking about run-of-the-mill bickering.

"Plus…" I shiver. "Cole isn't normal. Sometimes I think I'm just a trophy to him, like he'd mount me on his wall."

"He's an artist." Erin shrugs, unconcerned. "We're all fucking weird."

"Not this weird."

"And you still haven't fucked him?"

"It's complicated—I don't want to lose him as a mentor."

That's not the only reason it's complicated, but it's the easiest to explain.

"I don't know where you get your willpower. I'd be down on my knees the first time we were alone in a room together. He's so fucking sexy, the way he doesn't give a fuck about anything or anyone..." Erin laughs. "Maybe that's why I never find love. Show me a philanthropist, a teacher, and a complete degenerate, and I'll pick the guy who steals my purse every time. I never did find my ID, by the way. I swear somebody took it."

I'm not really listening to Erin—I'm stuck on her second sentence, remembering how I *did* drop to my knees in front of Cole, resulting in the most humiliating moment of my life.

I got him back. Then he got me back. Now I hardly know where we stand.

Whatever Cole might say, going to this party does feel like a date. It's not like New Voices. The Artists Guild Halloween party is a rager. It results in more random hookups than your average swinger convention.

My phone buzzes with a text from Cole:

I'm out front

"I gotta go," I tell Erin. "I'll see you at the party."

I snatch up my purse and hurry down the stairs, knowing better than to keep Cole waiting.

He's standing outside his car, his arms crossed over his chest, already impatient.

I can't help laughing at the sight of him: he's dressed as a Greek warrior, but painted head to toe in mottled gray and white so he looks like a person turned to stone.

"How long did that take you?"

"Not too long. I rigged up my own airbrush."

Cole is well known for designing custom machinery for fabrication. By all accounts, he's an engineering genius. I haven't seen any of his inventions because he still hasn't brought me to his personal studio. It's the one place on earth I'm most curious to go—better than a secret tour of the Vatican.

"I want to see it." I give him a not-so-subtle reminder of his promise.

He ignores my hint, opening the car door for me in a way that somehow manages to feel bossy rather than chivalrous.

"I'm surprised you didn't dress as Perseus," I say.

"I thought this would amuse you more."

"Oh, it does."

Another joke for my benefit... I'm not sure whether to be gratified or disturbed that Cole is making this level of effort. I'm flattered as fuck, but I know there's always a reason with him—something he'll want in return. Cole doesn't do anything just to be nice.

We climb into his Tesla. Always prepared, Cole has laid a plastic tarp over his seat so the gray paint doesn't damage the leather.

As he pulls away from the curb, he engages the autopilot.

"I'm surprised you trust the computer to drive for you," I say. "I thought you were too much of a control freak for that."

Cole shrugs. "This car has eight cameras constantly looking in all directions and an algorithm that updates daily. It's superior to a human driver—even one as careful as me."

"Well, what do I know? I don't even have a driver's license."

"Are you serious?"

"Why would I? I've never had a car."

He makes a disgusted *tsk* sound. "You should still know how to drive."

I grin at him. "If autopilot keeps improving, maybe I'll never have to learn."

Though he's barely touching the wheel with his index finger,

Cole keeps his eyes on the road. He only pulls his gaze away for a moment to run those dark eyes up and down my body, murmuring, "You're stunning."

I'm glad the green makeup hides my blush. "Erin said it was too much."

"Erin is conventional. The blend of grotesque and sensual is alluring."

"Well…thanks."

I never imagined I'd be flattered to be called *grotesque*, but here we are.

We pull up in front of a tall brick building in Russian Hill, the party already in full swing. Bass thuds across the lawn, and eerie violet light spills out from the windows. As we enter through the front doors, we step into a thick fog and hanging sheets of artificial cobwebs.

♫ *"Devil's Worst Nightmare"—FJØRA*

Sonia grabs my shoulder, already well on her way to drunk. It takes me a second to recognize her because she's dressed as Beetlejuice, complete with a plunging black-and-white-striped suit, corpse makeup, and her gray bob sprayed lime green.

"Congratulations on selling your painting!" she cries with a valiant effort not to slur her words in the presence of her boss. "I wasn't surprised, but I'm damn happy for you."

"I know you are." I squeeze her shoulder in return. "You're my fairy godmother after all."

Cole looks put out. "Then what am I?"

"I don't know." I look him up and down. "You're more like…the goblin king in the middle of the maze."

"What does that mean?" He frowns.

"Haven't you seen *Labyrinth*?"

I can tell by his scowl that he hasn't.

"You're missing out!" Sonia cries. "David Bowie in those tight pants...it's classic."

Cole gives a dismissive shrug. He hates not knowing things. "Do you want a drink?" he asks me.

"Sure—whatever they have. I'm not picky."

He disappears into the crowd, searching for the bar.

Sonia cocks her head to the side, regarding me with a curiosity that cuts through her inebriation.

"Do you know why Cole smashed his solar model?"

I stare. "Are you talking about the Olgiati?"

"The one and only."

"You're kidding. Isn't that worth like...all the money?"

"Three million at least. He shattered it with a golf club. Busted it into a billion pieces."

My stomach churns. I hate the thought of something so unique being destroyed. "You think he did it on purpose?"

"I know he did."

"Why?"

"That's what I'm asking you."

I shake my head. "I have no idea why he does anything he does."

"I thought you might...it was the same day he hung your painting on his wall."

Now I do understand, though I try to keep my jaw from falling open so Sonia doesn't see it.

Fucking hell...he smashed his favorite glasswork because of me?

My skin goes clammy wondering what he would have done with that golf club if I were standing in the room with him instead. Suddenly, I feel like I got off light with a nonconsensual tattoo.

Sonia's eyes narrow. "Spill it."

Thankfully, Cole reappears with a hard cider in each hand.

"What about me?" Sonia complains.

"You're drunk enough already."

I gulp my cider, trying to calm the pounding of my heart.

"Take it easy," Cole says.

Whenever he barks an order at me, it makes me want to do the exact opposite. I wasn't going to take another gulp. Now that he said that, I take three more in quick succession.

Is it because I want to see that stiffening of his face? The way his pupils expand and his jaw flexes, creating a beautiful tension on the bow of his lip...

He grips my arm with iron-hard fingers. *"Don't fucking test me."*

Why do I like that?

Why is warmth flushing all the way down my legs?

Jesus, I'm so fucked up.

The alcohol provides me with newfound bravery. And newfound honesty.

I want Cole. I want him like money, like success, like achievement. I want him much more than I want other supposed necessities: Safety, for instance. Or sanity.

"Dance with me," I say, pulling him out in the press.

♫ *"Sinner"—DEZI*

I'm curious to see Cole dance. While I have no doubt his taste in music is as refined as the rest of him, that's not the same thing as having rhythm.

That question evaporates the instant his hands make contact with my skin.

Cole's touch is electric. For all his coldness, his actual body burns like a nuclear reactor—destructive heat radiating from the inside out.

I'm terrified of the energy in him. I have no illusions that it's under my control.

Cole pulls me against him. His hands slip around my waist, his thigh presses between mine, and our hips align. He holds me at the base of my neck and the small of my back. I'm a rabbit in his hands: helpless, heart racing.

He lets his lips graze against the side of my neck, his hot breath singeing my skin.

"I shouldn't give you what you want when you're being bratty... I'm not going to dance with you at all unless you behave yourself."

"I came to this party with you, didn't I?"

"You didn't do that for me," he growls. "You *want* to be here with me. You *want* to be dancing with me."

"So do you," I retort.

"Of course. I don't do anything I don't want to do."

"Never?"

"Fucking *never*."

I'm jealous. The freedom, the confidence to be that selfish...I envy Cole. No one owns him. No one controls him.

"Do you ever get lonely?"

"No. But I do get bored."

"I'd rather be dead than bored."

"So would I," he says, after a moment's pause, as if he hadn't realized that before. "An eternity of boredom sounds worse than death. And heaven sounds pretty fucking boring."

I laugh. "You can only stand so much plucking on a harp."

"We lack creativity when we describe heaven. The Greeks had more interesting mythology. Medusa, for instance. A beautiful woman with a head of venomous snakes...that's a powerful image."

"No one could look at her, or they'd turn to stone."

Cole stares into my eyes, his already as dark as wet black rock. "You don't want to be looked at?"

I hold his gaze. "Men never want to just look. I wish I had the power to do something about it."

More and more people arrive, cramming into the already crowded space. The more people want to dance, the tighter Cole and I are pressed together by dozens of bodies on all sides.

I'm sweating off the green makeup, and Cole's chalky stone is rubbing all over me. Neither of us cares. Soon we're both covered in muddy paint, our bodies sliding together.

Cole rubs his thumb across my cheekbone, over my lips. He licks the paint off my mouth.

I kiss him back, the earthy paint coating my tongue.

The heat, the scent of Cole's skin, and the chemical taste make my head swim.

"How have I never tasted paint before?" I murmur.

"Probably because it's made of awful things…"

"Like Mummy Brown?" I laugh. "They used to grind up real mummies…"

"You don't want to know what I use for *my* paint…"

I can never tell if he's joking.

Maybe he never jokes at all…

The pounding beat throbs through our bodies. I'm so dizzy, I doubt I could stand up if Cole weren't holding me.

I shouldn't have downed that drink so fast.

I've never felt this level of attraction to someone. I know without a doubt that Cole is taking me home tonight. Fuck, I might not make it to his house…I might not make it to his car…

I'm grinding against him, feeling the thick swell of his cock pressed against my hip.

I let my hand graze over his cock, my fingertips stroking the head with only a little fabric between us…

"Bad girl…" he growls in my ear. "You can't keep your hands off what you want…"

"Why should I?" I squeeze his cock hard. "You're the one who says whatever I want must be good…"

"That's true for me. It might not be true for you…"

I finally do what I've been wanting to do since that ink-black hair of his first brushed against my skin. I thrust my hands into it, filling my fingers with those soft, thick locks, gripping and pulling hard to yank his face toward mine.

"I don't care if you're good for me."

I kiss him deep and hard. I kiss him like he kissed me at the art show—like I'll eat him alive.

I fuck his mouth with my tongue like I wish he'd fuck me with his cock: deep, filling him all the way up.

We only break apart to breathe.

Cole's eyes blaze darker than I've ever seen them. "Come with me."

His hand is locked around my wrist, dragging me toward the door.

We're leaving together, and we both know where we're going.

Until a beefy figure steps in front of us, blocking our path.

I don't recognize him at first. He's dressed as Rambo with jungle camouflage on his face and a black mullet wig covering his sandy-blond hair. The size should have tipped me off. Not many people can fill a whole hallway with their bulk, blocking it off like a cork in a bottle.

"Shaw." Cole gives Alastor a curt nod while trying to slip past, my wrist still clamped in his grasp.

Alastor Shaw has no intention of letting us go that easy.

"Cole!" His booming voice cuts through the pounding music. "I thought I'd see you here. I heard you got some new student. Is this—"

He peers over Cole's shoulder, trying to get a good look at me amid the smoke and streamers and dim purplish light. He breaks off midsentence, the strangest flow of emotions passing over his face:

First, shock.

Second, disbelief.

And finally…what looks like pure glee.

"There she is," he breathes.

Cole drops my wrist, breaking the bond between us.

"She's just renting a studio in my building," he says.

The grin only spreads across Alastor's face. He looks unutterably happy for reasons I can't understand.

"I bet she is. I heard you're mentoring her."

Cole is silent.

I don't know what the fuck is going on. He's never seemed embarrassed of me before. My face is burning, and I want to speak up, but the tension is so thick that for once, I keep my mouth shut.

"She's nothing to me," Cole says, so quietly that I can't actually hear him. I watch the words form on his lips and carry across to Alastor, slashing me deep along their way.

Now it's me who takes a step back from Cole, my heart cold in my chest, a steak tossed in the fridge.

Alastor only laughs. "You brought her here. You're wearing matching costumes."

Cole steps between me and Alastor, putting me directly behind his back. He stands face-to-face with Shaw, almost the same height but not even close to the same weight, one slim and dark, the other broad and blond.

"She is my student," Cole says. "And she only learns from me. So stay the fuck away from her."

"You're so territorial." Alastor smirks. "You need to learn how to share."

"*Never*," Cole snarls back at him. "Keep your distance. I'm not fucking around."

Grabbing my wrist once more, Cole drags me past Shaw, always keeping his own body between us.

He hauls me all the way outside into the cold October night. He won't release my wrist until we're several blocks away.

"What the fuck was that?" I demand.

"What," Cole says.

"Don't even fucking try that. Don't try to pretend that was anything close to normal."

"I loathe Shaw, you know that."

"I've seen you interact with plenty of people you despise. That was different. You were stressed. He upset you."

Cole wheels on me, angrier even than he was with Alastor.

"I'm not *upset*. I don't give a fuck about Shaw."

"Or me either, apparently."

Cole raises his hands in front of my face. They tremble with the desire to throttle me.

He points one finger at me instead. "Stay away from him."

The order pisses me off. I wasn't trying to buddy up to Alastor Shaw—in fact, I find him obnoxious. But Cole has no fucking right to tell me whom I can and cannot speak to, especially in the art world. He wants to be the only one who can help me, the only one who can influence me.

"Why?" My eyes lock on Cole's. "Afraid he'll teach me something you can't?"

Cole's hand twitches. He wants to grab me by the throat. "I'm not fucking joking, Mara. He's dangerous."

"Oh, he's dangerous?" I sneer. "Like *you*?"

I'm facing him down. Daring him to admit what he's hinted at a dozen times. Daring him to say it out loud.

Cole's face goes still and smooth. Bleached by the last remnants of paint on his skin, he's pale as a skull.

As I watch, he removes the last mask. The last vestiges of humanity.

He shows me his real face: utterly devoid of emotion. No life at all in those pitch-black eyes. Teeth white as bone.

Only his lips move as he speaks.

"You think you know what you're talking about? I filet people with precision. This guy does what I do *badly*. You have no fucking idea what I'm capable of."

The air freezes. Sweat turns to ice on my skin.

I can't speak. Can't draw breath. Can't even blink.

He could kill me… He really could. I see it on his face.

And I'm too scared to move.

Instead, Cole turns and walks away, leaving me there alone.

27
COLE

Shaw knows.

The look of triumph on his face was unbearable.

He had no idea she was still alive.

He's been out wilding the past few weeks, not paying attention to me, his work, our mutual acquaintances, or anything else that should have tipped him off.

That's what happens when he goes on a frenzy: he disappears from the art world until the madness passes. Until he's ready to act sane again.

He killed two girls. That means there's one more to go.

He's never satiated until he takes the third. Then he goes quiet—sometimes for months at a time.

That's his cycle. I've watched it happen.

He's predictable. And I can easily predict what he'll do next:

He'll try to take Mara as his last kill.

He'd love the symmetry of that—he was the one who gave her to me, and he could take her away.

He might do it just to see how I'd react. To see if he could truly make me snap.

I don't know how the fuck to stop it from happening. Even I can't watch Mara every minute, every hour. If Shaw is determined to hunt her, how the fuck can I keep her safe?

Especially when she's reckless and stubborn, determined to get herself killed. I saw the look in her eye—ordering her to stay away from Shaw only makes her want to defy me.

So I terrified her on purpose.

She thinks she isn't scared of monsters? I'll show her a fucking demon out of hell.

It worked. She didn't come to the studio yesterday or today. She must be fucking terrified if she stayed home when she's aching to work on her painting.

She's home but not actually alone. I'm watching her right now through the telescope. Watching her lie in bed reading.

She finished *Dracula*. Now she's started *The Butterfly Garden*. I'm not familiar with that one, but if it interests Mara, I want to read it. I want to know everything in her head.

I've been following her continually. It won't be enough.

Alastor won't give up that easily.

I could kill him.

That eventuality has always loomed between us.

He knows too much about me, and I, about him.

I've been tempted many times before.

I almost followed through after he deposited Mara in my dumping ground. I should have done it then.

I'm not afraid of Shaw. But I've put myself at a disadvantage: it's not just me versus him. I have to protect Mara, too—if I want to keep her safe for myself, for my own use.

I'm spread thin. Covering too much ground.

This is exactly why I always avoided these kinds of entanglements. Mara complicates my life in a hundred different ways.

Yet here I am, neglecting my own work so I can watch her.

It's addicting. All-consuming. When I'm not near her, when I can't see her, it has a literal physical effect on me. My muscles twitch like I've had too much caffeine. The craving builds and builds until I can't think about anything else. I lose all my powers of focus, my mind straining after her.

Watching her creates the opposite effect. The drug courses through my veins, and I'm soothed, relaxed, purposeful once more.

Several hours pass. It's late now, past midnight. I should go home and sleep in my own bed.

I stay because of the nagging sensation that she's not safe, not even asleep in her room.

Shaw's going to do something, I know it. He saw us at the party together. He's going to take some action, leave some sign to let me know I didn't fool him for a second.

He must be over the fucking moon right now. His plan worked better than he ever could have dreamed.

All he wanted was to entice me into killing Mara. He never imagined I might form an attachment to her.

And, as difficult as it is for me to admit...that's exactly what I've done. I'm fixated on her. Obsessed with her, even.

Which gives Shaw all the power he could desire and more. I've put my attachment onto something fragile, something impossible to keep safe and under my control.

It's exhausting. This level of focus is draining.

I'm starting to realize that what entices me most about Mara is the contact high I get when I'm near her. She feels things so intensely that it makes me feel them, too.

I have no control over that effect. I can't choose what to feel and what not to feel. Mara infects me against my will.

Right now, she's so sleepy that she can barely keep her eyes open. Her head keeps nodding forward and then jerking up again while she sits propped up on the pillows, trying to sneak in a few more pages of her paperback.

Watching her lashes flutter and her head slowly sway is making me sleepy, too. I'm leaning against the windowsill. Nearly drifting off...

A shadow moves under the trees behind Mara's house.

I jerk upright, pressing my eye against the telescope, swiveling the lens to look down instead of across.

I only catch a brief glimpse of the figure disappearing around the side of her yard, but I know it's Shaw. Only he possesses that bulk, that heavy tread.

And only he would be lurking on her street, staring up at her window.

I push aside the telescope, slipping my arms into my coat.

I don't like playing defense. I'd rather be hunting than waiting.

Shaw has exposed himself, coming out alone at night.

I've got a knife with me—my garrote, too.

I can end this right now.

I descend the stairs of the Georgian, leaving all the lights turned off. I slip through the front door, closing it behind me with the soft *snick* of the lock settling into place.

At the far end of the street, Shaw's hulking frame is just turning the corner.

I trail him from a distance, knowing I'll have to stalk him with much greater care than usual. Shaw may be impulsive, but he's not stupid.

He likes to think we're the same species—lions hunting gazelles.

Shaw's an animal, but I'm no fucking lion.

I'm myself. Me. The only thing like me.

It'll be hard to trail him unseen. To sneak up on him. To take him down without serious injury. It benefits me nothing to kill Shaw if I bleed out right next to him.

So I follow with the appropriate level of respect.

Shaw walks rapidly, his head down, his hands in his pockets. He's dressed in dark sweats, his hood up, like he's out for a nighttime jog. Really, he's concealing his most memorable features, including that shock of sun-streaked hair.

He weaves, crossing over several streets, cutting through alleyways, jumping a chain-link fence. I can't tell if this is his usual mode of travel, the most direct route wherever the fuck he's going, or if he suspects that I'm following him.

I know he hasn't actually seen me, but he came to Mara's house on purpose. He knows damn well I could have been watching.

He could be luring me somewhere right now.

The question is…do I want to be lured?

Plenty of women thought they were snaring Shaw when they flirted with him, when they enticed him back to their apartments. They ended up beheaded on the beach.

Predator and prey, hunter and hunted…it's not always obvious which one is which.

The puff adder puts out its tongue, mimicking the movement of an insect. A toad that believes it's hunting soon becomes the snake's dinner.

This intuition solidifies as Shaw leads me into the grittier part of the Mission District—where every window is covered in iron bars and nailed-up plywood, where the graffiti covers not only the walls but also the doorways and awnings. Where half the buildings seem perpetually under construction, propped up by scaffolding, under the shadow of which squatters congregate and petty drug dealers run their businesses.

I have no fear walking through an area like this. Criminals know who they can rob and who they should avoid at all costs. Only the young and foolish would approach a man with Shaw's bulk.

I'm something else: a dark figure that repels even a curious glance. Gliding along like death, like famine, like plague in their midst.

Shaw pauses outside a ramshackle building, one of several in a row. They might have been apartments once—now they're all condemned, their doors chained and locked.

After glancing to both sides, Shaw takes a key from his pocket, opens the padlock, and slips through the door.

I hesitate on the opposite corner, pondering my options.

He might be waiting inside for me. Hoping to attack me in this isolated place.

If that's his plan, I'm not averse. I want to end this thing between us. I want it over, one way or another.

Or he might truly be unaware that I'm following him. In which case, I want to know what he keeps inside that building.

It feels like a trap. But also like an opportunity.

Stay or go? I've never been so torn.

If I go home, tomorrow I'll be right back where I was, staked out by Mara's house, racked by the paranoia of when and where Shaw will attack.

That's what pushes me to cross the road, to follow Shaw inside the crumbling tenement.

Inside is black as pitch, water dripping from the upper levels. The stairs are crumbling, large gaps between the risers. Moldering boards and stale urine assail my nostrils. Beneath that, the stench of putrefaction. Could be rats that died in the walls. Or something else...

I stand perfectly still, listening for Shaw.

All I hear is that drip, drip, drip of water and, farther up, wind groaning through open rafters.

I let my eyes adjust until I can make out enough detail to walk without tripping over the piles of old construction materials and the mounds of shredded tarp and old blankets where addicts have slept.

Shaw isn't on the main level. I'll have to climb the stairs.

I make my way up slowly, careful not to dislodge a single pebble. Any sound will echo in this desolate space.

I'm not afraid. But I am aware that I could be walking to my death or his. The next few minutes could decide.

The light at the head of the stairs is dim and slightly purplish.

That's how I know Shaw has laid a trap. He's mimicking the light at the Halloween party. Taunting me with references to Mara.

Still, I climb. I'm committed to this course.

I step into the space at the top of the stairs, a vast open cavern, all the walls knocked down.

In the center hangs a figure, suspended in space.

Not Shaw.

It's a girl, strung up like an insect in a web. Her arms and legs are outstretched, pulled to their farthest limit. Even her long hair has been bound at the ends and pulled all around her head in a dark corona.

She was alive when he tied her into the web—I can tell from the welts around her wrists and ankles where she pulled and struggled. She even tore out some of her hair.

She's dead now. Shaw cut her wrists and her throat, letting her bleed out. The puddle beneath her is so dark, it looks like a hole through the floor.

Because Shaw has never been subtle, he's woven snakes all through his web. Actual snakes, as dead as the girl. He wrapped several around her limbs, stuffed them in the gash in her throat, and even twined them in her hair.

The message is clear.

What's not clear is where the fuck Shaw went. He must have gone out another way...

Before I can look, I'm jolted by the last sound I want to hear: the crackle of a police radio.

Fuck.

Fuck, fuck, FUCK!

It's too late to go down the stairs—they're already inside the building. I hear them swarming in, trying to be quiet but failing miserably because cops are fucking awful at stakeouts.

Shaw called them. He trapped me in here with his latest kill. And I walked right into it, in the stupidest mistake I've ever made.

If I can't go down, there's only one way out.

After shucking off my coat, I wrap it around my arm and punch through the window. The cops hear the noise. They come thundering up the stairs at full speed, shouting.

I'm already climbing out, scaling the rusty drainpipe running up the side of the building. The metal is eaten through like lace, crumbling under my hands. The screws rip out, and the whole pipe comes away from the wall. I seize the gutter, swinging out into open air.

I haul myself up one-handed, my palms cut and god knows what strain of tetanus coursing through my blood.

The rooftop is hardly any better. It's nothing but flat concrete—nowhere to hide, not so much as a chimney.

The closest building is fifteen feet away. The gap between plunges twelve stories to a bare concrete alley. Not even a fucking dumpster waits below to break my fall.

Fifteen feet.

If it were ten, I could jump it.

Fifteen is dicey.

The next building over is slightly lower—that could help.

Through the broken window, I hear the cops ascend to the room. Discover the body of the girl. Fan out in search of me.

I've got seconds at most.

I back up to the far side of the building and sprint toward the ledge. I run as hard as I can and launch myself into space.

I fall forward and down, my arms stretched in front of me. When my feet hit, I tuck into a roll and tumble across the roof before coming to a stop sprawled flat on my back.

Not fucking far enough. Sirens howl, cop cars pulling up on both sides. They'll spread across the area in moments.

No time for strategy or planning. I leap to my feet and sprint again, running for the next building in the row.

Run, run, run, run…JUMP!

The third building is lower still, by two stories.

I crash hard, my right ankle buckling beneath me. It twists with an awful popping sound. Electric pain shoots up the outside of my leg.

Forcing myself up, I hobble to the edge of the building. This one has a fire escape still in place. Using the railings as a crutch, I limp

down as fast as I can, cursing my ankle, cursing that I've put myself in this ludicrous position.

Outsmarted by Shaw…what a fucking humiliation. I should let the cops put me out of my misery.

Hitting the ground, I limp through sickening pain, driven on by pure rage, by the desire to live through this so I can wreak my revenge on Shaw, so I can make him pay for this.

This is his fault.

His and Mara's.

It takes over two hours to shake off the cops and return to Sea Cliff. Some of that time is me hiding in a filthy alleyway, crouching under a pile of moldering trash bags, ankle too swollen to run another step.

The ignominy of this is almost too much to bear.

I spend every second imagining how I'm going to peel the skin off Shaw's flesh, inch by inch. Death will be a mercy I won't give him until his screaming soul is snatched from my grip.

I've never been so relieved to walk through my own front door.

The next hour is me standing under a boiling shower spray, scrubbing my own skin as if I, too, should be flayed.

After that, the thinking begins.

I'll kill Shaw, that much is certain.

But how the *fuck* am I going to do that when I'm already injured? Even at my peak, Shaw is more than a physical match for me. I'm smarter but he's bigger. An eight-pound difference matters in boxing—Shaw's got fifty pounds on me.

He knows I'm coming, too. He'll be watching for me. Waiting.

Mara remains a constant point of vulnerability.

Shaw's primary goal will be to kill her.

He's jealous. Fixated. He knows I want her—which means he wants her more.

Taking her from me will be a greater triumph than putting a knife in my heart.

I can't possibly keep her safe. Not for any significant length of time.

Mara weakens me. I chased after Shaw on impulse, believing I had to act quickly to protect her. Now my ankle is puffed up like a snakebite, and I can barely stand.

She weakens my mind. My decision-making. She warps my goals, making me think I care about things I never gave a fuck about before.

I can't protect her. Her death is inevitable.

But I'll be damned if Shaw is the one to do it.

Mara belongs to me.

I'm the only one who gets to kill her.

28
MARA

Rain thunders down outside the laundromat, drumming on the roof.

It's late on a Sunday night. Most everyone who had laundry to do finished hours ago. Only one load remains rotating next to mine: a jumble of dingy gray socks, which I assume belong to the tiny Asian grandmother asleep against the vending machines.

I'd rather not be doing laundry either, but it's been weeks since I stopped wearing underwear. I'm down to my last T-shirt, emblazoned with a print of Mia Wallace, complete with the bloody nose. Joanna makes movie T-shirts for spare cash on the side. She's so good at it that she could probably afford to rent a room in a much nicer place. I think she stays because she worries we'd burn the place down without her. Or at least Heinrich would.

Under the T-shirt, I'm wearing floral boxer shorts, striped hockey socks, and a pair of battered flip-flops. It's not my greatest look, but the sleepy grandma doesn't seem to mind.

I lean against the dryer, watching my darks tumble around and around. The motion is soothing. The warmth of the dryer seeps into my body, loosening the stiff muscles of my chest, making me melt against the convex glass.

I'm trying to decide what the fuck to do about Cole.

I can't keep avoiding him.

I'm itching to get back to my painting, back to that gorgeous studio that acts like creative catnip, whipping me into a frenzy as soon as I step foot through the door.

Or maybe it's Cole who puts me in a frenzy.

The number of ideas I used to get in a year, now I get in a week. In my sleep I see streams of images, colors so rich, you could eat them, textures that make you want to roll down them like a velvety hill...

I know exactly what I need to do to finish my devil.

But to do it, I'll have to walk through Cole's door.

I don't think we're playing a game anymore.

I filet people with precision...

He does what I do badly...

Jokes and threats? Manipulation? Or the pure, unvarnished truth?

Cole implied Alastor Shaw is a killer.

He *more* than implied that he's one, too.

He does what I do badly...

We're talking about two of the most famous men in the city. Artists, for fuck's sake.

Rival artists.

Or perhaps...just rivals.

You were given to me...

I jolt up from the dryer, the warmth of the tumbling clothes giving way to the chill that grips the back of my neck.

Two men. One heavy and rough. One slim, light, almost silent...

Convulsively, I clasp my palm over the wriggling scar running up my left wrist. I can feel it under my thumb, thick and hot as a snake.

I spoke to Alastor Shaw the night I was kidnapped. I met him at the show, before I went outside to vape with Frank. We only talked for a minute before Erin interrupted us.

Erin said she fucked him in the stairwell. How long did that take? Quick enough that he could have seen me leaving? Quick enough that he could have followed?

It only lasted a minute. But it was nice…

The pieces fall into place with sickening speed.

He could have snatched me up a block from my house. Stuffed me in a trunk. Bound, blindfolded, and pierced me, then slashed me open and left me on the ground to die…

No. Not to die.

Left…as a gift.

A gift for the man who would follow.

Where was Cole going that night? What was he doing?

Someone knew he'd be there. They knew he'd find me.

And what was the point? What did they expect?

My heart is racing, the steady *whum, whum, whum* of the dryer like a crank operating my brain. Forcing it to keep running. Shoving it toward the inevitable conclusion of these thoughts.

He expected Cole to finish me off.

That was the gift.

That was the temptation.

BUZZZZZZZZ.

The alarm to the dryer sounds, making me shriek.

The little Asian grandma pops up like a jack-in-the-box before bustling over to retrieve her socks. She bundles them all into a string bag, then slings the bag over her shoulder, heading toward the door, waving to me as she leaves.

I wave back, feeling like I'm floating, feeling like I'm one of the many pieces of trash running down the gutters outside, carried away by the rain.

What happened that night never made sense because I was too close to the picture. I could only see the tiny individual dots. Taking a step back, the whole image pulls into focus.

There were two psychopaths in the woods that night: Alastor and Cole.

Alastor brought me there.

Cole was supposed to kill me.

But he didn't.

I fucking survived.

And the whole palaver afterward, my *Great Expectations* rise to success with my secret benefactor Cole working behind the scenes... what was that? More of their fucked-up game?

I pace up and down the narrow aisle between the machines, listening to my clothes rumbling away on both sides.

This all sounds insane.

But it's the only thing that makes sense. The only thing that explains what I know I saw.

Two men.

Two psychopaths.

I stop dead where I stand.

I've seen all the indications with Cole. The way he swaps personas at will. The way he uses his money and influence to manipulate people...including me. The way he doesn't truly care about anyone or anything.

That's not true. He cares sometimes. He cared when he smashed that solar model.

I shake my head hard, irritated with myself.

Rage isn't the same thing as caring.

My chest is tight. It's hard to draw a full breath.

I keep thinking about the girl's body on the golf course. And the others on the beach...

How many has it been now? Six? Seven?

The Beast of the Bay.

I told myself that had nothing to do with me. I was cut but not torn apart. Not actually killed.

Now I think I was supposed to be.

Is Alastor the Beast? Is Cole?

Is it both of them?

The rain pours down harder, shattering in the street, sending up silvery sparks.

I've reached the end of the aisle. The plate-glass window is covered in peeling decals proclaiming, *Suds Your Duds, Coin-Operated, 24-Hour Self-Serve.*

Through those blistered letters, I see a figure across the street. Tall and dark. Standing still on the sidewalk without any umbrella, looking directly at me.

♫ *"High Enough"—K.Flay*

Cole has been stalking me all week. I've seen him on the street outside my house and at the café across from Sweet Maple. He knows I've seen him, and he doesn't care. He hasn't tried to bang on my door or force me to eat brunch with him again.

He's just watching. Waiting.

Standing guard.

The chill runs from the nape of my neck all the way down my spine.

I finally understand.

Cole's not watching *me*. He's watching for Shaw.

Stay away from him. He's dangerous. I'm not fucking joking.

It's too dark to see the details of Cole's face, especially with the rain plastering his hair down over his eyes.

He can see me, though. Brightly lit, clean, and dry, framed in this window.

I press my palm flat against the glass.

How can I be so afraid of someone but never run?

I don't want to run from Cole. I want to stand still while he comes to me, and then I want to reach up and touch his face. I want to pull off the masks, one by one, until there aren't any left. And whatever's underneath…I want to see it.

He terrified me, the night of the Halloween party. He did it on purpose, deliberately flashing his fangs to scare me away from Shaw.

Why?

Because he wants to keep me safe.

No matter how insane that sounds, it's what I believe.

Cole wants to keep me safe. It's why he's spent countless hours watching me when he has the whole city at his disposal, when he could be doing anything else.

I walk back to the dryers, checking the remaining time.

Twelve minutes.

I lean against the glass, my eyes closed, my whole body rocked by the hulking industrial machine. These dryers are probably older than I am, each one the size of a compact car.

The bell above the door lets out a gentle chime.

I keep my face pressed against the glass, my eyes closed.

I hear him coming up behind me. No one else would hear those careful, measured steps.

I can even hear the lonely sound of his breath entering and exiting his lungs.

Without turning, I say, "Hello, Cole."

His reflection is a ghost in the glass: wet black hair plastered to his cheeks. Dark holes for eyes, fixed only on me.

Rain drips from the hem of his coat to the linoleum tiles.

"Hello, Mara."

He swoops in behind me, pressing me against the dryer. His body is soaked and frigid, the hard muscle of his chest locked against my back. Against my belly, the dryer rocks and hums, spreading warmth all the way through me into Cole.

He traps me there, a moth on a windshield.

His heart pounds against my shoulder blade. His hot breath burns my neck.

"It's time for you to stop hiding," he whispers. "It's time for you to come home."

His scent is everywhere around me, not washed away by the rain, only enhanced by it.

If Cole's so bad, why does he feel so good?

Who knows what the rabbit feels when the hawk pins it to the ground? When those claws close around its body. When the hawk lifts the rabbit into the sky...

Maybe the moment of capture is bliss.

My body thrums against the dryer. Cole presses my chest, my belly, my hips against it. Grinding me into it. Never letting up on the pressure for even a moment.

"You want me to come to your house?" I gasp.

"Yes," he growls, his chest rumbling like the dryer, the sandwich of heat and pressure making my head spin.

"No." I close my eyes, shaking my head.

Cole grips my hips, digging his fingers in. He pushes me harder against the glass.

The vibration is having a certain effect on me. My skin flushes, my pulse quickening, my thighs twitching with that rushing sensation you can only hold back for so long.

"Why do you always have to be so difficult?" Cole growls.

I turn my head slightly so we're cheek to cheek, mouths an inch apart. "I want to see your studio."

I can feel his irritation. Hear his teeth grinding.

"Fine," he snaps. "Tomorrow night."

This is madness. I shouldn't be going to his studio *or* his house. I should be calling the cops.

But the cops won't believe me. They never have.

Is Cole a mentor or a killer? Is he protecting me or hunting me?

There's only one way to know for certain.

Cole slips his hand down the front of my shorts. He finds my pussy slippery and throbbing. Desperate for his touch.

I moan.

He shoves me against the dryer, grinding my hips against the door. His cock presses between my ass cheeks. The warmth and the rumbling surge through me with every turn of the clothes. It only

takes three thrusts with his fingers, three pulses of his hips against my ass, before I start to come.

I moan and shake, grinding against the dryer. Cole holds me in place with his wet, steaming body. Pressing me tight against the vibration.

"Seven o'clock tomorrow night," he growls in my ear. "No fucking around this time. If you're one minute late…I'm coming to find you."

I can hardly hear him over the dryer. Over the hot liquid pleasure pounding in my ears.

All in a moment, he's gone. The buzzer sounds, the dryer stops, and I'm standing there with my legs shaking, realizing I'm definitely fucking crazy.

29

COLE

As I make my preparations for Mara's arrival, I go back and forth a hundred times on how I should kill her.

I've never been so indecisive.

I've always known exactly what I should do, as if it already happened.

Mara clouds my mind. She darkens my ability to see.

If I remove her from my life, I'll go back to the way I was before. I'm sure of that.

The problem is…I don't know if I want to go back.

Mara warps who I am. But in the moment, when I'm with her…I like it. I see things I never saw before. Feel things. Hell, I even taste things differently.

She's electric. I touch her, and the current runs through me. She lights me up, turns me on, fills me with energy.

The cost is the loss of control.

Control has always been my highest priority. The thing that made me unique. The source of all my power.

I can't give that up. I can't become like everyone else.

In the end, it's Mara who made the choice: I invited her to my home. She asked to come to the studio instead.

She wants the artist, not the man.

My art is death. It always has been.

I'll make it a beautiful death. A pleasurable one. She deserves that at least.

The minutes tick by, seven o'clock drawing closer.

She won't be late this time. Her desire to see my studio is too great. It's what she's wanted most all along—just like Danvers.

I spent all day on the preparations. Planning is the foreplay.

At precisely seven o'clock, Mara arrives at the studio. I hear the motion notification and walk toward the door, then open it before she's pulled her finger back from the bell.

♫ *"Black Magic Woman"—VCTRYS*

She turns, startled, her hair and dress swirling. The dress is diaphanous, black as a shroud. She looks like a witch. She *is* a witch.

Fear and eagerness add a sharp edge to her scent. She licks her lips, red and slightly chapped. I can almost taste their texture, like the rim of a cocktail glass—salty sweet and granular.

"Are you going to let me in?" She tilts her head, her eyes slanted on either side of that upturned nose.

Each angle of her face reveals a mood, always something new to be seen. I never finished reading her, and I suppose I never will.

I step aside. Her hair caresses my forearm, sliding across the back of my hand like a whisper, like a kiss.

Old-fashioned lamps throw pools of golden light down from the walls. Mara steps in and out of these pools, sometimes shadowed, sometimes glowing. She twirls slowly, her skirt belling out around the stalks of her legs. Her mouth opens in awe. "All this space is yours?"

"No one alive has seen it—except me and you."

"Secrets are lonely."

"Only people who want company are lonely."

"Only people who are scared of other people want to be alone." Mara's quick smile shows all her teeth.

I draw closer, watching her eyes widen, watching how she has to force herself to stand still as I approach. The impulse to flee is always present. Mara's instincts are good…but she never listens to them.

"Which of us is scared right now?"

She looks up at me. "Both of us, I think."

My stomach clenches.

"Yet we're both here," she says. "Are you going to show me what you're working on?"

"I haven't made anything since *Fragile Ego*," I admit. "But I plan to start something new tonight."

A shiver runs across her shoulders—this time, pure excitement. "You're going to let me watch you work?"

"You're going to help me. We're going to do it together."

She can hardly breathe. "Right now?"

"Soon. I want to show you something first."

I take her to the adjacent room, where I keep the half dozen sculptures I never completed. The ones I could never quite make right.

I think of them as aborted fetuses. Unable to grow as they should. Abandoned by their creator because they died in the womb.

They're ugly to me, and yet I can't let them go because I know what they should have become.

Mara walks among them, slowly examining each one. It pains me for her to see them, but I have to know if she sees them as I do—ruined and unfixable.

She's silent, looking at each piece from several angles, taking her time. Her brows knit together. She chews on the edge of her swollen lower lip.

Mara's always biting at herself. It makes me want to bite her, too.

"These are the ones you couldn't finish."

"That's right."

She doesn't ask why. She sees the imperfections of each.

To a random person, they might look just as good as pieces I've proudly displayed. To the discerning eye, they're as dead as a fossil. Worse, because they never actually lived.

Mara pauses by the last sculpture. This was my most expensive failure—I'd been working on a chunk of meteorite dug up in Tanzania. The thing weighed two tons when I started. I had to design a custom plinth to hold it.

"This one can be saved."

I shake my head. "Trust me, I tried. The material alone cost a fucking fortune."

She runs her hand lightly down its spine, making me shiver, as if she were stroking my own skin. "You were making a figure...."

God, she's perceptive.

"Yes. I considered moving away from abstract. But I'm no Rodin, clearly."

"You could be." Mara looks at me, her hand still resting on the meteorite. "You could be whatever you wanted to be. That's not true for everyone—but I think it is for you."

My jaw tightens, resentment swirling. "You have too much faith in people."

I leave her, striding back out to the main room. Where my table waits, with all my tools.

Trusting as a lamb, Mara follows me.

She sees the table under its surgical spotlight. She sees the tools laid out next to it: the chisels, mallets, hammers, knives. And she sees the bare space where the raw material ought to reside.

I turn to face her, wondering how long it will take her to understand.

Mara crosses the space slowly, not looking at the table. Only looking at me.

"I really don't," she says. "I don't have any faith. I learned early that some people have no kindness inside them. No mercy. They're broken, and they can only find pleasure in hurting. Even when it makes no sense. My mother's like that. She's the scorpion that would sting you even if you were carrying her on your back. Even if it meant you'd both die. She just can't help herself."

I'm standing right by the tools. My fingers are inches from the knife.

"I'm good at seeing, Cole. I saw who she was at an early age. And I see who you are, too."

Mara steps directly into the brilliant beam of light. Every detail of her person is illuminated: every freckle, every glint of silver and thread of black in those wide eyes.

"I know it was Alastor Shaw who took me. He dumped me in the woods for you to find."

My hand freezes above the blade.

"He wanted you to kill me, but you didn't. You didn't kill me that night or any of the nights that followed. And it's not because you haven't killed before. It's because you don't want to do it. You don't want to hurt me."

My fingers twitch, brushing the handle of the knife.

"You've been watching over me. Protecting me. Helping me. You might have told yourself it was for your own enjoyment, for your own fucked-up reasons. But you care about me, Cole. I know you do. I've seen it. Maybe you don't want to care. Maybe you'd like to kill me right now to stop it. But I don't believe you will. Too much has happened between us. You've changed too much."

Slowly, she slides the sleeves of her dress down her arms. Baring her delicate shoulders and her small round breasts. She lets the dress drop all the way to her feet and steps out of it. She's naked underneath, her body glistening under the light, the silver rings glinting in her nipples.

The tattooed garden runs down her right side, caressing the underside of her breast, twining across her ribs, ending at the point of her hip. She wears it proudly, my mark on her skin.

And I wear hers: the white snake and the black. I thought the snakes were her and I, good and evil, locked in battle. Now I wonder if she meant for them both to be me...

She takes another step toward me. Naked and unafraid.

I never get used to the sight of her body. The tightness, the wild energy that courses through it. The moment I touch her, that energy will pulse into me. Sliding my cock inside her would be like strapping into an electric chair.

Her eyes lock on mine. "You won't hurt me."

Now it's me who licks my lips. Me whose voice comes out in harsh rasp: "Are you willing to bet your life on that?"

Mara climbs on the table before lying down beneath the light. Her naked body glows, exposed and vulnerable. "I'm here, aren't I?"

Her scent rises off her skin. I see the veins running beneath, all that hot blood pumping fast with every beat of her heart.

She raises her knees. Lets them fall open slightly, revealing the soft pink folds between. My mouth waters helplessly.

I stoop and lift the restraints attached to the table legs.

Perhaps there is some mercy in me because I hold up the manacle, giving her one last chance.

"Are you sure?"

She looks into my eyes, believing she sees something there. And she holds out her wrist to me. "I want you. And you want me."

I close the manacle around her wrist, hearing it lock in place. "Now I have you."

30
MARA

THE TERROR THAT SURGES THROUGH ME AS THAT MANACLE CLOSES around my wrist is like nothing I've ever known. I'm Mia Wallace now—stabbed in the heart with pure adrenaline.

Every nerve fires up, my senses screaming. Cole's breath flows across my skin. I feel the heat of his hands long before they touch me.

He clamps my wrists down to the table, then my ankles. Slowly, he turns a crank, winching my legs apart.

I gasp as the cool air hits my bare pussy. I want to shriek, I want to squirm, but I force myself still. Cole is a predator. Fear will only ignite his worst instincts.

He looks down at me. He's never been more beautiful than in this dazzling light. He really is a dark angel, biblical in power and wrath.

Those black eyes crawl over every inch of my skin. His upper lip tightens, baring his teeth.

"You know I watched the video of you fucking that guy."

I hold his stare, unembarrassed. "That's why I brought him to the studio. So you'd have to watch."

"How many times do you think I watched that tape?"

I swallow hard. I hadn't considered that he'd view it more than once. "I don't know."

Softly, Cole says, "Over a hundred, Mara. Over and over and over again."

My skin goes cold, then flaming hot.

He strokes the hair back from my forehead with disturbing gentleness. "Why do you think I watched it so many times?"

"I…I don't know."

I'm afraid he was stoking his fury against me.

Already this encounter is taking a turn I didn't predict. It's hard for me to remain calm.

"It was to learn." Cole lets his fingers trail down the side of my face. "I watched it over and over to see what you like, Mara. To learn your preferences. This body of yours is so responsive…"

His fingers slide over my collarbone and down to the top of my breasts. My nipples stiffen, standing erect as if begging for his touch. *Please, just a little closer…*

"You're a thrall to what you love. The things you hate repulse you," Cole says in that low hypnotic tone. "I knew if I learned everything I could about you, there's nothing I couldn't make you do…"

Gently, ever so gently, he grips one of the silver rings in his fingers and rotates it through the tight point of my nipple. The feeling of that cold steel sliding through my flesh makes me moan. I can't help it. I can't stop it.

"You can't possibly imagine what I know about you…" Cole says. "I know what you read, what you eat. I know how you touch yourself when you think you're alone. And I know every song you listen to. All your favorites. I compiled a list and made an algorithm to search for exactly the type of song that carries you away…"

He pauses, taking his phone from his pocket and setting it next to his tools. With one long, slim index finger, he sets his playlist in motion. The music that floats out of his expensive speakers is not what I expected: light and ethereal instead of dark and pounding.

♫ *"Spells"—Cannons*

I can't control how music makes me feel.

My body relaxes, every muscle loosening. My eyelids grow heavy. Despite my predicament, despite the danger I've put myself in, my mind drifts across the swells of the first verse.

"I made something for you." Cole's voice comes from somewhere down near my feet. "Custom machinery."

I try to force myself to focus. I do *not* like the sound of that.

Cole switches on his machine. A low buzzing sound cuts through the music. What the fuck is that? Is it a drill?

Craning my neck, I see he's holding some kind of device shaped like an oversize microphone. The head is soft and bulbous.

"It's like the dryer." His lips curve. "Only much, much better…"

He presses his tool between my legs, right against my pussy.

The effect is instantaneous. I fall backward into a deep, warm bath. The vibrations are a hundred times stronger than the dryer. Tied to the table, I can't close my thighs or pull away. Pulsing waves flow through me, all the way up through my torso and down through my legs. The vibrations run across my scalp, down through my fingertips and into my toes.

"Ohhhh goooooddddddddd…"

The words come out of my mouth without action, without thought. There *are* no thoughts in my head, only explosions of colored paint.

I've never owned a vibrator; I could never afford a good one.

The one Cole built is heavy and powerful. The soft head molds against my pussy, warm like living flesh.

Cole runs it up and down my slit. My legs are pulled apart, my clit exposed. Each stroke sends another tsunami of pleasure crashing over me.

Sometimes he holds it in place, pressing against that sensitive bundle of nerves running from my clit down to the opening below. The pleasure builds and builds until it feels like it will drown me. I thrash and squirm, tied down, unable to escape, until the wave finally breaks, obliterating me completely. I'm dashed apart, washed away.

Until I slowly, slowly come back to myself again. And it all starts over.

The whole area is becoming more swollen and sensitive by the minute. I'm becoming aware of nerves that hardly existed before, firing to life under the continual stimulation of those low, insistent rumbles.

"I tested all kinds of frequencies…" Cole murmurs, his eyes fixed on my face. He's watching my expression as my eyes roll back, as my cheeks flush and my lips part. He's taking note of exactly what feels the best, constantly adjusting his technique so the pleasure ramps up and up, never diminishing, never stalling out. "I even went back to the laundromat to compare."

Through the warm floating waves, I realize I've made a huge mistake.

I underestimated Cole. I underestimated his creativity…and how far he's willing to go.

Too late.

I'm no longer in control.

The next orgasm hits, rolling me over and over. Tumbling me through an endless cycle of warmth and pleasure. I'm groaning like an animal, noises coming out of me I've never heard before. The groans are low and desperate. I can't get enough of this. I'll die without it.

The pleasure draws back, only briefly. Before the orgasm is done, the next is building. No break in between. No refractory period.

The vibrations run through every nerve of my body. Every part of me is becoming as acutely sensitive as my clit.

Cole presses the vibrator against me with one hand and reaches up with the other to massage my breast.

"*Oh, my fucking goddddddd…*" I groan.

My whole body is melting.

Cole's hands are living creatures with a mind of their own. His fingers undulate on my flesh, each point of contact exquisitely soft.

He's not squeezing like most men, not groping—he's exploring. It feels like he has a thousand fingers, a thousand hands. He's touching me everywhere at once.

He moves to my other breast, keeping the sensation equal, keeping it spread across my body. He seems to understand that I don't like things uneven, hate unfinished loops.

His fingers move across my flesh, separate but coordinated, falling like rain.

The vibration pulses through me, filling me with energy, filling me with sensation.

Cole tugs gently on my nipple, careful of the piercing. He's giving me the intensity I need, taking me to the point of pain.

My breasts are as sensitive as my pussy. Maybe even more. The vibrations concentrate in my chest beneath his hand. My nipple feels as engorged as my clit, as capable of giving pleasure. The orgasm begins in my chest, not between my legs. Cole tugs on my nipple in slow, rhythmic strokes as if he's milking it. It's makes me come helplessly, irresistibly, stronger than before.

He closes his mouth around my other nipple, suckling one, tugging on the other. There's no table beneath me anymore. I'm floating in pure liquid pleasure.

"*Cole...*" I don't know if I'm moaning aloud or only in my head. I'm begging him not to stop.

Cole keeps the vibrator pressed against me while he comes around the table up toward my head. He unzips his trousers, freeing his cock.

It falls out in front of my face, heavy and brutal, pale as marble and thick with veins. The head is already leaking.

I look at that butter-soft skin, that clear drop of fluid gleaming on the tip.

My mouth waters. My lips are swollen, aching to be touched. Desperate to suck on something.

Without him asking, without him moving toward my mouth, I

tilt up my chin, parting my lips, stretching my tongue eagerly for a taste.

I close my mouth around the head of his cock. The burst of liquid salt is the most delicious thing I've ever tasted. It floods my mouth, that rich and complex mix of his skin, his pheromones, his sweat, and his come.

It's exactly what I like.

I suck gently at first, swirling his cock around in my mouth, running my tongue all around the head. Trapped inside his trousers, his cock could only fill so much. Now that it's free, it straightens out, growing so hard that it feels like there's too much burning flesh to be contained within such silky skin.

His blood pulses through the bulging veins beneath my tongue. Every time I take him deeper into my throat, I'm rewarded with another burst of come.

He thrusts into my mouth in time with the rolling strokes of the vibrator. Each shove of his cock is accompanied by a deep press of the vibrator right where I need it. The harder he presses, the harder it thrums, sending shocks through my every nerve, an endless loop from brain to groin.

He grips the base of his cock, stroking it into my mouth. His fingers brush against my lower lip. Nothing has ever felt better than his index finger against my lip. I open my mouth wider so his hand presses hard against my mouth, so his cock delves deep into my throat.

I want to be fucked in the mouth like I want his cock deep in my pussy. Nothing else will satisfy.

He pumps into my throat, the heavy head of his cock hitting all the way back, to a sensitive patch of flesh that's never been touched before. Maybe this should make me gag; maybe it would have before. In this moment, it feels like I have a G-spot in my throat. Like the head of his cock rammed down there is the only thing that can make me come.

The next orgasm starts, and I'm moaning around his cock, I'm coming with it deep in my throat, my desperate groans creating their own vibration against the head.

Now it's Cole who can't stay quiet, Cole who begins to shake and shudder as come flows out of him, thick and rich, the most satisfying thing I've ever swallowed.

He fucks my mouth hard. I look up at him, realizing that at some point, he took off his shirt. Every muscle stands out on his chest, his arms, the flat expense of his stomach. I look up at that perfectly carved figure and that face that wears no mask—that shows the full extent of his greed, his hunger, and his lust for me...

I look up at him, and I think, *He's not human. He's so much more...*

I drink his come like a gift.

I'm so dazed that I hardly notice when he pulls away. I only feel the absence of his taste and scent, of his warm cock against my tongue. I want it back.

I whimper like a baby, begging him for more.

"Patience," Cole says.

He's loosening the restraints that pin me to the table. I think he's going to lift me and carry me somewhere, maybe to a bed in some hidden room. Instead, he rolls me onto my stomach and tightens the chains once more so I'm tied facedown instead.

He slots the vibrator underneath me so he doesn't have to hold it anymore—it's pinned in place under my body.

This feels good, but not quite as good because it's only making light contact with my clit. I can't get enough pressure.

Still, I'm light and floating. Flushed with chemicals from all the orgasms that came before.

I didn't know you could have that many. I always stopped after one or two.

I don't have the stamina for this. I'm panting like I ran a marathon. I've never even run a 5K.

Cole moves around behind me.

This position feels even more vulnerable. I squirm on the table, wishing my legs weren't winched apart, my cheek pressed against the wood, everything exposed to his view.

I hear the whisper of cloth and realize he's taking off the rest of his clothes. My heart beats faster.

Cole pauses to press his finger to his phone, switching the song. The change in mood hits me like a slap.

This is no soft, floating ballad.

The new beat is steady, insistent. The voice comes in, young and deceptively innocent, but with an edge of menace.

♫ *"Bad Things"—Cults (on repeat)*

My muscles tighten; I grit my teeth.

Cole climbs on the table before sitting on the back of my thighs. He's heavy. I'm reminded of how tall he is, how strong. How easily he could overpower me even if I weren't tied down.

Every time he shifts, his throbbing cock brushes over me, touching my thighs, my ass, like a tentacle, like a battering ram testing for weakness.

My heart is racing too fast. Maybe Cole feels it. He begins to massage my back with long, slow strokes, calming me.

He plays my body like an instrument, seeming to understand better than I do which places are tight, which are sore. His strong hands grip and manipulate. I'm completely in his power.

I've never let a man tie me up. I never trusted anyone enough.

Now I've put myself under the control of the most terrifying person I've ever met. It's suicidal. His hands knead my muscles like he's tenderizing the flesh. Preparing it for slaughter.

Leaning over me, pinning me down with his weight, Cole murmurs, "Have you ever been spanked before?"

I'm sweating. Squirming. Realizing how thin the line is between nerves and hysteria.

"No. And I don't want to be."

Cole lets out a sigh of disappointment. "Don't lie to me, Mara. I hate it when you lie."

He sits up, his hand coming away from my back, then returning to my ass with a sharp smack. The impact ripples through my flesh, sharp and corrective. I jolt, trapped in place by the metal rings clamped around my wrists and ankles.

"Don't!" I shriek, panic rising in my chest. "I told you I hate that."

"How could you hate it if you've never experienced it?"

Cole brings his hand down again hard in the same place.

He's not holding back. The blows are hard and cruel. My flesh burns in the shape of his handprint.

I'm filled with a thick, squirming sense of shame. My cheeks are as hot as my ass. I blink hard to hold back the tears threatening to fall.

"All right!" I cry. "I was spanked. Is that what you want to hear?"

SMACK!

He slaps me on the other side, even harder. It makes me jump because I wasn't expecting it. I thought he'd only hit one side.

"I already know that," he says, low and dangerous. "It's fucking obvious."

SMACK!

He hits me again on the left side, making the whole cheek ripple, sending shocks all the way up my back.

Cole is viciously strong. The slaps are hard. They really hurt, especially when he hits the same side twice in a row. I find myself grinding against the vibrator, desperately seeking a little pleasure to ameliorate the pain.

"Please." My voice sounds childish and pathetic.

"Tell me how he spanked you."

I'm crying. The tears are silent, but I feel them running down my cheeks, falling onto the table.

SMACK!
SMACK!

SMACK!

He's not going to stop. Not until I tell him what he wants to know.

I'm sobbing, my eyes squeezed shut, admitting something I've never told a human soul.

"He'd make me go put on my school uniform. The plaid skirt and the shirt and the socks. No underwear. Then he'd make me lie across his lap, and he'd pull the skirt up around my waist and spank me hard."

Cole goes still on top of me, absorbing this piece of information. "How old were you?"

"Seven when it started. Thirteen when he stopped."

"Why did he stop?"

"A teacher saw the bruises when I was changing for gym. I tried to hide in the bathrooms to change, but that day they were full, and she made me change in the open."

Cole is silent for a moment. Then he says, "Did he touch you?"

I swallow the bile that rises in my throat. "The point wasn't to touch me. It was to make me cry."

Another pause.

"And did you?"

This is the part that shames me worse than anything. The thing I hate to admit.

He'll know if I lie.

"Yes. He wouldn't stop until I cried. If his hand didn't work, he used his belt. I tried not to break. But I always did. Every time."

I'm bawling now; I'm so fucking ashamed.

I tried so hard to be strong. To beat him at his game. But I never did, not one fucking night.

Cole shifts behind me. I think he's going to hit me again. Instead, I feel the warm, smooth, infinitely pleasurable sensation of him sliding his cock inside me.

My pussy is hot and thrumming, the vibrator still buzzing

against my clit. Cole's cock fills me all the way up, pushing down against the vibrator, giving me that deep, intense pressure I've been craving. The vibrations run through my body into his cock. The oscillation is inside and outside me, back and forth.

I sob again, this time with relief.

Slowly, gently, Cole begins to thrust.

I can't move my hips. I can only squeeze around him, clenching him tight.

The vibrator has engorged my pussy all the way along its length, all the way around my opening. I can feel every millimeter, every part of me that grips him, every part of me stroked by him. His cock rubs the inside while the vibrator buzzes on the outside, creating a friction so intense, so pleasurable that I'm crying again, tears of joy this time, from a sensation I can hardly stand.

I come, my pussy clenching and twitching around his cock, his weight pressing me down against the vibrator.

"Don't stop, don't stop, don't stop," I beg.

He doesn't stop until the orgasm is over. Then he pulls his cock free, sitting back again, his ass against my thighs, my pussy still spasming.

I'm a fucking mess. I'm glad my face is pressed against the table so he can't see the tears and mascara smeared everywhere.

Gently, but with deep, soothing pressure, Cole massages my ass cheeks. Soothing the pain. Soothing the spanking.

"It's all right." His voice is low and caressing. "It's going to be okay."

I press my cheek against the tabletop, my face crumpling.

He draws back his hand and spanks me again, but this time it's lighter. With the vibrator pushed against me, buzzing and thrumming, sending pleasure waves through my body, the slap doesn't really hurt. In fact, it almost feels pleasant.

Smack!

Smack!

Smack!

He's spanking me in time with the beat.

The slaps don't frighten me anymore. I know when to expect them. Instead of hurting me, they feel satisfying: a deep itch finally scratched.

SMACK!

SMACK!

SMACK!

He's ramping up the intensity, but it still doesn't hurt. The pleasure of the vibrator drowns it out. My ass is throbbing, probably bright red, all the blood rushing to the surface of the skin. It becomes more sensitive with every slap. But the pain stays even with the pleasure, a carefully balanced combination, like watermelon and salt.

My pussy throbs; my ass burns. Even before he puts his cock inside me again, another orgasm's building, rising, begging to be released.

Cole shifts, gripping the base of his raging cock. He presses the heavy head against my ass.

"No, wait!" I gasp.

He doesn't wait.

He runs his cock up my soaking wet slit, drenching the head, and then he presses it right into my ass.

"*Aghhhh!*" The groan rips through me as Cole pushes me down hard against the vibrator, his cock ramming slowly, surely, all the way inside my ass.

I can't move. I can't escape. He's got me pinned down with his knees on the back of my thighs, his cock driving all the way inside me, eight inches deep.

I've never been fucked in the ass before. Never even had a finger in there.

The sensation is so intense, so all-encompassing, that it feels like I'm being turned inside out. I can't breathe, can't move. I'm impaled.

He shoves his cock all the way in until his hips are flush against my ass. Then he holds his cock there, forcing me to take the whole thing, forcing me to adjust, millimeter by millimeter, to his outrageous girth.

I'm sweating, I'm panting—I can't stand it.

The only thing getting me through is the vibrator acting like an anesthetic, turning what could be intense pain into intense pleasure instead, through the magical alchemy of its relentless buzz.

In fact, if I rock my hips just the tiniest bit, my ass clenches around his cock and a pulse of pleasure rocks through me like a hammer strike. Each tiny movement feels like I'm being fucked by a horse—stretching, straining, at the absolute limit of what my body can handle.

Cole moves with me. Not rough, not hard—slow, incremental strokes in and out of my ass, wrenching another deep groan out of me.

I'm coming harder than before. Coming from the stimulation of nerves that have never been touched, that have no idea what kind of signal to send. My brain is bending in half.

Finally, Cole pulls out. It feels like giving birth—like three feet of cock is sliding out of me.

"*What the fuck,*" I say.

Cole massages my ass cheeks, kneading deep into muscles that get used all day long but never seem to find relief.

The song is starting over. I realize it must have started over several times—he's playing it on repeat.

I understand what's about to happen all over again, and I have no control, no ability to stop it. Usually, that sense of powerlessness would make me snap. Would make me scream and cry and fight with all my might.

But I'm lulled by the vibrator and by the countless orgasms flooding my body with pleasure chemicals.

Already I'm arching my back, presenting my ass to him. A Pavlovian response as my body seeks another round.

I can almost feel Cole smiling as he raises his hand before bringing it crashing down on my ass.

SMACK!

SMACK!

SMACK!

I think I'm crying again. While I beg for more.

"Harder." I sob. "Hit me harder."

SMACK!

SMACK!

SMACK!

Between spankings, Cole leans over and murmurs in my ear, "It's okay to enjoy it. You don't have to be embarrassed. Let go of the shame. Take the release…"

The words drift through my head. I don't know if it's Cole speaking or my own thoughts echoing…

I want this.

I need it.

It's the only way.

SMACK!

SMACK!

SMACK!

SMACK!

SMACK!

"Now you're not in trouble anymore," Cole whispers. "You're a good girl."

Already I'm anticipating the intense tearing and filling of his cock. He slides it back in my ass. I groan with pain and relief. With gratitude.

He fucks my ass slow and steady to the beat of the song.

I'm gonna run, run away, run, run away
Run away, run away and never come back…

I don't know if I'm crying or moaning. Begging out loud or only in my head.

I don't know how many times we've done this.

The song repeats over and over. The cycle does, too. He massages me, spanks me, fucks me, makes me come. Massages me, spanks me, fucks me, makes me come.

I have no sense of time. No idea how long we've been doing this. It could be hours or days.

I don't want it to stop. I don't want to be anywhere but here.

I've been drawn to Cole from the beginning. My body always wanted him. Only my mind was afraid.

Cole's lips touch my ear. I shiver with a deep and awful pleasure.

"It's okay for bad things to feel good. You can take pleasure from whatever you want."

I'm drugged with pleasure, drugged with pain. Drugged by the music. Time has no meaning. The only thing that feels real is Cole's voice in my brain:

"These ideas of right and wrong, good and evil...who taught them to you? Your mother? She's the worst person you know. Was it the priest at church? Your boss at work? Who decided these things?"

SMACK!

SMACK!

SMACK!

"It's up to you what's good and what's bad. This is your world, your life. *You* decide what to feel."

I'm floating through the air, weightless, rotating in space. I realize he's untied me. Released me from the manacles.

But I don't want to stop. I'm not finished yet.

Cole lies down on the table, his cock jutting up like mast, still rock-hard, still ready for me.

I mount him, my knees on either side of his hips, my hands on his chest. Slowly, I lower myself on his cock. It's easy to do—my ass is already stretched and ready.

I slide onto him until he's all the way inside me and I'm looking down into that flawless face—feminine and masculine. Evil and good.

I start to ride.

I ride him with his cock all the way up my ass. I ride him harder and harder, keeping time to the song.

> *Run away, run away and never come back*
> *Run, run away, run, run away, run away*
> *Show 'em that your color is black...*

When I know I'm right on the edge, I lift his hands and put them around my throat. I let him choke me, his fingers squeezing harder and harder until black sparks burst in front of my eyes, drowning out the music and the room, drowning out everything but pure sensation.

The last orgasm is so much more than pleasure. It's a detonation inside me that blows me apart, shattering everything I used to be.

I'm blasted to bits—*la petite mort*, the death of Mara.

I don't know if I'll ever come back.

Or what I'll be when I do.

31

COLE

WHEN WE'RE FINISHED, I CARRY MARA INTO THE SHOWER. I BATHE
her slowly and carefully, washing her hair, massaging the shampoo
into her scalp.

I wash every inch of her. Her chest, her back, her arms, her legs,
and even the tiny spaces between her toes.

She submits to me completely. Allowing me to move and manipulate her. Leaning her head back against my chest, her eyes closed,
utterly exhausted.

I don't know when I changed my mind about killing her.

Maybe it was the moment she lifted her hand and let me close
the manacle around her wrist.

Maybe it was even before that, when I opened the door and saw
her standing there in that black dress. She's beautiful, infinitely more
beautiful than the Olgiati. I can't shatter her.

I wrap her in a soft, fluffy towel and carry her into the living
quarters attached to the studio. I rarely sleep here, so the space has
the stark cleanliness of a hotel room, the blankets pulled tight across
the bed from the last time the housekeeper visited.

I lay her down on the crisply starched pillows, asking her, "Are
you hungry? Thirsty?"

It's not like me to be nurturing. In fact, I don't think I've ever done it before. I enjoy testing out personas, seeing how they make me feel, the effect they have on other people.

Tonight my motivations are different. I want to revive Mara because I want to talk to her again. I want to know if she has any other ideas for the unfinished sculptures. And I want to know how she feels about what we did.

More than that...I want to hear whatever she decides to say to me. Typically, I know exactly what information I'm trying to extract from someone. Mara surprises me with insights I hadn't foreseen. Letting her speak freely is more rewarding than manipulating her.

She's a continual puzzle.

She came here tonight already knowing the dynamic between Shaw and me. Already knowing what I am.

She put her life in my hands willingly. Freely.

She trusted me. Believed in me.

I should be disgusted at her idiocy. At her fatal mistake.

But somehow she was right. She knew what I would do better than I did.

I've never been in this position before. I'm cut loose. Floating in space. Unsure of anything.

I check the fridge in the small kitchen. It's filled with drinks and snacks. Usually, the housekeeper ends up throwing away the food and buying more because I forget to eat while working.

I make a plate of fruit and cheese before pouring two glasses of Riesling, nicely chilled. Mara has sat up in the bed, her wet hair in a rope over one shoulder, her eyes silvery with the reflected light of the television.

"Do you want to watch a movie?" she asks.

Smiling slightly, I set the food before her. Mara has an incredible ability to treat the bizarre as normal. To continue in her daily life no matter what happens to her.

She tears into the food, stuffing BellaVitano and raspberries into her mouth.

"I'm starving," she says unnecessarily.

I eat the same thing as her in the same order. Tasting the sharp, nutty cheese and the tart raspberries as one food. Sipping the wine in between, letting it pop in the back of my mouth. Closing my eyes like Mara does, focusing on the food.

"It's not better than sex," I say. "But it's damn good."

Mara laughs.

I don't know if I've ever made her laugh before. I like the way it rolls out of her, throaty and pleased.

"Better than sex with some people," she says. "But not you."

I feel a warm burning in my chest. Is it the wine? "You're a responsive subject."

"Have you ever done that before?" She seems curious, not jealous.

"No. Not like that."

"Neither have I," she says.

That's obvious if you're familiar with men. They're not that creative.

"What movie do you want?"

She shrugs. "I was just looking through Netflix."

"What about the one you mentioned at the Halloween party? Is it on there?"

"You don't want to watch that. It's old."

"Yes, I do. Put it on."

She finds the film, which has an illustrated poster like a fantasy novel from the '70s.

It's a classic "portal into another world" story. I watch it like I watch everything—carefully, as if there's going to be a test later.

"You think it's stupid." Mara finishes off the last of the berries, sucking the juice off her fingertips.

"No. I understand why you liked it when you were little."

Mara nods. "I would have done anything to disappear into another world. Watching it now, I guess it's kind of creepy how she's a kid playing with toys and David Bowie's a grown-ass man.

I guess I wished I had someone powerful who gave a shit about me."

I look at her profile—elfin like David Bowie, not soft like the youthful Jennifer Connelly.

"He's not exactly taking care of her," I point out. "He's seducing her. Manipulating her."

Mara turns her head, staring at me steadily with those metal-edged irises. "I don't want to be taken care of. I want to be seen."

My heart rate spikes as it only does for Mara. Not when I'm angry. Not when I'm violent. Only for her.

I was an ambush predator. I lived by concealment, camouflage.

What would it be like to strip myself bare?

It feels like destruction. Like immolation.

Could the pleasure of intimacy outweigh the danger?

This is a question perched on a cliff. No peering over—I'll only find the bottom by jumping.

Mara stares right back at me, ferocious, unashamed. Certain of what she wants and how to get it.

I've never held back from what I wanted. Not for morals. Not for laws.

I'll be damned if I'll do it for fear.

I've taken a life but never shared a life.

I lift my hand off the covers, crossing the space between us, cupping the curve of her jaw while my thumb rests on her full lower lip. "I see you."

"I know you do," Mara replies quietly. "And I want to see you."

"Be careful what you wish for."

She doesn't blink. Doesn't hesitate. "It's not a wish. It's a requirement."

32
MARA

Cole drives me home early in the morning. I'm planning to catch a couple of hours' sleep, then head over to the studio to work.

The intimacy between us is fragile but real, a thin rim of ice across a lake. I don't know if it's strong enough to bear weight just yet...but I'm already walking across.

He pulls up to the curb, flipping the car around so I can exit on the passenger side.

"Well, thanks for...whatever that was," I say, half smiling, half blushing.

I touch the handle of the door, planning to climb out.

"Wait." Cole grabs me by the back of the neck, pulling me back. He kisses me deep and warm, with just a hint of a bite, before releasing me.

The kiss makes my head spin. His scent clings to my clothes: steel shavings, machine oil, cold Riesling, expensive cologne. And Cole himself. The man and the monster. Layered together like sediment, like cake.

"I'll see you later," I say breathlessly.

"I'll definitely see you." There's a hint of a smile on his lips.

Knowing he watches me on that studio camera gives me a perverse thrill. I wonder what he'll do if I slowly strip off my clothes while I'm working. If I paint completely naked. Will he come join me?

I'm floating up the sagging steps to the row house.

It's so early that I don't hear a single person creaking around on the upper floors. No scent of burning coffee just yet.

That's fine—I'm too tired to chat. I can barely haul myself up the three flights of steps to my attic room. I may need to sleep more than a couple of hours. My body is so obliterated that the thought of my mattress and pillow have become intensely erotic.

I grasp the ancient brass handle and give it a twist. It slips through my hand, stiff and unyielding.

"What the fuck," I mutter, turning it again.

The door's locked. From the inside.

In my sleep-befuddled brain, all I can think is that I accidentally locked it on my way out or the handle is broken. Everything in this house is so decrepit that the shower, the furnace, the outlets, and the stove are constantly on the fritz. We've long since learned not to bother trying to call our landlord. Either Heinrich fixes what breaks, or we live with it.

In this case, I may be able to fix it myself.

Poking the edge of my thumbnail into the lock, I jiggle the handle until the tumblers click.

"*Yes*," I hiss, pushing the door open with a mournful creak.

I'm hurrying in, anticipating the long fall onto the mattress.

The bed is already occupied.

Not just occupied—drenched. The sheets, blankets, and mattress are soaked and dripping. Water pools on the bare boards all around.

And there on the pillow…Erin. Red hair spread out in a halo, damp and wavy. Skin paler than milk. Flowers framing her face: green willow boughs, scarlet poppies, forget-me-nots as blue as her wide-open eyes.

I'm crossing the space, falling beside her, feeling the water soak into my skirt as I lift her cold white hand.

I look down into her face, somehow believing that she can still see me, that I can bring her back if I keep calling out her name.

My shouts echo in the tiny space. They have no effect on her. No squeeze from her fingers. Not even a flutter of an eyelash.

She's dead. Hours gone. Already beginning to stiffen.

I drop her hand, overwhelmed by its rubbery chill. It no longer feels like Erin or anything attached to her.

"What's going on?" someone says from the doorway. "Why are you yelling?"

I turn toward Joanna. She stands there in her pajamas, her hair still wrapped in her silk sleeping scarf. I'm grateful it's her and not one of the others because she keeps our house running; she always knows what to do.

Except right now.

Joanna gapes at Erin with the same stunned expression as me. She's petrified, ten thousand years passing in an instant.

She doesn't ask if Erin's okay. She saw the truth sooner than I did. Or she was more willing to accept it.

Frank comes up behind her, unable to see because Joanna is blocking the doorway.

"What are you—" He cranes his head over her shoulder.

"Stay back," Joanna barks. "We need to call the cops."

I wait downstairs with the others, my whole body tense, listening for the sound of sirens.

Carrie huddles up with Peter, crying softly.

Frank thought we were playing a prank on him. He wouldn't go downstairs until we let him look inside the room. Now he's sitting over against the window, his skin the color of cement, both hands pressed against his mouth.

Melody keeps pacing the room, until Heinrich snaps at her to stop.

None of us are talking. It might be shock, or it might be the same reason Joanna is staring at me from across the room, somber and silent.

They know this is my fault.

Nobody said it. But I can feel the tension, the glances in my direction.

I don't need an accusation to feel guilty.

Erin is dead because of me.

Shaw did it, I know it. He must have come here looking for me. When he found my room empty...Erin was the next door down.

"Why was she in your bed?" Joanna asks, cutting through Carrie's soft whimpers.

"I don't know."

It's not hot enough that Erin would have gone in there to sleep. Shaw must have carried her in there, before or after he...did whatever the fuck else he did to her.

"Did any of you hear anything?" I ask the others, not meeting Joanna's eyes even though her room is right next to Erin's.

"I heard a thud," Carrie says miserably. "But I didn't know— everybody's so loud all the time. I didn't think anything of it. I just went back to sleep."

She dissolves into sobs again, huddled against Peter's shoulder. She's getting snot all over his sleeve. Peter just pulls her closer, cradling the back of her head with his hand.

"What about you?" Heinrich says to Joanna.

"I had my earplugs in," Joanna says irritably. She's always irritable when she's upset, choosing anger over vulnerability. It's why nobody fucks with her.

"Where were *you*?" Melody demands of me.

Melody is the newest roommate. I don't know her as well as the others. She's skinny and pinched looking, her short black hair sticking up in all directions. Her slippers slap against the linoleum as she resumes her pacing.

I don't know if she meant to sound accusing, but now she, Joanna, Frank, and Heinrich are all staring at me.

"I was at Cole Blackwell's studio."

"All night?" Melody persists, her head jerking toward me like a bird trained on a worm.

"Yes," I say stiffly. "All night."

Usually, this would stir up a barrage of intrusive questions from Frank. Only this level of awfulness could keep him quiet.

Our last two roommates, Joss and Brinley, come stumbling down the stairs, blinking sleepily. The sisters are wearing matching robes but not matching slippers.

"What's going on?" Joss asks.

"How come there's water dripping into our room?" says Brinley.

Before anyone can answer, two cruisers pull up in front of our house, followed by an ambulance. The lights are on, but no sirens announced their arrival.

"What the hell?" Joss says.

My phone vibrates in my pocket. Pulling it out, I see Cole's name on the display.

I pick up, turning away from Joanna's frown.

"Why are there cops at your house?" Cole demands.

I hurry out of the living room, my phone pressed against my ear and my voice lowered so the others won't hear. "How do you—"

"Never mind that. What are they doing there?"

"He killed Erin," I whisper into the phone, my hand shaking as I try to press it close against my ear. "He killed her, Cole. In my fucking bed. I came home, and I found her—"

"Who have you told?" Cole interrupts.

"I—What do you mean?"

"Don't tell the cops anything," Cole orders. "Not a fucking thing."

"I have to tell them! He killed Erin. He killed all those other girls, too, I'm sure of it."

I'm hurrying deeper into the house, trying to prevent any of my roommates from overhearing. Already the cops are banging on the door. I've got to get back out there.

"They're not going to be able to do anything," Cole says. "You'll only make it worse."

"How can you possibly—"

"What are you doing?" Joanna says.

She's followed me all the way back to the dining room. Her arms are folded over her chest, with no hint of the usual friendliness between us.

I end the call abruptly before stuffing the phone back in my pocket. "That was Cole."

Joanna jaw shifts like she's chewing on something I can't see. "The police are here," she reminds me. "They're going to want to talk to you."

I follow her back out to the living room, sick and guilty. Cole said I should keep my mouth shut, but there's no way I can do that. Erin is dead. Shaw killed her. He needs to be locked up, today, right this minute.

I follow Joanna back to the living room, where two uniformed officers are already in the process of interviewing my roommates.

Joss and Brinley are just now hearing that Erin's body is upstairs. Joss keeps repeating, "Are you serious? You're saying she's *dead*?" like she might not be hearing right. Brinley is hyperventilating.

The medics hustle up the stairs. They're not going to be able to help Erin. I remember the feeling of her rubbery flesh, the stiffness of her joints. My stomach does a nauseating flip.

"Who found her?" one of the officers says.

"I did." I step forward.

The officer looks me over, quick and practiced. His face shows no reaction, but I'm certain he knows I'm nervous. I'm sweating, shaky with guilt and fear and absolute devastation.

"Do you know what happened to her?"

"No." I shake my head. "But I know who did it."

———

Ten hours later, I'm stuck in an interrogation room at the police station.

I've fallen asleep several times over the hours, so exhausted that no amount of stress, frustration, or burnt black coffee can keep me awake.

Every time I drift off, a cop comes barging into the room on some flimsy pretext, jolting me awake, then leaves again. That's how I know they're watching me through the one-way glass and how I know I'm definitely a suspect.

Officer Hawks has come back twice to ask me questions.

I've told him everything I know about Alastor Shaw but nothing about Cole. And I'm feeling pretty fucking shitty about that.

I told myself it's irrelevant. Cole didn't kill Erin. He was with me the whole time.

But he's killed other people.

I press the heels of my hands against my eyes, trying to block out the dreary interrogation room—the cold metal table, the depressing Styrofoam cup of coffee, the greasy shine of the one-way mirror.

I don't know if he has. I don't know what he's done.

Yes, you do. He told you.

I remember Cole's face the night of the Halloween party. How still it became, how hard, each line carved into the flesh:

I filet people with precision… He does what I do badly.

Maybe he was trying to scare me.

He was *definitely* trying to scare me.

But that doesn't mean he was lying…

So why did I go to his house last night? Why did I let him put his hands all over me? Why did I let him tie me down on his table?

Because he's not a soulless monster, whatever he might pretend. I see more than that inside him.

Shaw, on the other hand…

The door creaks open once more. It's Hawks, his uniform looking decidedly less crisp than it did this morning, stubble shadowing his jawline.

He sits down across from me, placing a folder flat on the table between us.

"Did you find Shaw?" I demand.

"Yes, I found him," Hawks says calmly.

"*And?*" I can barely keep still in my chair, from nerves and the effect of all that nasty double-brewed coffee. I'm tired and jittery—not a good combination.

"He recognized Erin once we showed him a picture. But he says he only knew her from a casual encounter six weeks ago. He says he hasn't seen her since."

"He's lying!"

"He's got an alibi," Hawks says flatly. "He was with a girl last night. We talked to her. "

"Then she's lying, too! Or she fell asleep or…something," I say weakly.

"Why are you so certain it's him?" Hawks twirls his pen between his fingers.

Hawks is on the younger side of forty, with an athletic build, black-rimmed glasses, and meticulously polished shoes. His tone is polite, but he doesn't fool me for a second. I've spent enough time around Cole to know when I'm being tested.

Slowly, for what feels like the hundredth time, I repeat, "Because Shaw is the one who snatched me off the street six weeks ago. The exact fucking night we're talking about—he fucked my roommate, and then he stole her ID and tracked me to my house."

"I have the incident report here." Hawks taps his fingertips lightly on the folder.

Heat creeps up my neck, remembering the pouchy-eyed stare of Officer Fuckhead—his insulting questions and the long silences after every answer.

"That cop was a troglodyte. I'm surprised he could type."

Ignoring that, Hawks remarks, "It doesn't say anything about Shaw in here."

"That's because I didn't know it was him when I made the report."

"Because you never actually saw him."

My flush deepens. "I didn't see his face. But I saw how big he was. I felt it when he carried me. And I heard his voice."

I add that last part desperately. I didn't actually recognize Shaw's voice at the time—he only said a few words, and his tone was flat, nothing like his usual charm. But I've seen how Cole can switch it on and off at will. I have no doubt Shaw is just as proficient an actor.

"Officer Mickelsen had some doubts about your account of that evening." Hawks takes off his glasses and polishes them. Uncovered by the lenses, his blue eyes look reflective like the mirror. He can see out, but I can't see in.

"He was an incompetent piece of shit," I hiss, teeth bared.

"He thought you were making it up. He thought you did it to yourself."

I want to rip up that folder and fling the pieces in Hawks's face.

With great effort, I say, "Did you look at the pictures? Did you see *this?*"

I hold up my arm, yanking back the sleeve of my dress. Forcing him to look at the ugly long scar running up my wrist, still red and raised, livid as a brand. "I didn't do that to myself."

Hawks examines my wrist as if mentally comparing it to the photographs inside the folder. Unlike Officer Fuckhead, he doesn't mention the other scars, the old ones, and for that I'm grateful.

"It must have taken a lot of grit to pick yourself up and get out to the road, with all the blood you lost."

His voice is soft and low, his expression gentle as he looks from my wrist to my face. He's probably just buttering me up, trying to get me to lower my guard. Still, my shoulders relax from their hunched position.

"I got lucky. If a car hadn't come along to pick me up, I'd be dead."

"And why is Erin dead?" Hawks presses. "Why would Shaw want to hurt your roommate?"

This is where we venture into dangerous territory.

I can't talk about Shaw's obsession with Cole. I shouldn't talk about Cole at all.

Maybe it's wrong for me to protect him, but I feel compelled to do it. I've told Cole things I've never told to anyone, and he's done the same to me. Whatever secrets he's shared, I'm not about to spill them to the cops.

It won't help Erin either way.

"Shaw was hitting on me the night of the art show. Erin interrupted us. He attacked me later that night. I think he thought I was dead. When he saw me at a Halloween party, it fired him up again. He broke into my house, and since I wasn't there, he killed Erin instead."

"You were at your boyfriend's house?" Hawks says.

Now I'm the color of a stoplight. Calling Cole my boyfriend feels wrong on all kinds of levels. All I can do is nod.

"He's outside right now, raising a ruckus," Hawks says, watching for my reaction.

I have a shit poker face. I'm sure Hawks can tell exactly how much that surprises and pleases me. "He is?"

"He's threatening to call a whole team of lawyers if I don't let you out."

"I assume I can leave anytime I want. I haven't been put under arrest."

"That's right," Hawks says. "So why haven't you?"

"Because I care about Erin. She's not just a roommate. She's one of my best friends. And she was murdered in my fucking bed. It was my—" I swallow hard. "I feel responsible."

"You want to help," Hawks says, leaning forward across the table, his blue eyes fixed on mine.

I nod.

"Then tell me something..." He opens the folder before taking out a photograph, then sliding it across the table toward me.

The picture was taken from above, looking directly down at Erin. I've already seen everything it shows: her hands open on either side of her, palms up. The flowers scattered across her belly. Her red hair trailing like seaweed on the wet bed.

"Why was she killed like this, arranged like this?" Hawks points at the soaked bed. "Why was she drowned?"

"Drowned?" I say blankly.

"That was the cause of death. Someone wedged a funnel in her mouth and poured water into her lungs until she suffocated."

I shake my head slowly, staring at her pale, frightened face. The way she's posed puzzles me as much as it did when I first found her. Erin looks completely unlike herself, her face scrubbed of makeup, her body clad in an old-fashioned gown, silvery and beaded...

"That dress isn't hers." I frown.

"Are you sure?"

"She wouldn't wear something so..."

Slowly, I turn the photograph so Erin is lying horizontally instead of vertically. I squint at the willow boughs, at the red poppies...

"What is it?" Hawkes says sharply.

"It's...a painting."

"What do you mean?"

I let out the breath I've been holding, becoming more certain by the moment.

"He posed her like Ophelia."

"Are you talking about *Hamlet*?"

"Yeah. John Everett Millais painted the scene where Ophelia drowns in a river. This is what she looks like." I hold up the photograph. "Shaw recreated the painting."

Hawkes takes the picture from me and examines it anew, his expression skeptical.

"I told you!" I insist. "Shaw's an artist. He knows that painting."

"You're all artists," Hawks says, tucking the photograph back inside his folder. "You, Shaw, Erin…all your roommates."

"Except Peter," I amend.

"It doesn't point the finger at Shaw."

"Then what would?" I snap.

"Physical evidence."

"He's not stupid enough to leave evidence. You've never found evidence on any of the Beast's victims."

"You think Shaw's the Beast of the Bay?" Now Hawks definitely thinks I'm grasping at straws. "The MOs are completely different."

"It's Shaw," I insist. "I'm telling you."

Hawks sighs, pushing back his chair and standing like his back hurts. He presses the bridge of his nose with his thumb and index finger, then dons his glasses once more.

"Let's go," he says. "Before your boyfriend causes any more trouble."

He leads me out of the interrogation room, down the warren of hallways that wind through the police station.

Several officers stare at me as we pass. Their expressions are suspicious and unfriendly—angry that Hawks is letting me go.

"About fucking time," Cole barks the moment he sees me.

A warm rush of relief washes over me at the sight of him. His tall, stark figure, terrifying under the wrong circumstances, seems incredibly reassuring when deployed on my behalf. It's clear he's been terrorizing the officers, raising hell until they let me out.

The balls on him to stride into a police station and start barking orders. I guess that's what it's like being rich and privileged: you never feel nervous, even when you're guilty as sin.

I hurry over to Cole, letting him envelop me with his arm around my shoulders, shielding me from the glares of a dozen cops.

"Did they do anything to you?" he growls. "Did they hurt you?"

"No," I say. "Officer Hawks was perfectly polite."

That only seems to harden Cole's animosity. He pulls me tight against his side, glowering at Hawks.

"If you want to speak with her again, you can call my lawyer." He flicks a business card disdainfully across the information desk.

Hawks watches the card land but makes no move to pick it up. His cool-blue eyes sweep over Cole just as they did to me, taking in every detail. "I'll be in touch," he says.

Cole steers me out of the police station, out onto the street.

I'm shocked to see it's fully dark again, the whole day gone while I sat in that windowless room.

"What the fuck were you thinking?" Cole spins me around so I have to look directly into his furious face.

"I had to tell them about Shaw!" I cry. "He killed Erin! He was probably there to kill *me*. She's dead and it's my fault."

"And what good did it do?" Cole scoffs. "Did you see them leading him away in handcuffs?"

"No," I admit.

"Of course not! It's not his first fucking rodeo. Shaw is smart. He knows how to cover his tracks."

"Then what am I supposed to do?"

Cole takes hold of my face with both hands. He tilts up my chin, making me look into his eyes. "You're going to do exactly what I say."

I try to shake him off, but he's too strong. My face burns everywhere his fingers touch. I look into those deep, dark eyes that pin me in place, more powerful than his grip.

"You tried it your way," Cole says. "Now it's time to try mine."

"What does that mean?"

"You're going to move into my house, tonight. I'll send someone to pick up your things. You're going to stay with me, right by my side, every fucking minute of the day so I can keep you safe. And when it's time to deal with Shaw...that'll be my way, too."

"You want me to move in with you? That's insane."

"Do you want to stay alive? Or do you want to become Shaw's next painting?"

"Don't joke about that," I snarl. "Don't talk about Erin that way."

"It's no fucking joke. And it's no game. You pull another one of your stunts, running off without me, and Shaw will gut you like a fish. I'm the only one who can protect you. Unless you want to take a chance on Officer Hawks," Cole sneers.

I take a deep breath, considering my options.

They're few in number and unattractive to me.

What am I supposed to do, go home to the Victorian, avoid Joanna, sleep in the room where Erin was killed? Hope Shaw waits a few days before he comes back to finish the job?

On the other hand...

I saw Cole's face when he strapped me down to that table. When he took control of my body until I couldn't think or breathe, until he wrenched my deepest secrets out of me while I was limp and helpless, begging for more...

We won't be roommates.

More like teacher and student.

Mentor and protégé.

Sculptor and clay.

My breath comes out in a long sigh, a silvery plume in the cold night, my soul exiting my body.

"I guess I don't have a choice."

Cole smiles, his teeth gleaming in the dark. "Don't you ever believe that, Mara. We always have a choice." He holds out his hand to me, palm upward, his long, slim fingers pale in the moonlight. "It's time to make yours."

I take his hand, his fingers closing around mine. "Take me home."